THE WARGER
BUBBLE

A timeless tale

Foreword

The incredible journey in our story is inspired by the realization that reality and manifestations of reality are intriguing without limit for our minds to ever get a full grasp of. We don't understand in any depth, even a very fundamental property of nature – force. We don't know what a force really is. Any force for that matter - gravity, electromagnetic, strong or weak nuclear. How do any of these forces cause the effects that it causes? We don't know how and if any force caused the universe itself to begin. We don't know if there even was a beginning and we don't know how the universe is holding itself together from disintegrating after it began.

But we can reach beyond the chasm of our helpless ignorance by using that one power that we all possess and that same power which all men and women of science use in their quest for the truth – the power of imagination! A super power that only humans possess on this planet. In using that super power we realize how strange anything and everything is – if we didn't take anything for granted.

In my attempt to tell you this story I was all along aware how I owe my very being to so many people who came before me, people who told us things about the universe, people who spoke through their books and other means and had provided the way.

However, there are a few special people who mean a lot to my specific existence as a person. Some very special people in my life without who I wouldn't be

3

here and to them I dedicate this book. My late parents –Boxiram Chayengia, and Rekha Chayengia to whom I owe my existence and my values. My very special thanks go to three other very special people in my life – Late Geeta Taid (my eldest sister) and her husband - Padma Nath Taid, and Riju Panging Doley - my middle sister. Without the assistance of these three extraordinary people I would not have made past the formative phase of my life.

I am thankful to my two wonderful children, Neel Panging and Nishtha Panging, who have critiqued, edited, and shared their perspectives in the writing of this book.

I am thankful to my wife Dr. Jonali Baruah Panging, who has been through thick and thin in our conjugal lives.

~ Pankaj Panging (Author)

Contents

One – AB Initio   7

Two - The Unidentified Submerged Sphere   12

Three - Me and Songa   17

Four - Where it all Began - Year of the Glyphs   30

Five – Contents of the Glyphs   40

Six - The Trip to Austin   59

Seven – Kobayashi and Mirrang   72

Eight - The Great Propulsion Debate at IPNES   84

Nine–Austin to Genève   94

Ten – Mystery of Wallace   107

Eleven – Ghost of Wallace   110

Twelve – The Nebula in the Sky   122

Thirteen – An Anxious World   128

Fourteen – The Crew   135

Fifteen- Pegasus and C-Mind   141

Sixteen- The Launch   152

Seventeen- Higher Dimensional Universes   159

Eighteen– Astraea-B, the Landing   181

Nineteen - Day Four in Astraea-B   188

Twenty - Division and Conflict in Paradise   206

Twenty One – We are not Alone!   222

Twenty Two – The Settlement   239

Twenty Three – The Last Days in Astraea   249

Twenty Four– Departure from Astraea   263

Twenty Five – Return to Earth   289

Twenty Six – The Non-Welcome   304

Twenty Seven– Home that Wasn't   308

Twenty Eight – A Glimpse into the Forest   314

Twenty Nine – Geological Forensic   318

Thirty - The Restart   322

Thirty One - The First Contact   340

Thirty Two - The Relocation   345

Thirty Three - The Time Capsules   354

Thirty Four –Dad's Message   359

Thirty Five – Prisoners of the Future   377

Thirty Six–Nuevo Earth   393

Thirty Seven NErth-5   398

Thirty Eight- Droon Zoy   411

Thirty Nine – Life in the Nuevo Earth system   429

Forty - Life is Good, Too Good!   436

Forty One–Checking Out   444

Forty- Two – The Unexpected   456

Forty Three – To Eternity   461

One – AB Initio

Not everything that fell from the sky that afternoon was a fighter plane. One specifically, wasn't even a man-made object.

The vicious *dog-fights* far up in the air in-play between the Imperial Air force of Japan and the Royal Air Force of Britain would be outplayed by another spectacle that would unfold towards the later part of that afternoon.

This is the farthest East of India. The river *Suwansiri* flows through this land and drains into the *Brahmaputra* basin as it always did.

The name *Suwansiri* in the local dialect means – *a stream of gold*. It is no little stream in reality, but is a river of a decent size, a river that flows with clear water, so clear that at a good fifty feet into the river from the shore, one could see the pebbles on the river-bed - even to this day. The forest cover on the hills of the lower Himalayas that runs over the vast expanse of this region is as deep sylvan green as could be.

The year was 1944, the day – one of those hot and sultry days of June. Three years later, India would become independent from the British Empire. The most parts of a still colonial, but soon to be independent India were in turmoil, as Indians were in total revolt against an Imperial Britain – much weakened by the internecine World War that would not be concluded until after a year from that day. Battle *Kohima*, a ground battle to prevent the advancing Japanese Imperial army by the Indo – British forces, was raging less than seventy miles away to the south of here.

It was that time in India's history, and this easternmost corner of the country was having its share of that history.

The tribe that inhabits this region is known as the *Mishing* of the valley. To that tribe belonged Bhrigu, better known as Baangkong to his friends.

The late afternoon sky was buzzing with the sound of fighter planes approaching like a cloud of giant gnats, from either side of the war, followed by the sounds of rattling machine guns, determined to bring the other side down. Down below on the ground and by the river, Baangkong and his three buddies were looking up at the mortal combats for aerial supremacy. Suddenly, a resounding boom in the northwesterly direction forced their attention to a different patch of the sky away from the region of the main theatre of the aerial battle. A huge arc-shaped plume of water vapor appeared in that patch of the sky, like one that would be left behind by an ascending Saturn V rocket, except it was directed downward instead of upward. At the tip of that plume was a ball of fire. Of the several streaks of fiery splinters that showered out of that burning spearhead, one swooshed over their heads and that forced them to duck for cover.

The ball of fire plunged into the river in a big splash.

The bubbles after that splash were still bobbing. The vapor trail in the sky slowly evaporated to nothing.

The four young men in their late teens were naturally awestruck by the event that just played out in front of their very eyes. By then, the slanted beams of the Sun were barely squeezing their ways through the gaps in the hills from the other side of the river.

Baangkong, a well-built young man and a natural leader among men, instinctively dashed for the river and dived into the water headfirst with the intention to rescue the pilot in that mysterious craft that met with a fiery fate. Two of his three buddies followed suit. Baangkong swam up to the site and took a deep dive into the water. He popped out of it a couple of minutes later, gasping for breath, only to dive down one more time, by which time the two other friends caught up with him and they too took their dives into the deep.

By the time they dove back for one last time, the object sank halfway into the river bed. The flashy glimpse that they had of the object was that of a dark metallic sphere with three thick irregular lines, resembling three rugged claw marks from a large wild beast on the bark of a tree, indented parallel to the equatorial line of the spherical object. The object slowly began to disappear into the bottom, even as the dim bluish lights from the three indented lines were still blinking. The three lines blinked a few more times and gradually faded away. The water down under was already pitch dark and the whirlpool effect of submersion caused a pretty dangerous situation for anyone to be any nearer to the site. A minute later, the three waved back to their fourth friend who stayed dry on the shore. The fourth buddy of theirs, anticipating to hear something exciting, something queer, and partly out of concern for their safety, signaled them to come back to shore. It was almost getting dark by then, too dark to be swimming in a river this size. They began to swim for the shore. On reaching the shore, they corroborated each other's experience to match – that the sinking spherical object felt like a very strong metal to the touch with intricately designed gilded features. Its diameter was about the height of a city lamp post and it had three thick and rugged indentations in its center resembling three claw marks, and each glowed blue.

By then, a few dozen villagers had gathered there too, after they heard the boom and saw the ball of fire from wherever they were, to satisfy their inquisitiveness. The story thus spread like wildfire that Baangkong and his buddies did see something in the river bed. Something that vanished into the river bed. Something extraordinary, a very strange looking craft that was not among the descriptions of any of the fighter planes from either of the two adversaries of the war. The news reached the local District Commissioner, a colonial bureaucrat of King George VI of England. A day later, the Commissioner sent a team of professional divers and soldiers to investigate the site. They found nothing in that location. There was no machinery in those times to dig any deeper.

Just a week later, sightings of similar strange-looking crafts were reported in the Siberian wilds and few other places around the world. The story died down with the passage of time, and was forgotten.

Two - The Unidentified Submerged Sphere

The story remained forgotten, forgotten for twenty long years.

Eight years after that event, Baangkong married a very quiet and unassuming woman and fathered a male child after four years of their conjugal life. Eight more years later – in the year of 1964, another strange event would resurrect at the same location.

Baangkong told the story of the mysterious crash over a few evening meals to his then eight-year-old son – Denzing. Which father wouldn't? The elders in the village validated the story. Denzing remembered his father taking him to the site of the crash on a government motorboat once. That was after Baangkong got a job as an officer in the department of civil supplies in independent India.

There was nothing there.

Not too far from their idyllic village, an Air Force base was built by the government of independent India. That base was strategically located there so that India would be able to respond quickly to any potential Chinese aggression from the other side of the Himalayas. Every day, the Soviet-made, Indian *Mig fighter*-jets from that base made several mock sorties in the sky for combat readiness.

After school, Denzing would join his other shepherd buddies who did not attend school. In their quality times, they used to run through the bushes and with no particular intent. Armed with catapults in their hands and shells in their pockets, times like these were the times of total freedom for them. They would run aimlessly, doing cartwheels and handsprings on the sandy spaces between the bushes. At other times, they would sing bits and pieces of folk songs while the jingles from the cowbells coming from random directions provided the accompanying music. It was not at all uncommon for a first-time visitor to the village walking the banks of this river to get startled by the sudden emergence of a singing kid out of a tall grassy bush.

Every time a fighter-jet zoomed over them, leaving a long trail of vapor behind, young Denzing would look up, follow along the long white vapor trace as far as his eyes could. Whenever he looked up, his mind was filled with wonder, and he stayed that way until his neck hurt. Each time, a deep desire to fly one himself someday, grew.

And then the unbelievable happened. In the middle of the river where the crash was known to have happened, something was brewing under the water.

But after all these years?! After twenty-odd years!?

The water there was swelling up and up and up, and from within the foam, emerged a craft. Rising slowly at first, the craft then began to spin rapidly, followed by a few quick laps in increasingly larger circles over the water. At the end of a few such laps, it suddenly took off at an incredible speed, producing a sonic boom and in an instant vanished into the blue infinity. The mysterious craft was a dark metallic looking sphere with some intricately designed gilded features, its diameter about the height of a street lamp. The craft had three unmistakable markers in its equatorial region, three streaks of rugged indentations parallel to the equator that together looked like three claw marks of a large feral animal. The three markers glowed bluish, blurry yet bright.

Denzing and his buddies witnessed the entire sequence of the event, with fear and wonder in their eyes, and their ears still buzzing from the sonic boom. The cows that they were herding ran amok in all random directions, and the ownerless dogs were left barking relentlessly. The petrified boys slowly emerged from the cover of the tall shrubs, trying to make sense of the extraordinary visual that they had witnessed, as the water at that location from which the sphere rose was still churning in a whirlpool.

Observers from the nearby base of the Indian Air Force recorded that event as an inexplicable blip in their RADAR. It was entered as an unexplained phenomenon in their logs – dated and shelved.

One cannot predict which event in life prints an indelible impression on one's mind that inspires one's whole life from thereon. For Denzing, the visual of the spherical craft that emerged out of the river and flew away in a hypersonic speed was an indelible impression of his life.

He was among the eyewitnesses to the evidence of the kind of hypervelocity that the world of the human had not seen up to that time.

The eight-year-old Denzing would grow up to become a man. Based on his academic excellence, he was admitted to one of the top technology institutions in India.

In the year of 1980, Denzing left for the states to pursue an advanced degree in Aerospace after he got a full-ride scholarship to study Aerospace Engineering at UC Berkeley, California, USA. He graduated summa-cum-laude in his class and went on to earn his doctorate in the same field.

Three - Me and Songa

Where do I come in, in all of this? Who am I? How do I know anything at all?

My own story started in the year 2024, 12th of December to be exact - the day I was born - an insignificant and ordinary event. But what was to happen a decade later was not anything ordinary nor insignificant – the year of 2034.

I will go to that all-important year when the appropriate context comes. For the moment let me begin by giving this little intro of myself.

Let's start from the year of my eighth birthday instead - the year 2032.

By that year, I had finished one year of high - many would consider that as advanced compared to most kids of my age. Somehow I was just able to pick up on the things taught in school quicker than my peers did. I myself don't know how. Just lucky I guess. I might have got it from my dad, I guess. Dad worked as a Research Scientist at NASA in Clear Lake, Texas.

His dad, my grandfather, was from Seoul, South Korea and my grandma was from Florence, France. I've never met either. My dad was the youngest of a seven-child household, lost both his parents to natural causes when he was only twenty. Four years later he married my mom, a full-blooded American with some Native American ancestry in her lineage.

My dad was not done with learning even after his PhD and he would later go on to take a degree in Neuroscience to understand if there actually exists a model of intelligence. He wanted to know how the Biology of the human brain does create *intelligence.* He mentioned a book titled '*On Intelligence*' by Jeff Hawkins and Sandra Blackslee to me as one of the many books that he owes some of his views of the mind.

We loved to be by the sea!

When dad began working for NASA, we used to frequent the Galveston beaches whenever we could when the weather was permitting. The shores of the *Gulf of Mexico* were next door to us at Clear Lake - a suburb south-east of Houston. Mom too liked to stare at the gulf like us. She had friends in the area that she liked to hang out with. Half the time she would chat away with them, sipping a margarita at a seaside restaurant, but always within sighting distance from where dad and I lay low on our backs.

At the beach dad typically buried himself in a book, lying on a beach recliner.

I used to call him Songa, sometimes. His last name is Song, my last name too, of course that is where last names come from. For some strange reason I morphed his to Songa, and made it his name. He could care less.

I used to shoot all kinds of questions at him.

"*Songa, how do we really 'see' anything?*" My first question of the day.

And he always straightway jumps to respond, mincing no words.

"*That actually is a pretty loaded question. We 'see' through our brain, the eyes are just an important accessory to it. This machine that we call the brain is probably the most complex biological system that ever evolved on this planet. We don't yet have a solid understanding of how it works. We just have some inkling of it.*", he said, without raising his head from the book that he was reading.

And he continued. I know I triggered him and he would go on now. He likes to explain things to me and in detail.

"Al' righty... Let's do an exercise. Just drop the bouncy ball that you are holding..."

"What? Why? ...."

"Just do it. Drop it, but don't look at it!" he said calmly again.

"Okay..did."

"Now close your eyes and go get the ball from the sand."

I followed his instruction and after a little bit of struggle, I successfully retrieved the ball. Easy, of course!

"Got it."

"Great! How did you?" He asked.

"I don't know, I just did. Just like that, anybody could do it."

Then came his long explanation.

"You did not 'see' the ball with your eyes, yet in your mind you somehow 'saw' the whole thing.

You intuitively understood the laws of gravity so you looked for the ball in the downward direction and not up in the air. Your hand knows exactly how far down *in the vertical z axis that it needs to traverse from your current position on the recliner until it hit the sand. You used the prior knowledge of the recliner's height from the ground, walked the sand with your two fingers, mapped the surface below you, ruled out where the ball could not be, and finally settled on where it could be. Unconsciously, you considered the fact that this is sand and therefore even a bouncy ball would not bounce away that far. And your fingers, which do not have eyes of their own, knew that it is the ball that it touched and not something else. All the while it was your brain that 'saw' everything and not your eyes.*

So, you had a mental 'map' of everything - the recliner, the sand, the laws of gravity, the size and shape of the ball, etc. - all prior knowledge and you recalled all these so very effortlessly in retrieving the ball.

None of the knowledge that you successfully applied are stored as visual frames inside your brain, instead, all these are stored in some abstract forms, nicely inter connected and indexed for fast retrieval as we need them such that it feels like 'seeing' even when you are dealing with it by other sensory agents of your body. In other words, even without looking you picked up the ball from the sand successfully, and you did all that so effortlessly.

Isn't that so amazing?"

"Wow! I never thought about all that." Feeling enlightened I asked my follow-up question.

"So, every time we form a new experience, it is a stress on the brain to store it somewhere, isn't it? Does it not have a maximum storage capacity?"

"Yes. But the brain is very smart in handling all that, without us consciously telling it to do so. First of all, the brain stores things in a connected and relational way, building on top of prior experiences that are similar, rather than creating an entirely new set of memory for each new experience, every time. That is probably why we find it easier to understand the concepts that we are already familiar with than those that are totally new to us. It does all that automatically and very efficiently as well, I guess."

"What about the limit of storage?" I reminded him of the second part of my question.

"There must be a physical max. The brain deals with it either by recycling unused memory after a passage of time or by growing new cells. We remember and recall things that happened recently better than the ones that

happened in the remote past..... in general, because we lose some to make room for new experience. There of course are long term memories born out of childhood experience, etc., that are probably stored differently from the mundane stuff. We probably automatically know what is mundane and what is worthy of remembering depending on how much pain or joy an event associated with that memory caused to our body, to our feelings, to our success, and more simply, to our life"

"Cool! Is there such a thing as a unit of intelligence? Or a unit of memory?" I asked.

"My guess is there is. There must be such a thing as a unit of intelligence! Okay, know this - there is this little slug, just one **mm** in length, with only 358 neurons spread across its tiny body. It goes by with its life just fine. Just 358 neurons! True, it is not as intelligent as we are, but it performs the act of living just as well as we do. To me, there is some raw intelligence right there! In other words, there must be a unit of intelligence that needs a certain number of neurons to act together to perform one cohesive intelligent act – we just don't know what makes that one unit, yet.

Evolution has created this 'structure' of the human brain in a certain way to create our kind of 'intelligence'. Are there other types of **non-biological** '**structures**' that can engineer intelligence in another way similar to our biological intelligence? I'm sure there is – waiting to be discovered!" He explained.

"Okay. Question? So, beyond how the brain 'does' the act of 'intelligence' using the 'biological' arrangement of neurons, can we mathematically represent one unit of intelligence?" I asked.

"I'm pretty sure there is. There have to be some ways to model 'intelligence' using some elegant mathematics just as there is a mathematical diktat on how many electrons are allowed to occupy a specific orbit in an atom. Or just like how the Fibonacci series occurs everywhere in nature and such stuff. Yes, there could be some mathematical underpinnings to how the brain works that we just have not figured out yet. If we ever **do** figure that out someday, we may be able to claim that we actually have created true **artificial intelligence**. From that point nothing is stopping us in making AI unlimitedly smarter than ourselves. And to think that **Evolution** kind of developed 'intelligence' biologically and operationalized that underlying mathematics, and by itself? I guess that is absolutely amazing!"

That was Songa, explaining things to me.

I remembered how we talked all the time and we laughed for no particular reason sometimes. He calls me *Toot* – I never asked why, but I guess it sounded kind of cute!

"Okay, ready for a quiz now?" Songa asked me with a wink.

"Nooo... quiz...already?"

"This is going to be very easy though.. don't wanna try?"

"Oooohkayyy...."

"All righty, what thing can give a name to itself?"

"Aw wait...what?"

"What. Thing. Can. Give. A. Name.To. Itself?" he repeated the question, slowly, word by word this time.

After some head scratching and some ummms...I admitted -

"...I told you I am dumb...okay? Okay, you tell me?"

*"The **brain**! The **brain** calls itself – what? **Brain**!!"*

"Oh yeah...Gee..I never thought about it that way...I was thinking about all kinds of creatures."

"Honestly, I borrowed that joke from the net somewhere. I don't even remember who I should give the credit to."

That was Songa and I, and our little father-son moments.

We love the sea, love everything about it.

After all that heavy talk, I just stared listlessly at the bay. Even in that state of passivity, I said to myself, how my mind was aware of so many things, so many actions, and so many events that are constantly unfolding in front of me –

The opportunistic seagulls over the piers and everywhere, the anchored yachts, the distant fishing boats lurching this and that way, the sketchy human figures standing up on the surf boards far away from the shore - bobbing up and down and sideways, the group of beach toned people – children, men and a bevy of women, the row of bustling eateries perched all along the beach for a mile out. Everything. The amazing brain registers everything, all the time, even when one is not paying any attention!

I can stare at the sea for the whole day, doing nothing.

And I have to say one thing in passing - *'that something'* about the sea -unwinds my mind, always, every time.

When I stepped into my teen years, people said I had a matured mind of a thirty-five-year-old. I didn't feel any different myself, but I know that I do like the company of older people, I connect well with them better. I always felt that I had something to learn from them – always. I jelled well with older folks, some much older than me. I knew someone, someone who was sixty years old at that time. He and I talked a lot about science fiction stuff. He was the Sci-Fi buff of his time, grew up through the times of *Isaac Asimov* and *Arthur C Clarke*, the laws of robotics, yada, yada.

He admitted that he was awed by my interest in *Asimov, Arthur C Clarke* and *Carl Sagan* - these famous personalities from his generation, he thought. My generation was the super hero, the action hero, the restless, less science and more intense sci-fi action kind of generation. But I am an anachronism in my time, I guess.

The last memory of this kind of a *father-son and a day in the beach* talk between us was soon after I graduated college - at age 13.

Coming back home, to *Clear Lake, Houston* after finishing my baccalaureate, Songa and I would dash for the beach one last time.

That was in the year 2037. In the fall of that same year, I left home one more time to pursue my Master's and hopefully a Doctorate after that.

Those were the memories writ large and deep down somewhere in my synapses, neurons, dendrites and axons- all inside my mind, inside that wonderful human brain that I too am fortunate to possess one.

Nice to possess one, if you think about it. This brain of ours is a lot more amazing than we realize it is and give credit for.

And I was thinking, what if we could communicate with each other in the same form in which the brain stores our memories? I wonder what exciting possibilities that will open up!

The Glyphs

Four - Where it all Began - Year of the Glyphs

The all-important year of 2034. That was the year when everything began. It will not be any exaggeration if I said that our lives depended on what was 'discovered' that year, literally! Take that year away - and there is no us, we would be all dead – in a not too far future.

Dad's been evaluating a software product for NASA, a product built by a company called **Labyrinz,** based in Dallas.

This startup venture has a unique product called **Aries**. **Aries** prepares the data for deep visualization in as many as 36 dimensions. The program essentially encapsulates a series of algorithmically computed nodes that processes the ingested data for visualization. *Virgo*, an ancillary program to **Aries** takes the processed output from **Aries** and displays the result as a *Scalable Vector Graph* in more than three dimensions.

NASA needs a product like **Aries** and **Virgo** to visualize the tons of data received from **Kepler**, **TESS** and **Spitzer**. Just for a refresher - **these** are three space based telescopes that scour the sky for exoplanets. Add the **James Webb Space** telescope to the list, slated to be launched into space to replace Hubble. **JWS** is expected to generate its own tons of data in the near future, which will need a good tool to sift through.

Aries and **Virgo** together are one of the few competing products that meet NASA's criteria.

The program ships with a mathematically generated test dataset that the user can play around with to evaluate the product.

This software product has nothing to do with any real physical dimensions. It just is a tool to visualize a series of multi-featured input data.

But somehow, something happened here that tied up this unknown tech startup's product with the destiny of our existence itself.

It was a beautiful fall evening. Dad had been trying out the two software with a copy of the evaluation version of the software installed locally on his computer.

What he would discover in doing his evaluation of the software would ensure that the rest of his life is governed by that finding. At that moment he was just puzzled by a strange happening. He called up Liu, one of the resident planetary data scientists of the Planetary Science Division of NASA. Dr. Liu and dad go way back, longer than their professional association of working as colleagues at NASA.

"Hey Song, how are you?" Liu was on the other side of the line.

"Hey Liu, good, good. How is it going for you?" Just the usual conversation starter.

"Not too bad, wassup?"

"Hey, I keep getting these glyphs on my monitor. Like some Egyptian Hieroglyphs. No clue what the heck these are.......Need a second opinion from your smarty mind. Shall I share my screen, if you are free to look now?"

"Sure! Yes, I'm online now, go ahead!" Liu replied.

After the screen share program was initiated and Liu was able to see dad's monitor, dad pointed to some glyphs that were blinking on his monitor and faded away several seconds later only to pop up again after a while.

"See these things, even if I completely disconnect the internet, these still continue to appear on this machine....!"

"What are they? Looks like a glyph, no?" Liu asked.

"Yes, they do look like glyphs. They first pop up in the size of twenty by twenty pixels followed by some alert, grow twice as big then automatically get saved into a particular folder on my desktop. I did not even create that folder", Dad explained.

"Okay?"

"They are all in this folder. Twenty-three of them!"

"Did you try rebooting and reloading any new software you might have installed recently?" Asked Liu.

*"I deleted the folder, rebooted the machine, uninstalled the two programs that I recently installed, **Aries** and **Virgo** that is, and I reinstalled them. Guess what? The glyphs appear again, from nothing, even when I disconnect the internet from this machine!"* Dad had done his due diligence on this before he called up Liu.

"Did you scan the system for Malware?"

"Yes. This system is secured. I keep it offline all the time except for now as I am sharing my screen with you." Dad responded.

"If it is not malware then what remains is what it is, no matter how unlikely it might seem." Liu threw a theory.

"*What is that?*"

"*The programs **Aries** and **Virgo** are doing it, somehow. Either a bug or logic bomb. I would call up the Vendor's representative for this product. They will surely know more.*"

"*Okay lemme try that*"

Dad called up and spoke to the CEO of **Labyrinz**, who, knowing the importance of NASA's clientele to their business, connected dad with the principal architect and engineer for the programs *Aries* and *Virgo* immediately. On the conference call the CEO introduced his principal engineer as Raul.

"*Okay, if I may share my screen with you, Raul?*" Asked dad.

"*Sure!*"

"*Okay, I am hanging up, in that case. Raul, please provide all the assistance needed to Dr. Song to resolve this problem, ok?*" The CEO excused and disconnected himself from the tripartite conversation.

After conferencing for a while with Raul, it became apparent that Raul had no clue about the issue at all.

"*Is it at all possible that the algorithms in your programs could produce something like these glyphs?*" Dad asked Raul, with Liu listening as well.

"*No sir, there is just no way that our programs could spin off any logic that can generate all these glyphs!*" Raul replied.

"*Hope it is not some self-aware 'Skynet' and 'Turing complete AI' that you guys have built!*" Dad was just joking.

"*Ha ha haa.. Yes, Skynet might have programmed it in the future, transmitted it to the past and planted it in Aries!*" Raul was just playing along from the other side of the line. The metaphor was of course in reference to the Hollywood blockbuster –**The Terminator** series.

"*Ha ha..Got it!*"

"*No, sir! No way!*" Raul made sure that dad would not perceive his response as insincere.

They both laughed at their own jokes.

"*Okay Raul, no problem. I will fool around and see if I discover anything. Thanks a lot for your time!*"

"*If you find anything that is doing all that, please let us know. I will be very curious to know, sir!*"

After they dis-engaged, dad spent the next two hours trying to recreate the circumstance that might have caused the glyphs to appear.

And he found something else!

So he called up Liu again.

"Hey Liu! If you are free could you come over? This is some crazy stuff here!" Dad dialed Liu one more time.

This was a Friday night, but Liu knew dad would not spoil anyone's quality time without a good reason.

"Sounds like something, huh? All right I will be there shortly." Liu lived not too far from our residence.

Dr. Liu came as promised and sat next to dad in his study.

"I tried opening these glyphs through a few of the well-known media programs. But won't be opened by any of the known media software that I had downloaded. Just as you had suggested the first time we spoke on this – I now believe that it got to have something to do with this software. But what and how? Then it dawned on me, why not try opening these glyphs using this new software. This software has a media display component to it as the manual says. So, just to see, just for fun! Guess what? It worked!" Dad explained.

"Okay? And what did you find?"

Dad maximized the window to cover the entire screen space of the curved 45 inch monitor. At its default view, the glyph under test appeared as one hugely cluttered hair-ball diagram, with thousands of tiny nodes blinking with different strengths.

"The cool thing about this software is you can magnify an image up to 75000 times. Okay, so, I'm zooming in, as you are watching!" Dad spoke as he magnified the view and the magnification level reached 60,000.-

"At 60,000 magnification level, this is not a glyph at all...guess what? ...whoa, these are actual neuron-like nodes, all complete with dendrites, synapses, and axons. Billions of them! And you know what? From the varying luminosity - they look - alive!!" Dad exclaimed!

"Whoa!" Liu was thrown off his feet as well.

As confirmed by the chief engineer of **Labyrinz,** *Aries* is just not capable of generating anything like what they were looking at, certainly not any **glyph** that on magnification shows billions of neurons and synapses! The *Virgo* interface is ancillary to *Aries* and can be compared to the Adobe Acrobat reader program in its functionality, it just displays things.

How such a display that they are looking at is even possible?

*"The question is, even if someone did generate these glyphs, how does one generate **anything** like that? Mathematically, I meant. What kind of a mathematical function would produce such an output? Someone must be a Math whiz-kid in the genius of Paul Dirac or Ramanujan to be able to come up with such a function!"* Said Liu, a Ph.D. in mathematics he is - knows a few things about mathematical functions.

They deliberated on this over and over again and every time just kept on hitting a wall in trying to find any rational explanation. Nothing they could come up made any sense. Every explanation eluded rationality.

"I don't think we should sit on this. We should get help. Not sure what kind of help or who I should even begin to look for to explain this?" Dad was in a real quandary.

"I guess you should ask a neuro-scientist more than any cyber security expert. We need the neuro perspective rather than any IT perspective!" Liu suggested.

"I guess I know someone in that case. He could be the right person" Dad remembered a name.

"Dr. Roy Wallace. NeuroScientist. The gentleman has quite a reputation in the field. I met him a few times at two different wedding parties. We have common friends. I guess I have to reactivate my social media accounts and find his contact!"

Dr. Wallace visits a medical research institute in this city on the second Thursday of every month. That happens to be tomorrow.

Five – Contents of the Glyphs

As per dad's request, Wallace visited our house that Thursday evening. Liu was there as well.

Dad's study is like a nerdy mess, always!

After the usual pleasantries and after introducing Liu, dad broached the topic.

"*Thank you, Dr. Wallace, for making this appointment in such a short time.*" Dad expressed his gratitude.

"*My pleasure! From what you told me over the phone looks like we've got a real curious case here.*" said Wallace.

Dad explained away, divulging the necessary detail, so that Wallace might not miss anything important. As the saying goes – never hide relevant detail from your doctor and your lawyer – in this case Wallace was potentially both.

"*Hmm pretty extraordinary. Let's look at it. Are you obligated to divulge this to NASA, I know you both work for NASA. I mean like reporting this through your official chain of command?*" Wallace asked.

"I have not told anyone besides Liu yet, and Liu has not either. Until we get to the crux of this thing, I thought I should hold on to it. So yes, NASA or anyone does not know anything yet." Dad replied.

"I have not told anyone yet either! Although I guess we will have to at some point." Liu clarified his side.

"Ok, no problem, just asking.. " dad was not sure why that would matter to Wallace anyway.

Dad initialized the programs *Aries* and *Virgo*.

"Dr. Wallace...ready whenever you are?"

"I am, please proceed!"

"Please sit here, and I will let you drive!" Dad made room for Wallace and handed over the mouse to him.

Wallace zoomed in at the first glyph...starting with the hair ball to haywire graph, he zoomed in by a factor of a few thousands, panned side to side, up and down and then the neurons started to show up. After several minutes of fooling around-

*"Whoa, my socks are just blown off my feet! These do not look like any moment-of-time-snapshot of neurons! These are **live** simulations of an active network of neurons! It is almost like looking inside into a person's*

brain at the microscopic level. Never seen anything like this before…this is just extraordinary!" Wallace could not help blabbering. He looked truly astonished, because he was!

The three exchanged a long thoughtful look at each other.

"Now, these things I suppose did not come with an instruction manual written in English that we can run our fingertips on and say, aha, this is what this is. So… we will need to reverse engineer this somehow to understand what it really means. Where do we start is the question, hmm?" Wallace was not talking to anyone in particular, it was more like a soliloquy.

"No clue!" Dad admitted. Wallace continued.

"Okay, just a wild theory here. Just a guess! Whatever it is this glyph is a message, and it is a sensible no-nonsense message that is conveyed in the way it is supposed to be stored inside our brains."

Dad came up with a valid point as well - *"I am thinking on the fly here. If someone is sending us this message, that someone wouldn't send a cryptic message without sending the key to decipher it. So, to your point, what if there is an instruction manual or 'read me' kind of a glyph among the twenty three glyphs that are in the folder? I am thinking, like how an engineer would do a thing. We would not ship a rocket to someone without packing in a detailed literature about its working. "*

For lack of another word, the term **'glyph'** was becoming the accepted term to describe these strange files.

Liu proposed something that looked sensible.

"What if we sort these glyphs by memory size? Might that bring out the obvious outlier in the mix?"

"Possibly! Yes! Surely worth trying. Let's see. I would agree with the idea that the 'instruction manual' would be somewhat of an outlier in the mix, among all these twenty-three files. Hopefully, it should be different in some ways from the rest." Wallace acknowledged the 'instruction manual' idea and the idea of finding it using the outlier technique. His eyes and eyebrows were still pulled together and his left hand still grabbing his mouth, in a deep contemplation.

After sorting by memory size -

"Okay, this here is the smallest file among all of them. It actually is way smaller than the rest."

"Let's open it to see if it is any different!"

Wallace began to zoom in on that specific file. It is the same kind of file except it was about a third as busy, in terms of the number of nodes and connectivity. There was the same endless web of neurons and synapses, in a hair-ball like visual, just a lot less dense than the others. It was not much help off the bat to deduce anything.

"I still have a gut feeling that this file is a special something!" Wallace still pinned some hope on that theory of an *'instruction manual'* file.

Wallace pulled his chair back and turned around so that the three of them were now sitting in a circle facing each other – thinking of a way out of this.

"Everything ultimately is a piece of information and if these are meant to be some kind of a message, there must be a common language here waiting to be found, I guess" Dad thought out aloud.

"The problem is where do we begin?"

"How about if we record our instantaneous brain activity as we think about something or when we look at a physical object and compare that with these neural patterns for a fuzzy match?"

"Sounds like a brute force method. This will involve investment of lots and lots of time in building what sounds like a common vocabulary." Liu made a valid point.

"Yeah, you're right! Taking back my words! Not the quickest way to do this. And also, yeah, just because we see a subset of similar neurons light up when we are shown a particular object, and that matches with any one section in this glyph, does not necessarily mean the message is about that specific object. So, never mind...I take back my thoughts" Dad admitted with a chuckle.

"No, no, please hold that thought. This actually could be one good way to diagnose this challenge. You have brought out the kind of complexity that is reflected in our human language. When we speak we use metaphors to mean something completely different than the object used as the reference in our communications, but the 'common vocabulary' approach definitely sounds like a valid one. Even if this approach demands a lot of time, it could be the only way out of this!" Wallace enriched that line of thought or at least he did not think that approach was ridiculous.

Liu was facing the monitor now and Wallace facing both of them as he turned away from looking at the monitor. There were tons of silence among them as they were thinking of an approach to crack this hard problem. One of the **glyphs** was still on display on the monitor behind Wallace and Liu was staring rather nonchalantly to one particular area of it.

Suddenly Liu looked pretty alarmed and confused.

"What happened?" Dad asked, looking at the terrified Liu.

"I don't know.. it's like I suddenly started to see images, like real live images, of the Earth, as if I am looking at the Earth that is slowly spinning in front of me ... as if I am descending slowly from a spacecraft while the Earth continues to spin in front me... whoa, whoa.."

Wallace and dad were totally confused by Liu's totally unexpected transformation.

"Are you saying you saw something displayed on the monitor?" asked Wallace.

"Hmm, no, not exactly on the monitor or not in the same sense as watching a 4k HD display on a monitor, what I thought I saw was as if everything was happening all around me, like it is real!" Liu is still a bit shaken.

"Did you see us and the other objects in this room?"

"No, I just saw the Earth in front of me. You all, this room, everything here, were all gone! Just the spinning Earth in front of me. I could not even hear your voices!"

".. take a deep breath, calm down", Dad comforted the still short breathed Liu.

Wallace comforted Liu with a calming touch on his shoulders. Liu was visibly terrified from the unexpected experience that he seemed pretty certain that he just had.

And after a few deep breaths, Liu said.

"It's all right, I am okay, just a bit shaken."

"Dr. Liu, can you recall every step that happened leading to this hallucination?"

Wallace asked, and continued.

"I am sorry to call it a 'hallucination' for lack of a better word, and that is the one term I am used to saying in my line of work." Wallace thought the word 'hallucination' might carry a bit of an umbrage.

"No, no, that is ok. It probably was a hallucination. But let me recollect.

Yes, I was staring at that specific area on the monitor. There, where you see that tiny but somewhat more prominent node? That node. Yes, the one with the little reddish kind of a halo around it - that's blinking a little quicker than the others." Liu pointed to that one specific node in the middle of the bottom right quadrant of the screen area.

"Take your time Liu, cool down!" - Dad comforted Liu.

"I am fine, I am fine. I just got caught off guard. I want to try one more time. I want to validate that it is what I thought it is, one more time." Liu asserted rather boldly.

"Hey bud, anytime you get alarmed, just give us a signal." Dad assured Liu.

"Keep talking to us if you see anything, Dr. Liu, and if you get a panic attack again, give us a hand raise, I will be resting my hands on your shoulder..... Remember, we are all here" - Wallace assured.

"Okay, I will..." Liu said.

Wallace's hands were on his shoulder and dad was as close to him as possible, providing psychological comfort by proximity.

"Don't worry, I will be fine....It is kind of like looking through a VR (Virtual Reality), I just did not expect that

to happen without wearing a VR device, which is what got me.", said Liu.

Liu stared at the same region on the monitor for several seconds and just as before he began to see things, again. He then began to speak like a commentator watching a live event as the presumed *'instruction manual'* glyph played out on the monitor.

Here is the transcript of what he spoke out slowly but clearly -

"*That is the Earth in front me like I saw earlier and I am zooming in.. (pause) There... (silence) ...I cannot see or hear anything in this room now. ...(pause) The Earth is rotating and I am still descending....now I hear the sound of the wind as I am descending slowly through the stratosphere, through the clouds. O' my God, this feels so real, I am feeling the air on my skin and on my face..(pause) I am going down and down.. I have touched down on this place. Some grassland. Tall grasses everywhere, I can still look over it.. (pause) Whoa, this feels so real.. I can feel the grass, the wind and the rustle....wait.. I hear something, that's a wild gazelle, running scared through the grass.... It just ran whizzing past my right side, and it is running fast and I feel like I am running right behind it as well. It is gaining distance on me, it is fast...it's like 200 feet ahead of me....whoa, now four tall guys appear from behind me, mostly naked, with spears, like we see in on the Discovery channel, now they all whizzed past me, now...(pause) I am just on close heels behind them, so close that I can even smell their body odor, and see their lean muscles twisting and turning as they chase the gazelle.. looks like they are chasing the gazelle to hunt it down. Appears that they have been on that chase for a while.. (pause) The gazelle appears fatigued now, it is losing ground ...wait , one of the men is pausing and getting ready to throw the spear at the gazelle now, and he does. The spear goes swoosh .., now I am flying in the air now- right behind the spear, the spear drilling through the air ahead of me going in slow motion and it lands on the target, right at the neck of the gazelle, piercing it....blood sprouting from the fatal wound. Ugh...That was too graphic...*

Now I look back, I see the men coming towards me and the gazelle.. it does not feel like that they can see me. But I can see them, these very tall men. Now I see the gazelle being carried away to some place, yes to some kind of a dwelling .. they all seemed to be headed back to their dwellings with the kill. Everything is fast forwarding now and now I see lots of people, waving to us, in anticipation. Uh oh.. everything stopped now, the images are fading away. I think I am back in this room now. I can see you all now..."

Liu withdrew from the monitor and began rubbing his eyes to bring himself back to reality. He opened his eyes after some time and seemed to be 'back'.

"Wow! That was so real, it's hard to tell which is the true reality - that or this."

Wallace and dad too were still recuperating from the shock of what they heard Liu describe all this time.

"But the question is why does Liu see all of that and we don't?" Wallace asked.

"Could it be because the monitor is more curved from our view than from where Liu is sitting? But that does not make any sense either. It is in fact precisely because it is curved that we should see it from the angles that we are seated." Dad thought out loud.

"The point then is," dad continued, *"why didn't I see it yesterday when I looked at it from where Liu is sitting now? Could there be some other contributing factors to it that we have not found yet? Could it because it needs to be set at a certain magnification level?"*

"Let me switch seats with you Dr. Liu, while keeping it at this current magnification level, if you don't mind?" Wallace volunteered.

"Sure, please!" Liu stepped away and made room for Wallace.

Ten seconds of starting later, Wallace began talking just like Liu did.

"I am seeing things now. Yes. There is the Earth in front me...everything...I am approaching the Earth from a spaceship, slowly.......It is so real."

Wallace described the same exact imagery that Liu did a few minutes ago, in his own words.

Several minutes later he withdrew and turned his back on the monitor to face dad and Liu. He let a few long breaths to calm his mind down.

"Would you mind me trying to get a taste of it as well?" Dad asked.

"Absolutely!" Wallace stepped out of the way for dad.

Dad went through the same procedure and saw everything just like the other two gentlemen had described.

It was incumbent on Wallace to find a rational explanation now, he being the presumptive subject matter expert in such matters. It seemed like he had an explanation now and he was working on an appropriate comparative to describe this experience.

"Well, this got to have an explanation ...let me get my head around this..." - Wallace said while he buried his face in his palms.

"I think I can make an attempt to explain here."

There was this strange mixture of awe, angst, curiosity, concern and confusion in the room. Wallace was struggling to find an explanation to this overwhelming vision. And he came up with this.

*"Okay gentlemen, this still is a theory. **Just** a theory.*

Think of a hypnotist. What does a hypnotist do? He first prepares his subject with the appropriate ambience. He begins by talking to his subject in whisper, while holding a clock in his hand that swings like a pendulum. That is the typical imagery that we get when we think of a hypnotist doing his work. Whatever his action may be, it somehow puts the subject into a deep trance shutting him from his surroundings, but the subject can continue to hear the hypnotist clearly. The subject hears only the hypnotist speak and no one else. Everything else in the surrounding does not exist for the subject. This is what that special node in the glyph is probably about. It prepares the mind to receive whatever input on the monitor that is to come next. It is equivalent to the ticking clock that a hypnotist uses." Wallace made a convincing explanation.

And he continued-

"Ordinarily, our awareness of objective reality is built from the inputs that we receive through our visual, auditory and olfactory senses. Our senses are only a means to receive these inputs into our minds. The brain eventually processes these inputs received from our senses by converting them into a completely different form.

So, those special set of blinking neurons that we started from prepared some kind of a back door in the brain for it to receive the information that was to come next from the rest of the web of neurons. The content of this glyph are in the form that is already pre-cooked for us –in the form of the true language of the brain, the way the brain probably communicates and understands things. Staring at those special sets of neurons for some time probably triggers a very specific area of the brain that we didn't know exists and that somehow facilitates the subsequent reception of these millions of blinking nodes directly into our brain by by-passing our usual sensory receptors!

Dad added his thoughts -

*"To your point Dr. Wallace, whoever has generated these glyphs got to have an in-depth understanding of how neurons work. So, instead of using **a** language, which is just a layer on top of that raw form in which the brain understands, it is communicating with us in the rawest possible form, at the level of the neurons itself. A language is just a mapping tool – a way to represent an actual real world object or an idea to a set of neurons that holds the representation of that idea or object. A language is just an additional layer. Have I got this right?"*

"That's it. You just hit the nail on its head, I believe!" Wallace was supportive of that theory.

"So theoretically, if we show these glyphs to a giraffe or a zebra or a lion, after we trigger its back door the right way, that animal should also be able to experience the same vision as we did. Assuming, those other animals have as many neurons as required to receive that information. So, using such a representation we should be able to communicate directly with most living

creatures that have a central nervous system equivalent to something like a brain." Dad added.

"..And each of these glyphs probably contains information that is independent of time and independent of any grammar. And it got to be very scalable too, in the sense that we can easily connect one event to the other which were not connected to begin with, without changing anything in the original events. Am I even adding any value to this, gentlemen?" Liu contributed his thoughts.

"I am sure you are. You both have brought out some solid points. That probably is how things work inside the brain. Unfortunately our language does not reflect that scalability that is already built into the information system of the brain. Our brain is a lot smarter than ourselves by design, even if it may sound like a convoluted paradox!" Dr. Wallace acknowledged.

After watching the next glyph for three more hours they paused to take a break. It did not appear that they were even one fourth of the way through that glyph yet.

Over several long discussions and few more such viewing that figured out that the so-called *'instruction manual'* glyph was just a trailer. And contrary to what they all theorized, every glyph had the same one *'back-door-to-the-mind'* trigger node, so that one does not need to start from the *'instruction manual'* glyph every time to watch another glyph.

"I think this is the limit of what I can take in one day." Wallace declared with a smile at the end of the elapse of several hours.

"Agreed. Hurts my brain too. We can continue from this point, tomorrow." Dad spelled out what was in everyone's mind.

"This is just the first two of the twenty-three glyphs besides the demo glyph. I wonder what must be in the other twenty remaining ones." Liu wondered.

It was almost 3 AM now. They were exhausted. What they just witnessed was a series of moments from the history of the world through the eyes of someone who saw some of the important historical events as it happened first hand. These twenty-three glyphs can be thought of as twenty-three different Netflix series, each of twelve episodes long, and each episode a two hours' worth of view. So far, they were barely done watching one, the trailer glyph and a half of another glyph. Twenty-one and a half more to go. Writing all those down will easily fill up a good portion of a section of world history in a library.

Six - The Trip to Austin

Dr. Wallace frequented our house a few more times in the next few days. In each of his visits he glued himself to the glyphs for hours, taking down notes in detail. Dad watched alongside him as much as he could, time permitting.

After three days of binge watching the first two glyphs, Wallace quit coming from the fourth day in a rather abrupt way. He could not have finished viewing all of the glyphs in the three days that he was here.

Wallace was gone, just like that. He wouldn't respond to any email or to a phone call. He even stopped coming to the medical facility in the city that he used to visit periodically.

For some inexplicable reason dad and Dr. Liu did not divulge the existence of these glyphs to anyone at NASA, up to that point. They felt that there must be something to these glyphs, a higher sense, a bigger picture that they have not found yet. And without them hitting that higher sense first they resisted the compelling justification to share it with more people.

Wallace was with them, he helped in a very important way. But now he is gone, uncontactable and untraceable. Something bothered dad about the way that Wallace disappeared. Wallace, like them now, is privy to some very strange knowledge. Who knows how he would put that into any use.

So far, they have watched only two of the twenty-three – mostly related to the history of the world and the history of technology. These were more like level setting our civilization from the perspective of an outside observer but as viewing things first hand as they occurred in the historical past.

What might be in the rest of the twenty glyphs?

Let me fast forward to the last two glyphs because of what it contained.

These two are the two larger ones among the list.

Out of some strange spark of curiosity dad and Liu decided to watch the twenty-third glyph even before all others before it. It could be months before every glyph could be watched, even just to skim through. Just so you know, the index here is based on the ordered timestamp of their download into dad's computer.

The last glyph was a bit unlike the ones that they have viewed so far. It showed lots of mathematical calculations and schematic process diagrams. Not anything quite within the domain of Liu's or dad's expertise. In the first few minutes of the run of the twenty-third glyph, it revealed one acronym written large in English in the background as – **IPNES**. **IPNES** is the acronym for *Interstellar Propulsion and the Next Earth Summit.* A society of the smartest minds on the planet. IPNES and NASA collaborate on many fronts.

More detail on **IPNES**, soon.

Turned out that Dr. Steinberg from the University of Texas at Austin is the current President of **IPNES**. Quite a reputation he got in the scientific circles, not just as a scientist but also as a diplomat for science. His ability to arrange funds for worthy scientific causes is well known. He and his fellow scientist - professor Kobayashi – are the duo who could convince any lawmaker to set aside any needed fund for an important scientific program. Dad knew Dr. Steinberg slightly from a one off meeting, but they were not exactly in any communication with each other, just that one meeting.

The next major **IPNES** summit starts next Tuesday where the top hundred minds of the planet will gather to deliberate on some heavy duty science topics.

Dad sent an email to Dr. Steinberg the night before. There was no response to the email as of twenty four hours later. Dad did not have his phone number to reach out directly either. He called up Liu, again.

*"Liu, I guess it is time for a road trip to Austin. We will need to catch Dr. Steinberg before he leaves for the **IPNES** summit at Genève next week. I am just assuming that he has not been looking at his emails lately, so."*

Austin is a short two and a half hour trip from Clear Lake.

Dad and Liu decided to make that trip. An hour later they were on the road, driving to Austin. By 8.00 PM CDT they were inside the UT campus.

University of Texas Campus, department of Physics. The last graduate-level class of the evening got over an hour ago.

So everyone pretty much left the Physics building for the week. In one of the offices in the department the lights were still on. Someone must be working late on a Friday evening.

And incidentally, to their relief, that someone was Dr. Steinberg.

The President of **IPNES**, Dr. Steinberg, was getting his own paper ready for presentation at the upcoming world summit of **IPNES** at Genève, Switzerland, and was working late into the evening. He was all alone in the entire building, even the department secretary who usually stays long after, was long gone by then.

Dad knocked on the professor's door. A surprised Dr. Steinberg, not knowing who to expect, carefully opened the door.

"Our apologies to you for coming to you this way Dr. Steinberg, with no prior appointment. (cleared his throat) We did send an email to you. We assumed you might not have read it yet. We could not wait, because of the nature of this thing and we learnt that you are leaving early tomorrow to Genève."

"I am sorry I could not recognize you!"

Dad introduced himself and Liu, reminded the septuagenarian professor of the last time that he bumped into him at a conference in Austin.

"I remember you now. Oh, yes. Dr. Song. How are you? C'mon in. I was working on finishing a paper before I fly tomorrow."

"What we have to show you might totally influence your paper and all that you and the others are slated to discuss at Genève. Since it's this late, and we understand how valuable your time is, I would straightway rush to the point. If you allow us, could we show you?"

"Okay! Sure, please do!"

Steinberg would not have liked to be disturbed, but he sensed an exception here that might justify an interruption.

After taking a seat on the sofa facing Dr. Steinberg in his office lounge, dad began.

"Let me explain to you briefly what it is all about, Dr. Steinberg, while Liu would set up things." Dr. Song began.

"Okay, I am all ears."

Dad explained the reason why they were here and in this manner – a quick rundown of what it is all about. *"...so...these last few glyphs show us a lot of machinery that we have never seen before. It takes us through a tour of hundreds of engineering drawings and measurements and a lot of theories as well. There is this equation for example, resembling Einstein's General*

*Theory of Relativity, followed by many more such. This is all outside my field of work. At some point it shows us this acronym - **IPNES**, flashing in the background in large fonts.*

*We knew **IPNES**, of course, and knew you as its current President. We googled and learnt that the world summit was starting in three days, so we drove all the way here to meet you in person before you left. The Friday traffic delayed us somewhat."* Dad ended his briefing.

Liu was done with his set up which mostly involved getting the curved monitor from the car and to set it up inside Steinberg's office, followed by remoting to the machine that was at Dad's study back home to access the glyphs remotely.

Before the start of the journey dad tried to copy the glyphs to a portable external drive, but the memory size of each being a whopping few dozen gigabytes took him forever to do it.

Liu placed a chair facing the curved monitor for Dr. Steinberg to sit. He explained to him about the procedure such as where he should begin looking at the glyphs from when it loads and after it is magnified sufficiently.

"Now if I may ask you Dr. Steinberg, please look at this, here, yes, and begin by looking at this group of synapses, the ones that are blinking brighter than the others, and stare at it for like five seconds. It could be shocking to you at first as you will see life like illusions all around and you will feel immersed yourself in it. You will **not** *hear our voices or see us when that happens. And when you want to come out of it, just give us a signal or close your eyes for ten seconds or just look away from the monitor, everything will be back to normal after that."*

"Okay" said Steinberg. There was some apprehension in his mind, totally understandably so. He could not yet fully assimilate what he just heard from a couple of gentlemen who do look pretty decent and sincere otherwise. What he heard them say does not make any sense at all. These surely are good stuff for a fiction, but do not sound like there is any science in it. Science - he knows a whole lot more than most people on the planet.

As suggested by Liu he began to focus on the specific area of the first glyph where those special blinking synapses were. A few seconds later he pulled himself out by closing his eyes. After he recovered he was in total disbelief at what he just experienced and his eyes were rather wide opened trying to process that experience in his mind.

Just as dad and Liu expected, the **glyph** successfully established a perfect communication with Dr. Steinberg, in the language of his brain.

The last two glyphs talk about a new drive, a new propulsion system, unlike anything we have known so far. It claims of a true interstellar travel-worthy propulsion system that supposedly tears space-time apart, not just the space-time of our three dimensional universe but across several other dimensional existences. The cosmic limit of the speed of light does not apply to its working. What kind of science is that? Not anything we have ever known.

It was as if Prof. Steinberg lived his entire life for this one moment. The dream drive, the sets of equations, the required engineering to build it – all there in the two last glyphs.

Steinberg watched the last glyph for a good two hours, playing with the zoom and the pan controls, noting down the equations on a scratchpad.

Finally he bailed out of it. He closed his eyes, took a few long breaths to come back to the familiar reality from the other reality. That other reality that he was immersed in for the past two hours was completely indistinguishable from the reality that he experiences every day. That other reality had tons of knowledge for him to pick from limited only by his ability to absorb.

They were eager to hear whatever he had to say. And he said, while still rubbing his eyes -

"Gentlemen, if what you showed me is true and if this is the true nature of existence in a much deeper sense, mankind is forever indebted to you, and I am deeply indebted to you for choosing me to be the first to see this. I just can't thank you enough." He spoke slowly from the depth of his mind.

*"We really did not choose anything. Someone or something chose us and apparently they chose you too, because without the acronym **IPNES** flashing there in that glyph, we would not be here to find you."* Dad admitted. Dr. Steinberg continued -

"The glyphs talk of the existence of higher dimensions. Many of us were suspecting that the higher dimensions do exist. We just had no clue how to prove that experimentally. We speculated on the possibility that the force exerted by dark matter in our universe could actually originate in some higher dimension because

we could not understand them in the context of our own dimension of existence.

We needed this help, we just could not have figured all these out by our limited human mind.

Okay.. It's getting late for tonight. Wish we had more time to talk.

I will take this knowledge to the IPNES summit, for which I am going to Genève tomorrow- as you already know. Gentlemen, we might need you both to fly there too. Please book your tickets for any of the days from Monday till Friday. Your expenses will all be reimbursed. ` `

And he continued.

"*There is no point in working on my paper now, it just became obsolete by a thousand years*" He chuckled.

"*However, gentlemen, I am sure you all understand the extreme sensitivity of this stuff that you have here. Please keep it extremely confidential, including withholding this information from NASA for the time being. I know it is difficult for you to do given your terms of employment with NASA. I will reach out to the Director of NASA, a good friend of mine and he's an*

IPNES member as well. I will explain to him why you did not follow the usual chain of command to report this.

At Genève we will deliberate on this, and decide on the next step. We might have to keep all these glyphs in a secured vault."

Dad and Liu both nodded their consents. They felt relieved in their minds, knowing that **IPNES** is the right home for these strange **glyphs**. This might be why they have been waiting so far to report this - in a strange coincidence, yeah.

After some pauses, Steinberg came up with the necessary distraction of the moment.

"You guys have been on the wheels for a good three hours, why don't we all get some dinner at Texas de Steak?"

"That sounds like real food!" Dad remarked.

"Don't we have to reserve a table?" Liu asked.

"Not with Benny. Benny owns the place. We have been buddies since the beginning of recorded history. He will find a place for us." Steinberg winked and dialed a number as he spoke.

"All righty, know the address? Or you might just want to follow me in your cars?"

All that I have told you about the **glyphs** so far are based on what my dad will have told me in a very distant future, as I was not privy to the developments that happened while I was still a student, then, when it all happened. I knew nothing about them at that time.

Seven – Kobayashi and Mirrang

Let me take a quick break from our discussion. In that break let me present a conversation between two gentlemen and introduce the two gentlemen along the way, as well. The conversation happened in the same year of 2034 when the glyphs first appeared.

Somewhere in a small academic township in the state of California, two gentlemen were taking some time off from their work on a lazy Sunday afternoon – one, a renowned physicist, and the other a much younger academic, a first year undergraduate in mathematics. They were seated on a bench in the park, facing the pond that was in the shape of the letter **S**. The pond covered a good third area of the rectangular park.

This was much like the conversations that dad and I used to have, except this is more between a mentor and a mentee.

These two gentlemen were talking about- well ……..the universe.

"I will be too surprised if the universe had a beginning as we like to believe that it had." Dr. Kobayashi, the older of the two, started the thread of a new conversation.

Dr. Kobayashi is well known and respected in the scientific community.

"I don't quite get that?" Asked Mirrang, a final year undergraduate student who happened to work as a Research Assistant with Dr. Kobayashi. Mirrang's father and Professor Kobayashi are good friends.

His friends call him Mirr.

"Well, if you think about it, the notion that the universe has a beginning is even more unlikely an idea than the idea of not having a beginning!"

"Why?"

"Because it immediately begets the question - what was there before the beginning?"

"Hmm...how about..... Nothing?"

"From nothing to everything?.... and all in a fraction of a fraction of a second? That is even harder to wrap a mind around, isn't it? What was in that nothing that caused everything to burst forth into existence? Something? Then we land into 'something' that caused it. 'Something' that was already there in that nothing which means that the question just got pushed back a step further."

"Okayyy." Mirr was listening.

"Possibly, it is a cyclical universe - one that goes through repeated cycles of birth and death, of creation and dissolution, all the time, and across vast spans of time. With a long period of quiescent intervals in between. The notion of a 'beginning' is just how our human minds are wired to think of things. We think in terms of a 'beginning' of a process or of an event. What if we actually could get comfortable with the idea that there does not have to be a 'beginning' - of anything! No process we see in our daily life 'really' has an absolute beginning. Every beginning has a prior or begins from the end of another process! So, nothing begins and nothing ends, things just dissolve into other things.

"So, this universe came about from another prior universe that collapsed ...and the whole thing repeats, repeats and repeats, perpetually?" Mirr asked.

"Correct, that is what cyclical means!" Dr. Kobayashi responded.

"If it is cyclical, what will cause that reversal at the end of the current expansion phase of the universe?"

"I guess, we have not figured that out yet." - was Kobayashi's short answer this time.

There was some pause and Mirr asked.

"Is ours the only universe that there is?"

"For a very long time in the ancient times we used to assume an Earth centric universe. From that position we moved to the Helio-centric universe, and then to a single galaxy universe to now an infinite number of clusters of galaxy universes. So, if that trend holds, there could very much be an infinite cluster of universes out there, each with its own kinds of matter and each with its own laws of physics, no?

Just do this thought experiment? Think of several tiny explosions that are so far apart from each other that they don't affect each other at all. So, let's say each of these explosions created one universe, like the one we live in. In this scenario, all these universes still exist in this same three-dimensional existence"

"I guess, it's possible - since we don't have any evidence to the contrary!"

"If that is the case, also possible is the possibility that there are some other kinds of universes that are not really that far away, but right here, just happens to exist in another plane of existence.

Let's frame this argument as a question. Is anything stopping those other universes from existing in some totally different set of dimensions from our and from each other? Or, what is so sacrosanct about this three-dimensional existence of ours that no other configurations of dimensions are possible?"

"Hmmm...okay.. can't rule out that possibility either!" Mirr was not sure how to frame another question around that thought.

"It could be that there may be other kinds of matter and energy out there in those other universes from the other dimensions that we can never interact with."

"Hmm! Logical, maybe!" Mirr thought.

There was some pause in the conversation at that point - only the chirping of birds and crickets filling in the void of silence. And then Dr. Kobayashi broke the silence again.

"Interestingly enough, at least one ancient philosophy laid down a detailed treatise on this infinitely repeating cosmic life cycle and on the subject of the time scale of this universe. I am referring to ancient Hindu Philosophy. Some ancient Hindu philosophies suggest the existence of distinct Yugas, such as the Kalpa, Maha Kalpa, and Manavantara yugas. These are stated to be

extremely large time spans in the cyclical life cycle of **this** *universe. They did not leave behind any conversion table to translate that time scale to a modern measure of time."*

"Does it mean that the ancient Hindus or at least some of the philosophers in that culture were right all along?" Mirr had roots that go to that region of the world.

"Not saying that they were right on everything. The fantastic stories and beings mentioned in some of the same ancient Hindu scriptures may just be figments of their imaginations. But just on this specific subject of the cyclical nature of this universe, of the large time spans, and the probable existence of multi-verses and other kinds of worlds- the ancient Hindus did wonder about these ideas in their minds!

Something that we are arguably doing – now." Dr. Kobayashi made somewhat of a concluding point.

"Hmmm… !"

After another spell of a long silence Mirr spoke first.

"So, uncle, please make a bold prediction - How will this Earth and how will humanity eventually end?" Mirr sometimes addresses Dr. Kobayashi as 'uncle'

although they are not related through blood. Kobayashi knew Mirr since he was a child as Mirr's dad and he have been very good friends since their days at the University.

"I would say violently, just as many violent events caused our coming into existence, another violent event will cause our annihilation!"

"So, it will not be a smooth decline to total dissolution?"

"Probably not! The nature of the physical world is one of violent interactions followed by phases of quiescent periods in between. Many collisions formed this Earth and one or more collisions will end it. We exist in between collisions."

"Got it..." Mirr responded.

"Much before the next collision takes us out, we might need to find another planet to inhabit simply because there seems to be no collective will to arrest our population growth any time. The Earth cannot sustain so many of us.

The big problem of finding the next planet is of course the cosmic limit of speed, the speed of light of course. That limitation makes it impossible for us to reach that next habitable planet within any realistic human *lifetime! We will have to figure out achieving speed much **Faster than Light** somehow, without that talking of interstellar flight is just a flight of fancy!"*

"Yes!"

*"If we can invent our way to achieving **Faster than Light** velocity, we conquer death and become immortal as a species."*, Dr. Kobayashi winded up the topic.

"I never understood that, what does immortality have anything to do with speed of travel anyway?"

"There are two parts to that statement. One, by inhabiting other planets we reduce our chances of getting annihilated if a Global mass extinction event were to happen. The second part of that statement is ingrained in the act of traveling at near light speed itself.

Think of a beam of light, by the way that was Einstein's favorite vehicle of imagination, that tiny beam of light."

"Okay..."

"That one beam of light, a photon, ... leaves a beautiful star in Galaxy X, and travels towards us. Okay? It's a journey that will take a long, long time from the standpoint of our time scale because we are two millions light years away from that Galaxy X, for

example.. But for that tiny happy photon, which travels at the speed of light, time is - **frozen**. If that photon wore a wrist watch, it would seem as if no time has passed while it traveled the entire millions of light years that it traveled. It will feel that it is immortal and it probably is, in that sense."

"Got it..So, if we can travel at the speed of light we will feel that we have reached our destination instantaneously, because our biological clock stopped or slowed down too. Is that the correct understanding?"

"Probably.. at least theoretically.."

"What if we traveled at faster than light speed (FTL)? Will we be able to travel backward in time? How does that work?"

"I don't think we can ever go back to the past. That will mean that the grandfather paradox will apply. I guess by traveling at FTL we will just arrive at the destination early and quickly. It is like - 'Hey Mirr, your class does not start until after an hour, and you are here already? Did you take the FTL bus to school?'" Kobayashi laughed at his own joke.

How **FTL** distorts time is just not conceivable to our minds, no one knows it yet.

For now, the law of the universe still is –

Thou shall not travel faster than the speed of light!

It so happens that Mirr is the son of Dr. Denzing - if you remember him from the beginning of this chronicle.

Denzing, the unassuming Asian looking boy from a tiny corner of the North East of India named as 'Dings' by his friends at Berkeley, driven and motivated by his witnessing that one life-changing event as a child, worked his entire life to advance the cause of science, specifically, of the physics of Antimatter. One day in the future he will help build that Antimatter drive to achieve the kind of hypervelocity needed for overcoming the enormous interstellar distances.

The theory of Antimatter (**MAM**) was still on a scratch paper, and the Anti-matter propulsion system not yet attempted – and that starship was not yet built.

After decades of concerted efforts by some of the best minds in the game, backed by the will of a nation, **MAM** would eventually emerge from fiction and become a reality someday. The **MAM** propulsion system will be used for the last cruising part of an interstellar travel.

Science is a multi-generational effort. The life of a human being as short as it is, it will not be Dr. Denzing, but his son who will ride that **Matter-Antimatter** powered ship that Dr. Denzing will have helped develop.

Dr. Denzing, now in his late Seventies, has been working tirelessly on the **Matter-Antimatter** Interstellar propulsion system for the last thirty years as the lead scientist of the program.

The lab prototypes for **MAM** are already looking very encouraging in achieving the kind of hypervelocity that we would need for interstellar travel.

But the **principal propulsion system,** the kind only that can propel a starship through the vast distances of the cosmos in any reasonable human life-time, will still elude us at that time. If ever such a propulsion system becomes a reality, it will be a different beast altogether – a totally different beast.

Beyond the human mind, out of this world!

One day, I will know Mirr, know him as my fellow crew member and a trusted friend.

IPNES

Eight - The Great Propulsion Debate at IPNES

Songa - my father, once told me that there was one major conference, one very consequential meeting of the top minds that charted the course that humanity would take in its endeavor to find the next home beyond planet Earth. That conference caught the attention of the world.

The first conference in the series happened towards the end of the year 2020, before I was born, before the **glyphs** appeared.

This conference and the series of conferences to follow were some of the most consequential scientific deliberations in the history of mankind. This series that started in 2020 had nothing to do with the **glyphs** to begin with until 14 years later when the **glyphs** first appeared in dad's machine and landed at IPNES through Dr. Steinberg. From that point onward all future conferences would be dominated by the **glyphs**.

I thought it might be a good occasion to go back to the beginning of the series and talk about the very first conference in the series before talking about the upcoming 14th conference in the same series to be hosted at Genève - the one that would be the most consequential yet, and at which dad and Liu were asked to attend.

I felt that telling about this very first conference was necessary to appreciate how limited we were in our ability to travel to the next star before the **glyphs** showed us the way.

The very first conference was hosted somewhere in Paris, in a conference hall of a hotel, where several scientific luminaries from different countries gathered for a ten-day long event. The invitees were the top minds in the field of Astrophysics, Astronomy, Mathematics, Philosophy, Chemistry, Quantum Physics, and Biology. The conference was on the subject of- *Interstellar Propulsion and the Next Earth Summit.* Hence the name **IPNES**.

There were discussions on the subject of Faster than Light (FTL) travel as well. The point of this specific conference was to develop a 50-year long program – like *Orion*, to discuss the possibility of interstellar travel within a reasonable span of a human lifetime so as to find a new home for most species of Earth.

This initiative was inspired by three events.

The first one was the promising development in the field of Anti-matter production. Scientists were confident that by the end of the decade we will be able to produce antimatter in enough quantities required to power the acceleration of a large spaceship to achieve up to 15% the speed of light, assuming the material of the ship can handle that enormous speed.

The second event was a development in medical science that promised the possibility of increasing the average human lifespan by thirty years in the near future.

The third - the two Voyager probes soon after they left the solar system for interstellar space had sent us messages that indicated how hostile the cosmos is, even starting as close to home as just beyond our solar neighborhood. The two Voyagers reported back how a gigantic envelope of ionized plasma from interstellar space is pushing hard against the heliosphere of the Sun. And by extension, it gave us a chilling realization of how vulnerable we were to the onrush of deadly showers of interstellar materials including radiations should the protective shield of the Sun's heliosphere weaken for any reason. It was as if our fort was under siege by celestial elements waiting to breach the gate and raring to take a go at us, like the ancient barbarians would have been at the gate of Rome. By the time we would know what was coming it might be just too late to prepare for any defense. We need to be prepared and prepare in advance. That preparation must begin in advance – which is why this series of conferences was so imperative.

One kind of a preparation could be to build a ship that can take us to a safe world. The agenda of the very first conference therefore was to debate - on the direction of that preparation.

A crucial part of that preparation would be to strive for speed close to the speed of light, if not faster. At the least, we need to attain a good fraction of that speed if we really have to find a new planet to call home within the lifetime of one generation.

The eleven brightest minds were seated around the long oval table when the meeting convenor arrived.

I being the narrator of this tale will however take the privilege of shortening the participants' names by just their initials – just for brevity and for reasons that the specific names of the participants do not matter.

"Good evening gentlemen!"

"*Evening*" - responded the audience.

"*Gentlemen, I deliberately chose this time of the evening and not the morning, because I really expect our minds to wander free when we speak our thoughts. Even a mere scientific instinct is welcome, it does not have to be a proven theorem or in the thoroughness of a published paper. The evening is when our minds run free, unshackled, more than any other time of the day – as one psychologist friend would tell me.*

We will try to extrapolate much beyond what we already know within our proven collective wisdom. We will dwell in the realm where science and fiction could overlap. We are looking to get the faintest beacon of light, the tiniest spark that is hidden deep inside your brilliant minds. So nothing is off-limits."

"*Where are the bottles of single malt whiskeys for that to happen?*" Professor V quipped.

"*I would prefer Bourbons instead!*"

There was a general chuckling murmur.

"*We can't possibly refuse a chance to speak anything we like, especially in the evening and not being in the presence of our wives, can we?*" Dr. P's quip generated some laughter.

"*Agreed, agreed...*", the convener chuckled in agreement.

"*Okay, we would go round table on our responses, but please be free to speak out of turn. In our situation it is not the same thing as interrupting. So here is the first question to you all. Should we look to settle on another planet and is it even possible, considering the enormous interstellar distances and the speed limit of the universe?*"

"*What else should we do besides writing papers for each other in the twisty scholarly language anyway?*" that was a response from prof. G. Everyone chuckled.

The convener, an elderly gentleman, a famous astrophysicist himself, continued, "*Would you please take the first shot at the problem, professor?*"

"*Yeah, sure! We must keep looking into the cosmos and we must keep inventing. Should we look for the next planet for a home? Sure we should, whether or not we could get there. But in looking, we expand our horizon, we stumble into new discoveries. And in that looking we might figure out some way around the cosmic speed limit, who knows!*"

The august assembly spoke of several other things, exploring several different lines of thoughts. One thing I would reproduce here as it was pertinent to what would unfold in the future. Let's say it is also pretty interesting.

"Gentlemen, many of us at some time or other in the past touched on the possibility of the existence of multi-verses. To say in another way we at least cannot deny the possibility of such existences. What would be our thoughts on that - today? Anyone?" The convener broached the topic.

*"I would say, everyone. Everyone is a **multiverser** these days. You can't deny or accept what you can't prove or disprove, yet."* Prof. M spoke.

"I...agree! Could you say some more on that, Professor?"

"Yes! I reason it this way -

One fine morning I woke up to life on a lonely island, in the middle of the Pacific with no other islands for hundreds of miles in any direction, and I say - whoa - this is the only island in all existences! There cannot be any other island or other kinds of islands! How me-centric is that? In that sense it is possible that other existences exist. Maybe things in there are made of such matters that are nothing like ours. So different that we

- from any of our perspectives, just cannot fathom what those other matters could be!"

"Agree..."

"It is also possible that matters of this universe actually came from those other verses, they just got transformed. So every atom or particle knows where it came from if only it could speak. It might also know that under some circumstances it can still go back to where it came from! There may be pathways, a lots of them, we just don't know!"

I won't detail each of the conversations among all these luminaires. Instead I will just summarize what they talked about in the first day of the summit[‡]

So here are some of the notable points that came out of this first conference -

A – There are a very large number of potential Earth-like exoplanets just within 200 light years from the Earth.

B – The existing technologies cannot take us across the enormous distances to any of these candidate planets in any reasonable timeframe. Parker Solar probe, which is the fastest man-made object yet– will reach a velocity of 430,000 miles an hour by 2024 from its current velocity. Even at that speed it will take 1561 years to cover one light-year. So, to cover 4.2 light-years to Proxima Centauri B, our nearest stellar neighbor –will take a whopping 6556 Years.

C – The cosmic speed limit is a severely limiting factor for any possible interstellar travel.

D - Even if we could achieve a theoretical max speed comparable to the speed of light, the average speed will still be a lot less, depending on how far we aim for. That is because we will need to accelerate in the beginning for a considerable period of time and slow down for as long before reaching the destination.

‡ (*A transcript of the detailed conversations is in a separate supplement to this book*)

E - The possible engines of the future are Antimatter Propulsion, EM Drive, SEP drive, Fusion powered drive.

F - There are the popular drives from science-fiction such as – Warp Drive, Black hole drive, etc. We actually would need something in the order of these drives to truly overcome the enormous interstellar distances.

G – Multi-verses are a possibility.

Nine–Austin to Genève

Let us fast forward to the all-important 14th conference in the series, fourteen years after the first. Year 2034.

Like Dr. Steinberg had asked, dad and Liu were on a plane to Genève, come Monday. What dad and Liu will show in that conference will take the world in a different direction from there on – a fundamentally different one.

Dad played the twenty third glyph to all the attending scientists at IPNES at once as they sat facing a monitor each. It was rare to be able to shock an audience such as this all at the same time by any single new discovery. In this case it was equivalent to a series of extraordinary discoveries.

They all were just floored and flabbergasted.

After a day-long session of watching – Professor Steinberg addressed his colleagues in the conference before the conclusion of the day's session.

"Gentlemen, there are these gifts from someone to humanity, a gift to advance our civilization by thousands of years in one shot. Who are they, where

*are they, and why would they do that to favor us, we
don't know. We probably shall never find out. But
whoever they are, they want us to make that trip to the
stars.*

*So our quest for the elusive engine that we need to
travel the cosmos culminates here, at least for now."*

*"This is just, just, just unbelievable. I am still not back
in one piece."* Dr. Lorentz, gave words to what
everyone else had in mind.

*"We have to move these files or glyphs, whatever you
call it, to a secured vault. The power hidden in these
glyphs can be totally misused."* Dr. Chandra spoke.

"Gentlemen, was any copy of these glyphs made?"
asked Dr. Yakama.

"No sir, these are the only copies that there are." Dad
replied. Liu nodded in support.

*"Gentlemen, until we figure out what could be some of
the outcomes of revealing this to the public at large, we
all will have to take the oath of secrecy, to keep this in
absolute confidentiality. I am afraid, Dr. Song, and Dr.
Liu, and anyone else who has seen these already, must
also be sworn into secrecy. So I would say please ask
them to get on the next plane to Genève. We will cover*

their expenses." Dr. Tao, one of the much respected scientists opined.

Dad and Liu nodded.

Dad let the conference know about Dr. Wallace and how he could not be contacted anymore.

That was a cause for concern. A leakage in the form of Wallace, a loose cannon, has already happened.

This was already too much even for this audience to absorb in one session. The discussion would continue for the next few days. This conference would now be extended for several more days.

On the third day the executive committee addressed the question of how should any program proceed from there on.

"Gentlemen, we still have to decide on the important question of whether we should inform our respective governments, or if we should carry on any program we take up based on knowhow revealed in these glyphs outside of any government interventions and independent of any national politics. My personal opinion is we keep this to this group alone until we figure out otherwise." Dr. Tao brought up the topic.

"*While I agree with you Dr. Tao, I am also concerned with the question of how we can keep such a big, earth-shaking revelation a secret from the governments, and how we will be able to generate the kind of funds needed to develop this technology if the governments are not told about it?*", Dr. Reuben made a valid concern.

"*We have to develop this under the umbrella of some of the current initiatives such as the many well- funded programs that we are currently exploring. If the fund dries up we will have to make up some reason to funnel funds from elsewhere. Even crowdsourcing funds under some other alibi could be another option.*" Dr. Tao elaborated.

"*Hmmm..I think Tao has a point there!*", Dr. Johansen and Dr. Tao are childhood buddies and they do not address each other with the title of Dr. like most other professors prefer to address each other.

"*I think I agree..*" Steinberg threw his weight behind.

"*I am afraid, gentleman, we will need the server that contains the glyphs to be moved here, into a secured vault.*" Steinberg directed his statement to dad

"*Everything is in my home computer system. The programs **Aries** and **Virgo** that we need to view the* *glyphs are a third party tool that I am evaluating for NASA at the moment. So, we don't have the source code for these programs, we only have the executable programs."* Dad let them know.

"I am afraid we will have to talk to that third party and buy all the rights of that software. Has NASA made an offer to them on that software?" Steinberg asked.

"I don't think so. We are still evaluating a few other software." Dad replied.

"Okay, great. I will speak with the director of NASA. He is slated to come here tomorrow to attend this conference. So we will settle all that here. Good!" Dr. Tao spoke. He is the Co-Chair of **IPNES** with Dr. Steinberg.

In a very far future I will learn from a message that dad left for me that NASA brought all the rights of the two software from **Labyrinz.**

Explained in the twenty-third and in the twenty-second glyph was the science of **WARGER.** As we will use the terms **WARGER** energy and **WARGER** drive frequently, we will refer to the two collectively as the **WARGER** system in our further discussions. The name **WARGER** probably was an acronym, the **glyph** where it featured the very first time does not say what it stands for. The term came from the twenty-second glyph. It was in the background, as a graffiti on a wall. The science behind **WARGER** seemed far too complex for anyone – even for the bright minds at **IPNES**. It was given in the **glyphs** as a series of formulae, and in a collection of blueprints and engineering diagrams.

In the science of **WARGER** lay the answer to the deep connections between our dimension and the other dimensions or verses if we can call them as such. It had the solution for overcoming the enormous interstellar distances in a faster than light speed, effectively. Much faster, actually - many order of magnitudes faster! The way to achieve that, as the science of **WARGER** prescribed, was by generating the fifth force of nature – something that we did not know exists! It showed how the four forces of nature that we are familiar with transcend across dimensions. The four forces of nature that we are quite familiar with are -- *gravity, strong nuclear force, weak nuclear force,* and *electromagnetic force.* It showed us how to generate the fifth force to create an incomprehensible state of matter called the **WARGER** *bubble.*

Think of the *Tesla coil* – by the use of just one of the fundamental forces of nature - *electromagnetism,* it steps up the ordinary level of voltage to an extremely high electric potential that breaks down the surrounding air. If we extend this analogy to include three more of the fundamental forces of nature all acting in perfect synchronicity producing a resonance like situation where the fabric of space-time itself breaks down – we get the **WARGER** conditions. That broadly is the idea. But yes it goes deep, much deeper than that. Probably no analogy is appropriate enough to comprehend this force.

The **WARGER** theories also provided us with a deeper understanding of how these forces act at a distance without anything connecting the force source and the object on which they act.

It was as if whoever sent us these glyphs intended it for us to build a series of Arks to rehabilitate humanity in other planets without explicitly telling us everything about how that science works or how the universe or universes really works. But we could not have complained. At the deepest level, the nature of reality is probably such that a human brain will never understand fully. Never!

We just may not have the necessary hardware in our brain to understand it in any depth. Our brain is made of stuff from our three-dimensional universe and which probably is why it is not equipped to understand anything more complex than that.

From this point on scientists and engineers will join hands to build the first prototype of the **WARGER** drive using the blueprint provided by the last few **glyphs**.

The site for the first **IDP** was selected as somewhere near the Colorado Plateau, precisely because of its contours, the rocky foundation, and steep vertical façade that is needed for the specific design of the IDP port system. As per the architecture prescribed in the **glyphs**, a huge U shaped electromagnetic core will be buried deep inside the rock in a specific orientation to Earth's magnetic lines of forces. An identical core will start from the vertical side of the rocky façade and run at 30 degree to the surface. Both cores will run below the rocky surface of the plateau but well above the sea level.

This airport equivalent for the **WARGER** launch was named IDVLP – *Inter-Dimensional Vehicle Launch Port*, which later was shortened to -just **IDP**.

A few years later, while the **WARGER** System was being developed under the cover of other big ticket programs a lot of things had happened in the lives of some people who had any knowledge of the **glyphs**.

Dr. Liu, a planetary data scientist at NASA and a good friend of dad, had developed amnesia, to the point that he did not remember anything about any of the times that he and dad had spoken about the **glyphs** or any memory of the conference that he had attended. But not dad, for some reason, dad was spared from that mind delete.

The CEO of **Labyrinz** suffered from the same amnesia as Dr. Liu. The entire team of software engineers and architects of **Labyrinz** who built the two programs suffered similar selective amnesiac conditions. After the Genève trip dad called the CEO of **Labyrinz** and his chief architect Raul, one after another. They just did not recall any of the phone conversations that they had with him in that fall evening of that year of 2034!

The programs - *Aries* and *Virgo* with all their source codes were shipped to **IPNES** after NASA purchased all the rights to the programs. The source codes will stay in the secured vault of IPNES thereafter. Only the eleven top scientists of IPNES and dad had any access to the source code.

The development of the **WARGER** system will move forward undercover.

By the year 2042, two of the eleven **IPNES** scientists passed away due to natural causes. Dr. Steinberg was still strong at eighty-one.

Unbeknownst to us all, we were living on an Earth that was under a doomsday clock. We were the children of a time of threatening geological disturbances and of an impending global extinction. Except a very few people, dad included, no one knew anything about all that with any certainty, up to that point.

Dad became an **IPNES** member soon after the conference. He, like them, was oath bound not to divulge this to anyone.

The world summit of **IPNES** grew in fame and recognition worldwide with several million followers, mostly the younger generations –the ones twenty five and under. The world was told that **IPNES** was developing an Anti-Matter Propulsion Engine. The propulsion system that could give us the stars. This also was a fact that matter-Anti-matter drive (**MAM**), which dwelt in the realm of fiction until recently, was fast becoming the candidate for primary drive for interstellar travel thanks to several engineering breakthroughs during the last decade.

(Let me take a step back on that. MAM will be the second primary drive actually. Please note that I am not saying the word 'secondary' here - because it is not. You will know why as we move on.)

The weakest link in the chain now was the material of the spaceship and not the drive anymore. The ability of the material of the spaceship to withstand the kind of acceleration that **MAM** could theoretically generate would determine the practically achievable speed of the star ship as one whole unit.

MAM caught the imagination of the world. Every young man and woman would want to be part of that endeavor. Besides **MAM**, two other propulsion systems were also being developed on a war footing by other scientific agencies. The well-understood Fusion power drive and the SEP (Solar Energy Propulsion).

While theoretical Physicists from past and present perfected the theories of **MAM**, engineering the theory was up to the Jet Propulsion Labs at Pasadena, California. One of the leading gentlemen of that engineering effort was Dr. Denzing, reiterating it just one more time – I am sure you remember.

His son Mirrang will be one of the pilots of that engine along with Professor Taushi Saito and me, some day in the future.

All these experimental drives are linear – in the sense that they propel matter along the curvature of space-time, like going in a straight line from a point A to the point B - through space.

The real McCoy was the **WARGER** drive powered by **WARGER** energy.

The **WARGER** drive was different, it would not respect the vast linear separation of distances between two points in space. It would not create a wormhole nor warp space-time. It does things differently, very differently, as we'll see.

Our ability to engineer it would determine if our species survives in the event that we need to escape Earth.

The theories and the blueprints were there - given to us, the only question was can we actually build it?

A Quick Note

Just so you might want to keep in mind
....

The three domains of operation for the three phases of Pegasus.

WARGER phase – to overcome the enormous distance in the order of parsec or light years via higher dimensions.

MAM phase - for distance less than 1 AU to destination. (1 Astronomical Unit – distance from Sun to Earth)

FUSION phase – during orbital run and entry into the gravitation field of the destination planet until landing.

Ten – Mystery of Wallace

Let's dwell a bit more in the year 2034 - *the year of the glyphs*. That *year* deserves its own tag considering the earth-shaking impact that year would leave on the planet.

In a very far future and in an extraordinary setting, Dr. J Song - my dad, will tell me all about it.

Dad suspected Dr. Roy Wallace might have made copies of one or more of those **glyphs** during one of those long sittings. He also might have copied the two programs - *Aries* and *Virgo*, which he would need to visualize the **glyphs**. One without the other would be useless for him.

But whatever happened to Wallace?

I had told you once that Wallace had vanished after the last meeting with dad at our home and that dad tried but could not contact him thereafter.

No trace of Wallace was found anywhere and no dead body was ever recovered that could be identified to be his.

Coincidently, the FBI was hunting for him as well, for a totally different reason, or well, maybe not for a totally different reason. The FBI put him on the top of the list of the most wanted on their website.

If Wallace had defected, then the question remained – to which country did he defect to?

If he disappeared on his own volition, then he must have planned it carefully, leaving no clues behind.

The search for Wallace ran cold as soon it began. Wallace is far too smart to be so easily discovered if he did disappear on purpose.

Whoever Wallace might be pretending to be now, he probably has a very different agenda. He saw the power of this thing first hand, this *glyph* stuff that was in his very wheelhouse of Neuroscience. He could use his knowledge for good or for bad. Wallace had access to these large databases of many hospitals and clinical labs. How he might use his knowledge of the **glyphs** with that of his access to all the medical records of patients' scans is not fully clear.

Smart as he is, if he had a malevolent intent he could use his new found knowledge in any number of ways to hurt or harm.

For one thing, it is certain that he was not about the money, he had plenty of it, just from his day job. If he wanted to, he could monetize this knowhow by selling it in some form to many willing buyers in the world. The very rich ones, conglomerates, oligarchs, or even nation-states. No such sell-out had surfaced up to that point as per FBI's sources. Not saying that it will not happen in the future or have not already happened in secrecy.

Eleven – Ghost of Wallace

A cold December evening in the year of 2036, which was two years after the last IPNES summit that I had mentioned to you about.

The closing minutes at a premium local bar. Round Rock, Texas.

The man who had been frequenting this place lately, was seated in one corner of a restaurant, and was highlighting something on the paper that appeared to be a research journal article. Even when he was seated it was not difficult to identify him as a very tall man.

"Sir...do you want anything else? We will be closing soon." The waitress with a pretty face approached and addressed the man. She had a clear Aussie accent.

"Oh, uh..no ..no... thank you... please bring the bill...", the man sounded as if he was taken a bit off guard, as if he was rudely woken up from a dream. He instinctively tried to use both of his hands to cover the documents that he was editing.

"...Shall I bring the bill for today then?"

"Oh yeah.. sure...thanks", he responded in a soft low tone.

She left with a smile. And came back after some time with the bill.

"*Thanks.*" The man got up, collected his stuff, and got ready to leave. He looked at the bill and left some cash that should cover the billed amount, and put another one hundred dollar bill on top, which was meant to be a tip to her.

As he approached the door that he was headed to, the cold wind through the opened door reminded him that he forgot his jacket, compelling him to come back to pick up his sheep leather jacket.

By this time, the waitress discovered the big tip on the table.

"*Sir, a hundred dollars is too much of a tip for me...I cannot take it.*"

"*No, it is for you.. How do you know your service is not worth that much? Please take it... You can use it, you know ..The ...the.. Holidays are coming..*", he managed a smile, but he seemed rather indifferent beneath the twist of his lips.

The last man left in the bar was also done with his meal and signaled to her for the bill. She went back to her cashier counter, got the bill printed, and brought it back to him.

"By the way, do you know who that gentleman is? The one who just left you a hundred bucks for a tip?" The man asked as she neared him.

"No I don't."

"Wallace, Roy Wallace. A very successful Neuro Surgeon, Neuroscientist, a John Hopkins and a Rhodes Scholar. He treated me for a malignant brain tumor once."

"Oh, you know him? (Pause) He seemed rather pensive to me."

"Yeah, lost his entire family in a car crash. Happened in one late rainy night, about two years ago, (he) drove over the bridge into the river - the red river."

"Oh!"

"The cops had him for careless driving and manslaughter. The jury bought his side of the story, not the prosecutor's. The story goes that he and his wife had a big tiff. She was sitting next to him in the front seat and the two kids, a boy and a girl, in the back. It conflagrated to a point that he lost control and drove over the bridge. He got flung out of the open door from

the driver's side while the vehicle plunged into the river with the rest of the family.

He broke his ribs and his left hand in the fall but he survived. He alone survived. The rest of the family could not come out of the vehicle alive. The kids' seat belts got jammed. The wife tried to save them but in the process could not save herself. This is as per the police report of the scene. He woke up after a deep coma for a full week. Internal brain hemorrhage."

"Oh!"

"The thing is no one knows if he really killed his family or if it was an accident. The story also goes, that he is mildly Bi-polar.

The man let the story sink in. And continued...

"How do I know? Well, from a source who used to work in his lab. The source told me that he was working on a pretty extraordinary paper. On the possibility of a mind to mind communication. This was a little over a year ago and soon after he got acquitted for the accident, recovered, and resumed his professional work. Then he disappeared!"

"Okay" she was listening intently.

"The twist in this tale is that – this man that just walked out from your restaurant does not look anything like Dr. Roy Wallace."

"What! ..Excuse me, the restaurant is closed now and I have to leave." She clearly thought the man's story just got too far-fetched!

"No, I am serious!" The man insisted, calmly.

"Well, if you will excuse me for saying, but I am really not so interested!" She turned her back on him.

"Well would you be interested if I told you, the man you have been serving for the last five times is among the FBI's top most wanted list?"

That did it. She paused and turned back. And he continued.

"Yes, he is. He is on top of the most wanted list. And for good reasons, obviously! And we have good reasons to believe that this person you have served for the last eight times until tonight is the absconding Dr. Roy Wallace. We can't prove it yet. It is true that except for the height, this gentleman does not look, talk or behave like Roy Wallace at all, which is what we need your help for."

"How then do you know he is Wallace?"

"We don't for certain. But we strongly suspect Roy did some magic and transformed himself into this man, whoever he is. We just don't know-how. What is the basis of our suspect? Well, this gentleman is searching the net for the same exact stuff as Roy did before he disappeared. Kind of stuff that ordinary mortals would not care to. Our Psychologists have mapped his online profile. A ninety-nine percent match with Roy's! It could not be anybody else but him."

"Okay?"

"Yes, he blipped on our RADAR in the last ten days, after we were rummaging through tons of search data. We traced him to his current dwelling – a two bedroom suit in a Marriot. His nationality on record shows as Iranian and he is on a Visa here, as a tourist since the last eight months."

"Okay?"

"Yes. And you know, when it comes to Iran we are on an information black out. We are still trying to trace his stated address as printed on his Iranian passport. But I am sure he must have covered that trail as well too."

"Did you not raid his hotel room?"

"Sure we did. Nothing there. We did not find any papers or his laptop anywhere in his suit. Don't know where he hides the stuff."

"But if he is Wallace then why does he not look like Wallace as you say?" She asked.

"Exactly, that is what we are not able to figure out yet. The hotel managers, the room cleaning stuff, the concierge stuff, everyone who had any interactions with him - we have their testimony and we also have secretly recorded many of those conversations that he was in. He neither sounds quite like Wallace nor quite talks like him nor quite behaves like him. There are some similarities with Wallace but not a whole lot. We have plenty of past clips of Wallace speaking in Neuro conferences and other records as well as his patients' testimony. People who knew Wallace say they find some similarity between Wallace and this gentleman but a lot of dissimilarities as well. In other words the opinions are confusing and inconclusive."

"If so many of your sources could not link him to Wallace how can I, a foreign student, do anything?"

"Yes, you can do something, actually! We need to know the content of the papers that he is working on. Is he publishing in somebody else's name or as himself?

Please use your charm and get more information from the devil himself! But don't make him suspect you. And also, take as many pictures of the papers as possible. Can you do that?"

"I am really not sure I can!"

"There is nothing for you to be concerned about. I will always be around, in a different disguise every time. You will know where I am. You will need to make him drink a mild laxative compound. Use the time he goes to the restroom to take quick pics of all his papers. Use this pen camera. I will be listening to the conversation and should something go wrong, I will step in to intervene so that he will be distracted." He showed her a special pen camera and explained how to use it.

"I am really not sure yet..." She said very un-enthusiastically.

"By the way, you are a student here at UT, department of philosophy, right?"

"Yes", the pretty waitress with the clear Aussie accent was not sure where he was going to twist her now.

"Don't worry, at the FBI it is our job to know people! You have absolutely nothing to fear." The middle-aged man assured her as he read her concerns.

"Do you plan to stay and live in the US after you graduate or would you go back to Australia?"

"I have applied for a green card already. So yes, I want to stay here. There are not many opportunities in my hometown."

"I hear you!"

"But Sir, I don't think I can do it. I will be too nervous and if he is not the one who you think he is, it will be very unfair to him. I am sorry..."

There was a long pause.

"Would you want a rogue nation to get hold of an extremely powerful technology that they can then use to change the world order, and even exterminate people that don't agree with them?"

"Is this some kind of new formula for a hydrogen bomb?"

"No, it is much more powerful than that. Imagine a scenario where every military officer and every soldier, every young man in a rogue nation, or a terrorist organization, were to become as smart as Einstein was - overnight, and ...we are not, ...would that be fair to the rest of the world?"

She looked at him straight, trying to figure out what he was really trying to say!

"Yes, it is that situation here. Our assumption is that there is a major breakthrough involved here that has the potential to fundamentally change science and therefore is extremely important for us to know before our adversaries do. We suspect that Dr. Wallace has at least a partial answer to how biological intelligence works, that is our best guess yet. If that is true, we pretty much can solve some very pressing problems in the world! Would you not want us to be a part of that new science?"

There was this moment of silence between them and the man continued,

"Not only will you be doing the world a favor, but we will also ensure that you are compensated well for your service. What if you get a nice scholarship from the government that reduces your tuition for all your graduate studies to zero and gives you an additional thousand bucks a month for your living expenses until you graduate?"

There was a long spell of silence, she was trying to process what she just heard, and he was looking at her through

"But why me?"

"Because there are not many places that this guy visits and spends time this long as he does here. Besides, you arouse very little suspicion in his mind as I can see. And he actually talks to you. I have not seen him doing that to very many people!"

"Ok. What do I have to do?"

"Excellent, you will be doing a good thing not bad. I will be in touch, I have your number!"

The man got what he wanted and left.

As she began to wrap the day's work a breaking news was flashing in all the TVs inside the bar.

<Mankind's first attempt to inhabit Mars ended in a big disaster. Something caused catastrophic damages to the two settlements that were barely continuously inhabited for three months. The disaster caused the lives of the first twenty pioneers of program - Red Rock.>

In that news segment, Professor Chandra, an invited scholar and an expert in that domain was responding to the question posed by the host-

"...this is once again a chilling reminder to us that our principal adversary in inhabiting other planets is not some slimy bloodthirsty reptile looking predatory alien life forms, but the challenge of keeping our own technologies working in those hostile environments."

Twelve – The Nebula in the Sky

It started in the early evening of 4th of July, 2045. Let me take you back to that moment just for a second.

The 4th of July celebration would start any second at the top of the hour. Sixteen city centers in the metropolis would begin firing firecrackers into the evening sky, all about the same time, when the clock hits 8 PM. If you were one of the many hundreds of spectators looking up for a spectacular display and facing the South Eastern horizon, you would be in for a strange treat tonight. Around the same time as the firework began, another kind of firework, a celestial one, started.

There it was, in the South-Eastern corner of the evening sky, well above the horizon and where the dominant constellation of *Orion* the hunter lies. A nebula, colorful and bright, and big enough to be conspicuous even in this very light polluted city, appeared in the constellation of Orion. Later, and well into the night, the airwaves were all filled with the news and analysis of that colorful nebula in the sky.

Everyone will have an extended stay out tonight, pointing their own telescopes at that patch of the sky.

If you are any Astronomy minded and knew of the *Crab Nebula*, which was first discovered by a Chinese astronomer in the year 1054 AD, then you know such supernovae events are not so uncommon in the galaxy. The *Crab Nebula* is reminiscent of a supernova in the constellation of *Taurus* some 6500 light-years away from Earth. The *Crab Nebula* is an eleven light year wide remnant of a violent event. Even being that far away it can still be seen today with a telescope, if you know where to look.

The event that occurred in the sky as just seen for the first time this evening, from Earth, actually had occurred six hundred and forty- two years ago. A red supergiant, the 11th largest star in the night sky in the **Orion** constellation, a star so massive that if it is placed in the center of our solar system - Earth, Mars and the asteroid belt will all be inside this star and more - its outer surface might even reach up to Jupiter. That is how big of a monster this **Betelgeuse** is or was. It blew itself up into smithereens, in a massive supernovae explosion, spewing out massive chunks of heavy matter in every which direction.

Years later from that moment of the first sighting, all concerted observations at that patch of the sky will have revealed a more unsettling tale. Yes, the light from the explosion has reached us now and will continue to reach us, but the materials from the explosion, which are still traveling in all directions, though at a much lesser speed than the *speed of light*, are coming. We might get a shower of the stellar materials, or we may not get anything at all, considering the spread angle of that shoot out over such a huge distance. How that will turn out to be is in the realm of speculation. But, even that would be the lesser of the two concerns for us. The more serious concern would be from the gamma-ray blast to come. But not any time soon. No!

Let me explain.

That region within and around *Orion* is a star nursery, filled with plenty of star forming ingredients, and other smaller stars ; stuff abundant with all the raw materials needed for many, many star births. Considering the massive size of **Betelgeuse** it should turn into a massive black hole if our understanding of the life-cycle of a star is correct. It could already have morphed into one, and if that is the case, it could already be devouring materials from its nearby zone of influence and heading toward the **micro-quasar** stage.

It will not be until late 2080's that any solid data would be available to us to conclude either way. The conclusion at that point would be that the polar axis of that black hole so formed will be tilted towards us, in one of the many possible scenarios. If that ever happens everything in the path of that gun will get fried. Cosmic events take a very long time compared to a human life-span, so even if that happens it is still far into the future based on all our best science. To reach the **micro-quasar** stage and any Gamma bombardment to finally hit us, assuming we really are in its line of fire, would take centuries or even millennia.

The scientific community, in general, maintained a stoic calm. Any doomsday scenario for lack of more concrete evidence was just purely conjectural - they said in various press releases and media broadcasts. It is just another *Crab Nebula* and we've seen things like this before – so, no worry.

CNN, MSNBC, Fox, and all the major channels were buzzing with that talking point all through the night, beginning that night and will be so for many subsequent nights thereafter. A huge surge in the search for *Orion, Betelgeuse, black hole, supernova, etc.*

was recorded in all major search engines. And a surge in people searching for *End of the World* prophecies too. Places of religious worship began to see a huge congregation of devotees.

It is amazing how just one change of view of a patch of the sky can cause so much impact.

And this was just the beginning. For the conspiracy theorist and the doomsday prophets, this also was their time.

In a world of free-speech, where information travels at the speed of a finger press many times we just do not know who to believe. Some people will muddle the truth and misdirect many just for the kick of it, sometimes.

The Events Leading to the Launch

Thirteen – An Anxious World

The general populace of the world soon after 2046 was totally caught on to the scenario of a global extinction event. Speculations were rife on the possible date as early as the end of the year 2047. Others comforted themselves on that speculation as somewhere after two or three decades. Popular science personalities either discarded the doomsday theory or maintained a timeline longer than several centuries at a minimum.

To shake up the already sensitized world population, the end of the year 2046 saw several sightings of comets, the ones never before seen. Not *Shoemaker Levy* or *Haley's*, but two unnamed comets that came out of the blue and swooshed past us close to the moon's orbit. That did not help to maintain any calm and order. It took several months for the panic to subside. The year of 2047 saw another major cosmic event. Something dropped from the heavens in the size of a football field in the South China Sea, sending out Tsunami waves of a few hundred feet high and the deluge wreaked havoc up to twenty miles inland.

Life rolled on, not quite as usual when you know you are under the gun. The gun in question here was the incoming gamma-ray blast from the ghost of *Betelgeuse*.

But as abnormality had become the new normal two sides to the debate emerged. The skeptic side had good rational arguments based mostly on our own flawed past when it came to doomsday predictions. Doomsday predictions are nothing new, our world has seen doomsday predictions before. Many times in history actually. Even as recent as 2012, when conspiracy theorists propagated the idea of the end of the world based on the end of the ancient Mayan Calendar. Then there were the folks who liked to interpret every news-worthy natural phenomenon to align with the scriptures. Self-styled astrologers invoked ancient texts to profess the idea of the onset of a *proloy (creation-wide destruction),* a *Yugo* (era) terminating event, *the* equivalent of the *End of the World* prophecy.

To many of the optimistic folks, the nebula scare of *Betelgeuse* was just one of those superstition mills at work. The *Crab Nebula* comparison was invoked over and over again – and some argued that **Betelgeuse** at 642.5 light years, which is ten times as close compared to the *Crab Nebula* at 6500 light years away, may pose a slight probability of a hit but 642.5 **l y** still is an enormous distance and in the grand scale of our cosmic neighborhood the earth is not all that big not to be missed.

A year ahead of the appearance of the nebula, the **WARGER** program was already in an advanced stage of development, still under the alibi of the **MAM** program. The world still believed that this was all about some deep research on the Antimatter propulsion engine that is destined for Mars and Titan. The world was told that it was a two pronged goal – one, to rebuild the lost settlement at on Mars followed by a trip to explore Titan, to be powered by this new **MAM** drive currently in development. They were not quite wrong in saying either because Antimatter propulsion will also have been tested for the first time. **MAM** therefore was the perfect alibi. The scientists reasoned that this cover-up act was necessary primarily because no one understood how the science of **WARGER** really works, even with the equations given away in the **glyphs**.

The science of **WARGER** is beyond any human's comprehension. It's as if - a chimp trying to understand *Calculus*. I apologize to all the chimps out there but – I state this just as a matter of fact and with no malice toward any chimp. Everyone is a *chimp* in relation to something, anyways, so no shame in there.

Another reason why it was kept a secret was because the **IPNES** scientists did not want to take the risk of being embarrassed if the **WARGER** endeavor turned out to be one huge fiasco. But they could not ignore what was so graphically instructed in those revealing **glyphs,** either.

In any case, under the auspices of **IPNES**, scientists had to continue doing such experiments, desperate as they were to break the limit of the *speed of light* to find another habitat for humanity. We would not really find any planet worth inhabiting without breaking that cosmic speed limit first - period. The science of **WARGER** provided that possibility, that hope. A solution to break the cosmic speed limit.

At the same time the **IDP** and the starship were being developed, the ads were hitting the airwaves asking for recruits - to be the very first pioneers of the very first true interstellar trip. The risk was arguably higher than it was for the *Kon-Tiki* expedition or an Apollo mission.

A team of nine spacemen was the decided team size for this very first manned mission.

At the end of the 4th year of development, the prototype for the inter-dimensional flight was finally completed and was ready for a beta test.

The first four launches were experimental and unmanned. Small space vehicles, no bigger than an automobile, crammed with all kinds of recording devices to satiate the curiosity of a civilization, were launched.

The first unmanned prototype was programmed to make a quick entry into the 4th and the 5th dimension and return immediately, acquiring whatever data possible in that short time frame.

A quick re-entry was configured because we just didn't know how the higher dimension would twist the time dimension. We had the math but we didn't know for sure how accurate that would be.

The very first launch took off successfully as predicted by the science and the math, but that experimental vehicle never came back. The presumptive causes were identified and corrected. Three months later, the second one was launched and it reappeared in the shores of Spain a month later. A few more corrections had to be made. NASA and **IPNES** were much more confident that the third launch would be successful. And it was. The third unmanned vehicle re-appeared successfully at the pre-calculated location from the launch site after several months. A fourth successful one made us feel like a veteran of that technology now. It was manned by '*Shah* the Penguin. *Shah* came back in one piece after two years, and it seemed happy too. The data from the fourth successful launch and its successful return did show some strange visuals from the other dimensional existences. Not much beyond that. The need to send real humans is now imperative, if we have to make any real progress. If we have to rehabilitate humans we need a human trial.

In a very subconscious way, even to the very religious minded and the God-fearing ones, the data collected from these trips somewhat allayed the fear of a terrible afterlife because now we could actually go '*there*' and come back in one piece. Something which was within the exclusive domain of religious preaching and believers had always connected other dimensions as the places where divinities lived, so far.

Both NASA and **IPNES** were now ready for a fully manned mission.

NASA floated ads inviting qualified volunteers from all over the globe to be part of the first ever interstellar and inter-dimensional mission.

The responses to the ads were overwhelming, tens of thousands, from every part of the globe

About two hundred thousand applicants applied to be among the first nine. It was a challenge of a different kind for NASA - to sort out these applicants and narrow down to just nine, the best nine.

Fourteen – The Crew

Two years prior to the year of the scheduled launch of the first manned starship there was this global talking point – *who made it to the last nine?*

Those days the prime times were replete with the news that - NASA is inviting volunteers to man its first-ever manned inter-dimensional flight. The required qualifications for the mission were defined. One thing that was made clear from the start was that the risk to life was very high.

The math of this mission was calculated to be a forty-year long trip, assuming everything went as planned. This was right out of the theme of so many sci-fi movies. Yes, forty-year was a long time to be gone for anyone, a timeline by which most of the people the crew members had ever known may just be gone. It is not intended to be a one way ticket, but in a sense it is. That is why it is voluntary.

What is at stake is the risk of not doing anything. And as they say at NASA – *failure is not an option* - for this one mission it applied completely. Its success will determine where we will eventually be headed to as a species.

That news asking for applications from prospective crew members was the most translated and relayed news of all time in the history of all media news cycles.

NASA made it known that it is looking for the perfect team, a motley crowd, a truly diverse team, diverse in skills, age, race. The stated goals are manifold- not just one expensive trip to **Astraea B** and back. This mission is a social experiment as well. The objective is not just to see the other dimensions through the lenses of nine pairs of human eyes but it was more than that. Among the important objectives were – the proof of concept that extra-dimensional existences are real, interstellar trip is realistic within the lifetime of a human, and that we can actually inhabit another planet outside the solar system for longer than three months - in this specific case inhabit the exoplanet **Astraea**- B. The ultimate goal was to make humanity a truly multi-planetary species.

From **TESS'** data we knew that **Astraea - B** is an Earth-sized planet and hopefully Earth-like too.

The nine-member crew who finally made it to the mission were –

mission specialist and top mission advisor Taushi Saito, mission specialist Mary Bennet, mission specialist Elea Gruber, mission specialist Vladimir Ruskin, mission specialist Greta Thun, mission commander Michael Matteo, deputy commander Darius Slater, mission specialist P Mirrang, and I – otherwise known as Rex Song, just another mission specialist.

I guess each of us deserves a little bit of an introduction for you to know us better.

Professor Taushi Saito, PhD – Astro-Physics, Tokyo University. He is the principal consultant to Japan's space program.

Professor Saito is well known within the scientific community. What Nyquist-Shannon's information theory is to signal-processing, his Saito-constant and Saito-limit principle is to one niche area of Physics! A profound concept that is used in many areas including avionics and mega-structure building. At just forty four, professor Saito is an avid marathon runner as well.

Dr. M Bennet is an Astro-Biologist fondly addressed by her fellow biologists as *Lady Darwin*, for all the audacious trips she took across the seven continents. From the acidic hot springs to the dry saline desert, from the deep sea floor to the top of the Mountains, she has endured the toughest conditions in her effort to catalogue the toughest organic lives that survive in such extreme conditions – the extremophiles. She started the journey with us at the age of forty one.

Dr. Elea Gruber is a Physician and a former world class athlete. She was a three times Tennis grand slam winner, but her career got cut short because of an unfortunate incident. Someone of an imbalanced mind pushed Elea Gruber from a balcony. She fell shoulder first on the hard ground one story below, damaging some vital muscles and a knee, never to be competitive again at that level of athleticism of the sport. She did not let her misfortune cut her out of the will to do more. She later completed her medical degree at the age of twenty eight from a prestigious medical school in France to be a physician in the field of Sports medicine.

Vladimir Ruskin - Vladimir is a world class aerospace engineer who worked on several successful Soyuz Rocket propulsion systems as the team lead. He had the grand master level of skills in chess, but never went pro. Ruskin was thirty six when he joined our team.

Ms. Greta Thun joined the crew when she was only fourteen. A girl wonder and a whiz kid who built a monster truck in her garage mostly by herself. She also developed a compress-air powered ultra-light.

Michael Matteo - Flight Engineer and former Colonel of the US Air force. Commander of several space missions. He led the team of astronauts that put the DEED Telescope in space. Michael Matteo is kind of a celebrity among space enthusiasts. Matteo was forty when we started.

Darius Slater, Deputy Commander and a former Captain of the US Army. Commanded a few space missions. Veteran of many space travels and had spent a full one year in the International Space Station. He was thirty six at the beginning of the mission.

Dr. P Mirrang, a math prodigy and a luminary in the fields of numerical analysis and partial differential equations. He helped solve some of the equations that baffled even the IPNES scientists. He was among the few who understood some of the **WARGER** equations, at least to some depth. Mirrang was twenty nine of age if I was not mistaken.

Dr. Rex Song Jr – the name I go by. I already have told you about me. I was twenty four when the mission took off.

Incidentally, all of us here are singles some way or the other, either never married or divorced. So no immediate family of procreation for anyone. Greta was raised in an orphanage until her foster parents adopted her.

We took the stage on the night of the 31st of December, 2044, when the ball dropped at Time square, New York, symbolizing a new beginning for mankind.

We spent the next two years in different locations to train. Among those places were Washington DC, Star City Moscow (Russia), and Houston, to get trained in all aspects of survival in space-Team building, problem-solving, etc.

We knew our mission would take us deep into the other dimensions. A totally inconceivable future state at that time in terms of what we could expect to see.

Fifteen- Pegasus and C-Mind

I guess starship *Pegasus* deserves its own introduction, so you have an idea what it is like.

It is by far the most sophisticated, multi-modal powered machine ever designed by humans for interstellar travel. It does not look anything like the familiar, long elongated rocket with a shuttle that piggybacks on it. It doesn't not have to be because there is no gravity to escape from.

The science of **WARGER** works in a different way

Starship *Pegasus* was designed to carry several kinds of smaller auxiliary crafts, such as the RAVENs, all docked under the belly of the hull.

Its landing gears come out and retract into the twenty four designated locations in the underbelly to keep it stable while parked.

Towards the rear of its volume are structures designed to house the nine **WARGER** pack reserves- the Anti-Matter fuel chamber and the fusion chambers. All these drives are housed symmetrically on either side of the ship's longitudinal axis.

The ship measures four hundred meters on its longest side. When parked, the ship stands eighty-six feet high from the ground up to its highest point.

The central hub of the craft is a modular unit by itself that can be detached from the starship and can be a sizable starship by itself.

It is a work of art, a beauty to look at - this starship‡.

C-Mind alias **Cygnus**

C-Mind -alias Cygnus- is the starship's principal *Near-Autonomous Intelligent* system, its main brain. Think of it as the *Alexa* or *Echo* of your time, just a heck of a lot smarter and a totally different beast altogether.

C-Mind - is not a conventional supercomputer or a Quantum Computer or anything of those kinds. When developing C-Mind, the creators looked to nature for inspiration - our own brains mostly. One trillion artificial *neuron-synapse-dendrite-axon* units and all interconnected hierarchically structured according to the design that comprised the hardware of C-Mind. The hardware of C-Mind is hidden away at five distributed locations inside the starship, with one hundred percent redundancy built in by design.

‡(*For the inventory that the starship carried, please see the section - Extra - A Catalogue of Starship* **Pegasus'** *Inventory, at the end of this book.*)

C-Mind is the closest to how biological entities do '*intelligence*'. The blueprint of it came from the tenth and the eleventh **glyphs.**

Inside the main control room of the starship, C-Mind is represented as a floating plasma globe. It is just a hologram-like illusion that represents C-Mind not the actual C-Mind.

C-Mind gets activated by its nickname – **Cygnus,** the swan. C-Mind is the generic name for the system and **Cygnus** is its specific name. So if we had another ship and we installed another build of C-Mind on it, we might have to call it by another name. Calling C-Mind as *C-Mind* will yield no response - it is like calling a person as a *person* and not by his or her name. C-Mind understands the intent and the content of any communication addressed to it. It is also situational aware and judgmental. It has a personality.

What the starship's creators built was just extraordinary. They built the whole starship like one huge, intelligent, living organism. Through its millions of component parts that run billions of neuron-like sensors which send their signals to **Cygnus**. In a sense, think of the whole ship as one giant living system, except it was not built biologically.

C-Mind is pre-configured and predisposed with three inviolable laws

·   1st **Law – The safety and security of the starship is first and foremost**

·   2nd **Law – The safety and security of crew members is next unless they violate the 1st law.**

Why did the creator team of *C-Mind* program it that way? Why would they put any human life as of lesser importance to an inanimate object such as the starship itself?

This is how the creator team reasoned –

C-Mind is not a personal assistant robot. It is designed to navigate the starship autonomously in the higher dimensions, something no human can do because the rationale for navigation in the higher dimensions are buried deep in the math and science of **WARGER**. Human intervention would not help.

Humans will have differences of opinions and humans usually resolve it by mechanisms such as a majority vote or through conflicts where a winner emerges and at times that conflict might include violence. Many a times, a majority vote is simply wrong, which can jeopardize the entire mission, which in turn will jeopardize this huge hope for humanity that this mission and the starship represent. The mission's objective is deemed far more important than the life of its crew members.

Humans have faulty biases and reasoning based on individual pre-dispositions, influenced at times by lack of experience or the wrong kinds of experiences. That is something that can jeopardize the mission if it relies on human judgment alone or if *C-Mind's* judgment is made subservient to the human mind.

C-Mind's creators were not sure how the higher dimensions will impact the crew's minds. Will they be driven to insanity? If so, they might become the cause for self-destruction of the mission itself.

Therefore the two laws are instituted that way.

However, there was one exception that the creators programmed into *C-Mind* with regard to the **1st Law** – for one very specific routine kind of a scenario. The *fallback-caution-clause* as they called it. A human operator with the proper credential and qualification could override a decision of *C-Mind* in one exceptional mission-threatening circumstance – and that specific circumstance is when the **WARGER** *bubble* deteriorates or gets thinned out while still in the higher dimension. The decision of how to recoup the **WARGER** *bubble* in whichever dimension the starship might be in that specific moment is up to the commander. It is only on that account does this *fallback-caution-clause* apply. This is not the same as invoking the **3ʳᵈ law**.

But wait, did I tell you about a **3ʳᵈ law** yet? I probably did not.

There is a **3ʳᵈ law**. It really is **not** a law *per se*, but it is a **person**. Yes, the **3ʳᵈ law** is a person. The **3ʳᵈ law** is one specially designated person among the crew members bestowed with certain special rights and authorities. The person will operate in secrecy. No one in the team is supposed to know who that secret *Samurai* is ahead of time, not even the Commander until an extraordinary situation demands that the person steps forward. The **3ʳᵈ law** has a code, a very special code as given to him or her in confidence by the mission directing team that only he or she knows. When that code is used to login in via the console to the ship's core information system, C-Mind will automatically be overridden that includes the ability to supersede the first two laws. There can be only one 3rd **law** at a given time. To still preserve the confidentiality of the 3rd **law** after it is invoked, all the crew members are required to recess into their respective chambers while the 3rd **law** logs in to the system from inside the chamber – that way the 3rd **law's** identity is not disclosed. The commander of the ship must first open a small window of access for each member to login. So, in other words, only the commander can '**ask**' or invoke the 3rd **law,** the 3rd **law** can't invoke herself or himself.

Distribution of power - check and balance is the idea behind this arrangement.

However, during the **MAM** drive phase of a journey and while traveling in the *base-dim* (*short for our three dimensional universe*), *C-Mind* can be overridden by the human operator to a fully manual mode if the human operator had the authority to do so. This is not a use case for the 3rd **law** to be invoked. This is more like a routine thing.

Some more notes on the **WARGER** system -

The **WARGER** energy generator is the heart of the gigantic **WARGER** system. The machine's inner working to create the **WARGER** *bubble* is not well understood. The **WARGER** *bubble* is a sheath of pure energy of a totally different kind, built of the fifth force of nature that encumbers the entire starship, such that a virtual three-dimensional world is still maintained and contained within that *bubble*.

The name *bubble* is kind of misleading here as it might sound like an easily pop-able soap bubble. That sheath is not fragile by any means or measure. But it is the exact opposite of fragile. It is tough, unfathomably tough. Tough is not even nearly the right word to describe it. Let's just say that there is no substance in any universe that cannot be sheared by the **WARGER** *bubble*. The fact is that the *bubble* is a fusion of all four fundamental forces, morphed into a fifth force - a force not of this world, a force not at all understood. That force of the fifth kind can tear open the fabric of all space-times of all dimensions, given the right kind of magnitude and force-density. As this fifth force shears through the dimensions, it also propels the *bubble* 'forward' with its payload contained inside. The word 'forward' is pretty loaded in the context of **WARGER** science. The concept of forward or backward navigation through the higher dimensions is just say - a totally mysterious science as well. As long as the *bubble* is maintained, the payload inside is safe during its passage through the higher dimensions. If it ever happens that the **bubble** gets evaporated while still within any of the other dimensions, the starship gets exposed to the strange effects of other dimensionality that will cause a complete disintegration of the entire volume of space-time within it, instantaneously- Like dropping a cube of sugar into a boiling cauldron of water.

The **WARGER** *bubble* has a life span- it does not persist for forever after it is formed. Like a radiating black hole, it evaporates at a very slow rate, slow enough to last a full trip back and forth between the Milky Way and the Andromeda Galaxy. That is like a round road trip on one full charge of an electric car equivalence.

The **WARGER** machine consumes power in the order of one Giga Watt Hour to generate one **bubble** capable of wrapping around a spacecraft the size of seven Boeing 747 passenger planes by volume.

The IDP launch port is huge- three miles long in all directions. That is just the measure of the area of the port over the ground, which mostly will be to house the docked starships. The closest comparable is the large Hadron Collider, at Cern. What is seen on the surface just hides an even more massive web of structures underground. The whole thing is the **WARGER** ecosystem. This design of the **WARGER** system itself is one of the many secret sauces prescribed in the **glyphs**.

To accommodate for this massive size and to adhere to the design requirements, **IDP** (Inter-Dimensional Port) is built on the rocky mountain plateau and deep into the rocky foundation to minimize the effect of noise from stray cosmic radiations.

The **WARGER** machine can operate in the range of 20K to 896K in the Kelvin scale. Not something to worry about here on Earth, but that could be an issue in deep space, where extreme temperature on either end of the temperature scale is the norm. When heading back home, if there comes a need to re-generate the **WARGER** *bubble* in the cold void of space, the **WARGER** engine must first be warmed up with fusion power.

IDP has the built-in capacity to launch up to ten starships in a twenty-four-hour cycle, before it needs to recoup its energy reserve for the eleventh one, needing an interval of forty hours to recoup that energy.

The craft can also maintain a force-shield or a total duration of 20,000 hours at most. A force shield around itself is like that of the earth's magnetic field - except this one is also a shield of intense heat, capable of frying anything that comes into its contact. The shield is for use in emergent situations only and must be for a good reason as it is very expensive to maintain. There are four modes of the shield - low, medium, high, and maximum intensity.

Sixteen- The Launch

A few weeks before the launch, we underwent several psychological tests designed to bring out the deep hidden mind inside each of us - our fears, our biases, our instincts – the better or the worse side of each of us, and to train on how to face them.

The last pep talk was delivered by the mission Director, Dr. Amherst, thus –

"... The whole of humanity is indebted to you for volunteering to this mission that will take you beyond our existence where no human has ever gone before.

In one short sweep through the higher dimensional existence you will have covered an incredible distance in our plane of existence. For example, if you travel at one tenth the speed of light per hour for a few hours in the 5th dimension, you would have covered 10 light-years in our third dimension by that relative time. This is just to illustrate the point and is not an exact computation.

The algorithm for navigating in the higher dimensions is buried deep in the WARGER science that only Cygnus can process in its hyper brain which is why navigating is entirely on Cygnus.

When you exit out of the higher dimensions, you will be within 47 million Kilometers (about one third of an Astronomical Unit) to Astraea B. From that point, you will be propelling MAM power to the final destination.

The Astraea Binary Star System has five Earth-like planets all in the Goldilocks zone. Astraea B is roughly 1.1 times our Earth with a thicker atmosphere, and a stable climate. We expect the planet to be teeming with some kind of native life forms – intelligent or otherwise. If the life form there is intelligent a lot will depend on what stage of civilization they are at the moment. If that star is very old, which we know it is, we can pretty much suspect that they had more time to evolve than we had. If they had the right kind of evolution, they must be far more advanced than we are, in which case we will pose no threat to them. They will just be curious about us.

If they already are a Type 2 civilization they may have visited us but did not see a compelling reason to make the first contact or to insert themselves into our civilization. We just don't know either way. You will find that out for us.

There is nothing that I have told you so far that you don't already know – you had been briefed and it is all *in the ship's knowledge base system for asking, should you need to know more.*

As soon as you exit the higher dimension starship 'Pegasus' will beam a message back to Earth of your safe re-entry to the base-dim, which of course will take three hundred and forty-two years for the radio signal to arrive.

Every man, woman, and child wants you to be successful because our lives depend on your success. So, Godspeed ladies and gentlemen!"

It's an enormous burden that we would be carrying on our shoulders. I hope we get it right and make all the correct decisions along the way.

The high profile launch was scheduled in the morning at 10 AM Central Daylight US time, on November the 5th, 2046.

The moment of truth when we risk everything has arrived.

We emerged from the shuttle that brought us near the gangway that led to the starship's crew entry module. After we were seated inside the starship slowly began to levitate to about hundred fifty feet into the air just like a maglev train hovers over the rails. It stayed levitated as the **WARGER bubble** slowly began to form all around it.

The spirit of the people gathered outside even in this very cold weather was amazing - the same spirit as when Apollo 11 was launched almost eight decades ago.

All the while that the *bubble* was thickening my mind was racing through all kinds of thoughts.

Who knows what the other dimensions would be like!

Will the little green men be there to finally reveal themselves to us? Are there other kinds of beings, the ones who took part in the mythical wars of Ancient India shooting atomic weapons from the sky or are they also the ones that inspired all of Greek's mythology? Or all of these are just nothing, just-figments of our imaginations throughout the ages...!

When the actual liftoff happens, it will not be like a rocket blasting off in a trailblazing white plume of water vapor. Instead, it will be very quiet, with only hisses and pneumatic kind of sounds.

This enormous starship was already encumbered in a lot of white water vapor around the **WARGER** *bubble* as it was thickening to the desired measure. The heat from the **WARGER** energy is so intense that it literally causes the atmospheric moisture around the *bubble* to boil on contact with it, and that is what causes the white vapor to form.

In my mind I was trying to stay focused on the immediate task of our mission and away from the anxiety. If we die it will still be worth the attempt and I try not to think about it. I just hope if we die we die very quickly and painlessly.

Our best ally in any high-risk situation is our knowledge and our calmness as I remembered one astronaut of fame once said.

We settled down in our respective G-Chambers and in our G-suits harnessed to the seats. There is no escape velocity to overcome and no acceleration against Gravity. It should be mostly nothing except a few jolts and the next thing we know, we should be in another dimension. At that point everything around the starship would disappear, including the people that are cheering us now, the IDP port, the cloud, the sky, the Earth – everything. Everything disappears from our view!

The countdown began, and every person on Earth is watching this historic and monumental event with bated breaths.

At the end of the 25th minute the thick vapor plume subsided, and everything disappeared all around us, just like that.

Did we really travel to another higher plane of existence or did we just get obliterated?

We must have survived, how else am I telling you all this?

Through Other Dimensions

Seventeen- Higher Dimensional Universes

C-Mind began crackling.

C-Mind **<Hello Crew, we are in the 4th dimensional universe now.>**

Did we actually hear **Cygnus** say that – 4th dimension! Whoa!

It is going to take some time to absorb this news in our minds!

It couldn't just be me who was feeling this queer sensation while experiencing this tranquility all around me, this total sense of peace.

On Earth, even when you are alone, away from the hustles of the city with no noise or disturbances, you will still register a surrounding sound pervading all the air around you, like static on a TV of olden times. That is if you chose to listen. Maybe those were some kind of all-pervading cosmic background noises, who knows? The cosmic background radiation is everywhere in our universe.

But this is different – in the higher dimension that we just entered, the feeling is just something else. It is absolutely tranquil here, as if the brain is finally rested!

The **bubble** that encumbered all around us was no longer cloudy but was rather totally transparent in every direction. It must still be there all around us, tearing through space-times and taking us with it. Looking outside we saw nothing, there was nothing there, anywhere, in any direction. Not a single star. Yet, there was a general glow of light in every direction. The dashboard instruments were showing everything as normal. Somehow, the laws of Relativity of our world still apply to this craft as long as we are encapsulated within the **bubble,** where all properties of our three-dimensional world are still intact. We felt that we were static at one point in whatever universe we were supposed to be passing through. The view in front of the ship did not have any reference to measure our relative speed against. It was also hard to tell because we were not accelerating in relation to the bubble that we were enclosed within, so we did not feel the force of acceleration. The propulsion was happening in a completely un-understandable way.

After staring through the windows for who knows how long, we slowly regained our sense of self. We looked at each other, our eyes still wide and our minds still wondering.

Slowly we came to our senses, more or less at the same time! Unconsciously we started applauding, to this successful 'liftoff', still half unsure if this is all just some illusions or it is the *true* reality.

C-Mind **<I cannot understand why you make that noise!>**

C-Mind was referring to the sound of our applause.

No one cared to respond to C-Mind, too absorbed we were with this newly discovered reality that we were immersed in.

We got up from our seats and began to converge to one another, as if subconsciously trying to get assured of each other's physical presence in an alien existence.

"This is nothing short of the greatest miracle that I ever have experienced. Is this for real?"

Mission Commander Matteo's voice quivered as he spoke, out of a mix of a deep sense of excitement and angst, all playing at the same time.

"We need to find where our own universe is." Professor Saito was wasting no time to be back on business.

C-Mind **<Professor, let me display our relative position with respect to our universe. Coming up!>**

The main display began to show things now. The only way to draw a comparative analogy of a view from the higher dimensions to the lower ones is thinking in terms of three, two, one, and zero dimensions. Looking at a zero-dimensional object is like looking at the corner of the room where two walls and a floor meet, which is a point. We don't have to move our head side to side or forward and backward - we just stare at that point in one direction. To look at a one-dimensional existence from a three-dimensional existence is like looking at a line between the wall and the floor of a hallway - easy. If we need to look at a two-dimensional surface from our three-dimensional existence, it is like looking at the flat floor of the hall. So how would our three-dimensional world appear from a four-dimensional existence, if you would ask? The entire three-dimensional universe of ours is seen all at once and all through it. It's like looking at a living person and being able to see his entire body from inside out, all his organs, and from all sides, all at once. Another analogy would be to think of any of Picasso's work – extend that to an entire universe.

So our universe appears like a flat sheet of paper of infinite surface area and no thickness, all galaxy clusters are dotting on that infinite surface one on top the other so that the whole universe appears like a glowing sheet of paper with some portions brighter than the others. The only difference compared to a two dimensional surface is that the flattened three-dimensional world of ours would constantly change with the passage of time.

Let's call the three-dimensional world of ours as the **base-dims**, like we were doing at some point earlier, for brevity.

While we were getting our minds around the new reality -or should I say the one of the many views of reality, *C-Mind* was keeping a tab of our Earth in the flat universe of ours.

"*The blinking light right there is our Earth.*" Saito pointed to a spot on the huge monitor that *C-Mind* kept track of.

According to the configuration of the itinerary of our trip, we will go up three more dimensions before we go down and re-enter **base-dim**.

As registered by the ship's clock we have been cruising in the 4th dimension for a good fifteen minutes. Hard to tell what time that fifteen minutes translates to in the **base-dim**.

The ship's logging system records everything that happens.

C-Mind **<Entering the 5th dimension now.>**

The outside view suddenly changed. It was hard to describe it in any materialistic terms. There is no earthly equivalence to describe it.

It is time to look at the instruments now, to see if each of the engines and all auxiliary systems are working as well - in the new environment. We are on **WARGER** drive now and all the drive parameters are looking normal as indicated on our monitors. The system needs to keep giving a trickle boost to the *bubble* in case it gets weathered from the journey besides propelling the entire *bubble* forward as it cuts through space-times. We got busy in our respective works such as monitoring all the ship's parameters to ensure everything is good. There are thousands of parameters to watch out for, which most of the time Cygnus is expected to auto-correct. But we need to keep a watch for any sudden deterioration in any of the critical parameters and to bring the ship back to the *base-dim* if there is an emergency. Fix the problem and relaunch the ship back to the higher dimension again.

The **MAM** and the Fusion engines must also be monitored as we are not sure if and how things may change there too. Things could happen in the most unexpected ways in an alien environment which we may not be able to anticipate as coming, especially on a maiden voyage such as this. If the electromagnetic core that keeps the Antimatter fuel in separation happens to fail, we will go down in a gigantic explosion of pure energy. That electromagnetic core (E-core) must always be warm and on. What if a higher dimensional environment adversely affects the E-core?

Then the Fusion power system which powers the entire inside of the ship including powering *C-Mind* itself must also be in perfect working condition at all times. There are several redundancies to the Fusion system, in case one unit fails.

In other words we just can't substitute caution for anything – which is why four of us are here. Among the four of us we have redundancy in skills. I mostly am responsible for the main **WARGER** system, and am a backup on the **MAM** and the Fusion system. Professor Saito is my backup on **WARGER**, as well as for **MAM**. Prof. is our team's Plato, he is knowledgeable across many systems. Mirr is the primary specialist on **MAM**, while he knows Fusion and some crucial theoretical aspects of **WARGER** too. Vladimir Ruskin is our principal Fusion System specialist and is also primary for all auxiliary machineries. Greta is the backup for all auxiliary machines and any other kinds of problem solving as her problem solving skills are recognized to be unique.

Matt is our commander and an expert on terraforming the destination planet. He is the principal security officer of the ship.

Deputy Commander Slater is the backup for Matt on the same set of expertise.

Dr. Bennet is a specialist researcher in her field – Astro-biology, her main role comes in after we land at the destination. But for now she has a few experiments running inside the ship, such as monitoring changes to protein and DNA molecules in the alien condition. Dr. Elea is our health officer, an expert on contagious disease, hygienist for the entire ship and our primary physician to keep us safe from any disease or health condition as might happen.

That is everybody.

One thing suddenly dawned on me was that in my mind and so would be in everyone's I guess, I did not register a sense of the passage of time as we were cruising through the higher dimensions. As if the biological clock in each of us took a break while in the higher dimensions. It may be that *'time'* is a thing only in our **base-dim** and not in the other dimensions – a pretty rough and bold assumption that I am making here, not anything to back it up by any evidence as yet.

Far away in our forward view, some objects began to materialize. There were a few of them, they still seemed very far away. Those amorphous objects appeared to be headed toward us. It will be a while before we can determine what those things are. The objects appear fuzzy yet solid. Suddenly, something passed by, something huge, covering the entire front view of the ship in its passage. It covered our forward view for a good while until it was done passing.

"What was that?!" Deputy Commander Slater asked.

C-Mind **<Could not determine, Commander!>**

"We have been traveling for over thirty minutes now. We will need to apply WARGER's transformation for dimensionality to know how much time that translates to in the base-dim. The coordinates of the ship are

configured to go up two more dimensions before going down toward our destination!" I observed.

In a short run later *C-Mind* crackled again.

C-Mind <**Entering the 6th dimension now.**>

As the craft entered the 6th dimension, suddenly the entire field of view changed to what felt like taking a deep plunge into a clear lake. The medium out there certainly seemed like water, although it probably is not. There were streaks of light coming from all directions with no apparent source or sources. It was like the Aurora Borealis in every direction for loose comparison.

It could be plasma or could be something else too. Plasmas are a phenomenon in our universe, no guarantee that it will pervade this dimension too.

"There, that streak of light, that infinite line is our entire universe. What was a flat surface from the 5th dimension just a while ago, is now only a line from this level of existence - the 6th", Saito pointed to a particular line in the monitor as we ascended to the 6th dimension. *C-Mind* still kept track of our starting point- the Earth that we left behind. A blinking point on the monitor was the marker for Earth. Amazing

that the system knows to keep a tab on Earth for reference through all dimensional ascends.

"Commander Matteo, on that infinite line, 4 units to the right is about 340 light-years from Earth and that's where we are headed" Saito translated the display on the main forward monitor for all of us.

"But it is not taking us there yet. It is instead elevating the ship one more dimension up, to the 7th. That should be the last dimensional ascend." I said.

A few minutes later-

C-Mind **<We just entered the 7th dimension!>**.

Suddenly the outside ambiance changed again. It is all purplish foam everywhere around us now. In that foamy ambiance are tiny bubbles. As if we are submerged inside a soapy bubble bath and each tiny bubble could be a universe each. There are an infinite number of them out there.

"Is this actually the multiverse view of all the universes that there are?" Saito was as awed as we all were!

"This is just the mother of all the wildest of dreams!" Matteo added.

*"And.. it's amazing that the **Cygnus** can still locate our universe. It still has a pin on where our universe is! That one – that still flickering dot."* Darius Slater made a point.

C-Mind **<Thank you Slater! I take it as a compliment!>**

"It is a compliment, Cygnus." Slater let it know.

"Is this what reality really is? No wonder we couldn't even begin to understand the nature of any of the forces in our universe. Maybe the stuff that we experience as a force in our universe pervades all dimensions." Mirr recalled the conversation with his mentor Dr. Kobayashi from a few years back, when he still was an undergraduate student.

C-Mind **<Initiating descent into the lower dimension>**

A few seconds later, we felt something like a turbulence that we experience when we travel in an international flight through the jet stream. It was a little more intense than we were used to.

C-Mind **<Turbulences. Please hold tight, working on it!>**

Anxiety crept in, as the turbulence continued. The ship continued to descend through the fifth dimension.

C-Mind **<Going one more dimension down >**

Everything was happening on auto-drive. **Cygnus** is in charge and is faithfully executing the commands using the strange science of **WARGER** based on the configuration set to it.

As we went down to the 4th dimension, the turbulence magically disappeared.

C-Mind **<We are in the 4th now >**

"And the turbulence is gone too, just like that!" Matteo observed.

"Guess some incompatibility within the 5th caused the bubble to be turbulent. It is possible that the bubble is weathering and that might have been the warning of the onset." Saito sounded a warning looking at some of the changes in the configuration parameters of the bubble on his monitor.

As they entered the 4th, things began to look somewhat like our own universe. The dials also indicated numbers that can be translated to our universe now -we indeed have covered 342 light-years from home.

Our universe appeared as the same flat glowing sheet of infinite expanse below our line of view. There were other universes above us too.

On the flat expanse of our universe two points were now blinking. One, a locator for Earth the other for *Astraea* B. The distance between them on the screen at this magnification level is just about three feet. Three feet on the monitor translates to 342 light-years of spatial distance in between the two worlds!

C-Mind **<We are now in our base-dim!>**

The beep and the new visual in the main monitor brought us back to reality – the one that we are familiar with.

*"**Cygnus**, we will be on manual MAM drive from this point. Over to you Professor and Rex!"* Matteo gave his instruction.

C-Mind **<No problem Commander, but I could do this if you want me to.>**

*"No thanks **Cygnus**. We need to experience this drive on our own."*

The main screen, mirrored in all the smaller screens, showed that we just descended to our universe, the only universe we knew before we embarked on this journey. The familiar band of the Milky Way began showing up above us now. Planet **Astraea** B is not all that far from our own solar neighborhood if you think about the scale of the size of our galaxy. Just three hundred forty-two light-years, compared to the width of the Milky Way at 105,700 light-years.

The view on the forward monitor showed the **Astraea** Binary star system, with its five rocky planets in close orbit to each other.

"Wow, that's a beautiful view!" Greta spoke for the first time, *"I would love to ride my monster truck and my air bike there!"*

Elea Gruber and Dr. Bennet were amused at what they heard young Greta say.

"Matt, it says Astraea B is 47 million kilometers from our current location and it is approaching fast. The time to fire MAM is - now." Saito rephrased what is shown on the monitor so that everyone is on the same page.

The **MAM** phase from here will be all in manual mode.

"All right team, we will need to re-enter our G-Chambers. Please gear up in your G suits now. The

extreme acceleration of the Anti-matter drive will cause exacerbated pain on your chest, you all know the drill!"

Matteo gave a clear order.

Once Matteo and I initiate the **MAM** engine we both would need to hustle back to our G-Chambers. Failing to do that on time could be fatal, as the incredible acceleration could hurl any free object against us at a speed far greater than a speeding bullet. The ship is designed for this and everything is secured tightly to the body of the ship.

Starship Pegasus will accelerate up to the maximum speed of 940,000 Km/ hour…it will reach that velocity in about three hours. Upon reaching that max, we will be cruising the rest of the journey. The space between us and the destination is all clear.

The count down to that acceleration began, and the huge craft experienced a sudden jolt as it entered into the enormous acceleration phase generated by the **MAM** engine. The **MAM** engine fired all its chambers, accelerating the starship forward at an incredible translational velocity of 940,000 km per hour. At that speed, the remaining 46 million miles should take about two days.

After 46 million miles of cruising, the retro engines will fire at the specific moment to slow the starship down for the remaining distance to destination.

At the end of a 44 hours of hibernation, we woke up in our G Chambers. The ship was cruising at the maximum velocity. At constant velocity the ride felt smooth now, it should be that way for the next two hours. At the end of that period the slow down phase will automatically get engaged.

Almost eight hours of the slowing down phase later, the planet **Astraea** B started showing on our main view. A planet about a tenth more massive than our own earth. We will feel a bit heavy there for sure –like carrying a back-pack with twenty pounds weights in it.

If an alien race was watching us from **Astraea** B at this very moment, and if they had no clue about trans-dimensional travel, they would be totally freaked out by the sudden materialization of this craft from nowhere.

There are five rocky planets in the Goldilocks zone of the **Astraea** binary star system. The two binary stars Astraea 1 and 2 - are both red dwarfs. Red dwarfs are known to spew solar flares once in a while. These flares could potentially wipe out any atmosphere from its orbiting planets. The Astraea binary system has shown a remarkable exception to this general rule. All the five rocky planets are in the Goldilocks (G) zone. The five planets range in size from half to about one and a half times the mass of Earth. Two of the five have oceans, land, atmospheres, climates, and day and night cycles. The other three are closer to the stars and are gravitationally locked so the same side faces the barycenter all the time, making it a lot less suitable for our kind of life.

What must two Sun rise look like from any of the three planets, I wonder? It's probably a very beautiful sight with two Suns rising from two different points in the horizon at about the same time!

Because the Astraea stars are red dwarfs, they are much less warm. However, for **Astraea** B, which is our destination planet, the two binary stars together and its proximity combines to give it the equivalent amount of insolation as does our one Sun. We are now within the gravitational horizon of planet B, and we slowed down considerably to a mere few thousand miles per hour.

"*Switch to the fusion power mode to reach orbital velocity around* Astraea. *We will make four orbital swipes around the longitudinal plane of the planet and three swipes around the latitudinal planes. Based on the data we will settle on a location. Probably near water, near shore, and preferably on a small island.*" Commander gave his instructions.

These maneuvers will be all semi-automatic.

"On it, Commander." Vladimir Ruskin was quickly on it.

Several hours of orbiting the planet revealed that the planet has two distinct big land masses that are as far apart as can be. One of the two landmasses appeared all white from this far. Probably it is all permanent winter snow in that part. Unlike on Earth Astraea does not have any season. There were patches of snow covers in the other landmass that we are headed to. The rest is all filled with an endless ocean, with very few islands in the mid-ocean region.

The orbital runs around the planet did not reveal any sign of an advanced civilization. No glitter of concentrated light sources seen from space like that would come from a populated area if intelligent life forms did exist! This is thinking like ourselves, from our own assumption of how a civilization on a planet should appear from space. We just don't know if any other signs of intelligent life could exist that are not like ours in any sense.

"Hmm, looks like no sign of civilization going by the absence of any concentration of energy sources down there!" Saito remarked!

"What if this is a planet of another kind -of apes or baboons or worse yet, zombies ...." I was trying some humor.

"Oh yeah, if the choice is between zombies and apes I will take apes of course." Mirr joined me in the humor.

"If there are Mermaids, I will be okay with Mermaids!" Vladimir joined in!

"Mermaids can smell fishy!" Greta chuckled.

"Nah, they sit on a rock to Sunbathe for hours, they can't smell that bad!" Vladimir added.

"Well, what if it is a planet of the Amazonian women?", Elea joined in.

"I will be okay with that..", I chuckled.

"Be warned, in that case, I might end up being your queen and you all working for me!", Elea quipped.

"Let's enjoy these last few days as equals in that case..."

"I appreciate that we can still come up with some humor!" Matt was onboard with this lighter side of the conversations.

"Humor certainly helps to cope with anxiety of arriving at an alien planet, Matt!" said Dr. Bennet.

"What? Are you all saying that you have not landed on an exoplanet before, c'mon?!" Vladimir cracked up everybody!

ASTRAEA B

Eighteen– Astraea-B, the Landing

An island was chosen for the initial landing off the shore of the big continental landmass. An island three times the size of the island of Manhattan. There clearly is life out there, from the color of things as apparent from this altitude. Some kind of static life exists on the island, just not all green as in our world. But all the colors when we think of colors, like a mosaic of colors are down there. Are these the color of life on this planet? If static life exists so will mobile life, assuming both life forms are symbiotic at a fundamental level as how it is on Earth.

We landed on the sandy beach. Some kind of plant-like life form starts from about half a mile away from the beach into the inland.

The two Suns that shine on this planet emit radiations more in the redder side of the spectrum. So, a typical mid-day on this planet is like a late afternoon on Earth. With two Suns in the sky, the days are much longer than the nights. That makes up for the less insolation per unit of surface area. About a tenth of the land here has snow and ice here and there.

The air has about 30% oxygen. Nitrogen, Hydrogen, and Neon make up for the rest. That is about 9 % more oxygen than on Earth. We can expect that the presence of Neon will make our voices sound squeaky. The presence of Neon also makes the atmosphere more colorful and dramatic.

It will be at least two more days before we can get out of the ship. We need to get acclimatized to the new world. The gravity being a tenth more than it is on Earth, our bones will give up if we just stepped out now.

We were still sampling the air outside for microbial life forms.

Dr. Elea cleared us of any health condition that we might have developed during this short trip through the dimensions.

By the third day, we felt much more confident to step into the new world.

"We will not go out in person yet. Instead, we will deploy the robotic drones to scout the area first. Based on the data collected by these robots, we will deploy five TALONs to scout deeper into the forest." Matteo made his instructions known.

"I guess if there are any mobile life with any level of intelligence they have already seen us. We have either earned their fear or their anger by now, just by our large presence. I would therefore suggest we keep the craft hot and ready should we need to scoot in a hurry." Dr. Bennet knows about the nature of living things like nobody else.

A *TALON* is a semi-automatic fighting machine. They are designed to look like an Earthly carnivore. *TALON*s come in the form of one of these animals - a cheetah, a black panther, a mountain lion, and an eagle. This is just the outer cover- the skin. Inside, they are all metallic machines and built of steel wires for muscles, with a tiny but powerful engine to power its speed, strength and agility.

In the auto mode, they can walk and run, but can't fight like real animals. When set in semi-auto mode, they are operated remotely by a crew member. And based on how the operator simulates a virtual fight, the *TALON* makes those actual moves.

The eagle *TALON* can actually fly like a real eagle by flapping a pair of artificial wings. They come complete with steel talons for attack.

"All right. Let's get into some actions now. Let there be drones!" Matteo instructed.

"Doing it now, Commander" – Greta and I will man the robot-drones.

The two drones were let loose from under the hull of the ship.

I took my robo-drone to circle over the shallow water of the beach to get a quick glimpse of the teeming alien life in the water first.

Greta's drone headed straight for the forest. The life down below is a lot different from the most plant life we find on Earth. Going by the pattern of the color pigmentation, a specific color type might be one kind of species while another pigmentation could be another. The species of similar colors tended to cluster together in small groups. There seemed to be too many variations down there to describe in any detail. Difficult to say much from this altitude. There were spikey and thorny looking bushes too. A whole new taxonomy of life exists there waiting to be cataloged. That would be a lifetime of work for any Biologist.

The life form below did not show any response to the swift passage of the two drones even as when they flew low. It will be interesting to find out if they have any DNAs in their cells like all life in our world has. That will be in Dr. Bennet's wheelhouse. It is a field day out there for her.

Greta's and my drones are now flying together, side by side.

"Wait, wait, let me go back. I see some movements in that area..." Greta noted.

She lowered her drone over the area to be just over the canopy. Suddenly an octopus-like tentacle rose from within the forest and spat out some dark, inky substance, totally smearing the under the belly camera of Greta's *robo-drone.*

"Ugh! What just happened? I can't see anything below! My lower camera is totally blocked! Rex, can you turn around and see what's wrong. I need to gain some altitude to avoid another sneak attack!" Greta quickly took her drone higher.

I turned back to see what it was. All I could catch was a glimpse of a contracting tentacle that quickly disappeared below the forest cover.

"I guess I'll dunk my drone in the sea to clean up!" Greta turned her drone toward the ocean.

We made a few circles over the island. The mainland will be at least a hundred miles away from this island. We are not going there yet, as per Matt's instruction.

My drone recorded some series of movements in the forest down below. It must be some kind of an arboreal life causing those movements. In our world, a gang of monkeys swinging from one branch to another while doing their monkey business could cause such an effect. Who knows what equivalent of a chimp might be out there?

After another hour of surveillance we came back and docked the drones back into the mothership.

"Looks like the two suns are about to set at the same time!" Saito said.

"Cygnus, put the ship on low power and on full camouflage mode for tonight. We will take a good night's sleep and live to fight another day." Matteo said.

The starship will park on its landing gears on the beach, and its invisibility cloak will stay activated so that it will appear transparent to any prying alien eyes. The presumption here was that they too like us use light in the same range of the spectrum to see.

We need to rest well to see what this planet has in store for us.

Nineteen - Day Four in Astraea-B

As we got ready for day four in this alien world, Matteo already had the schedule for the day prepared for us.

"Okay team, we will do a few things on day four in paradise. First, we will take out our TALONs and scout the forest from inside. Second, if everything goes well, we will actually walk the planet without our full protective suits and breathe the air outside. We will take samples, and even take a dip into the sea if Elea thinks it is okay to do so.

And Vladimir may talk to the mermaids, if he wants!" Matt ended his quick brief.

Vladimir chuckled and said in his Russian accent – *"Mermaids do not appear on Monday mornings, you know!"*

"How do you know it is Monday here?" Saito joined in.

"Well, it's our first workday on Astraea!" he chuckled again!

"I get the taking-a-dip in the sea joke, but no one is dipping yet - not before we make sure it is safe to do so." Elea Gruber made an authoritative remark.

"*Yes ma'am!*" said Matt.

"*Okay, we will let loose two TALONs into the forest: The* **panther** *and the* **cheetah**. *Greta and Ruskin will be controlling them from here.*"

"*Slater, Professor, and Mirr will man the ship while Elea, Rex, and I will take the RAVEN for a spin over to the mainland and see what we've got in the high altitudes of the mainland.*"

"*Dr. Bennet will take control of the submarine drone, and explore what is under the ocean and do what she needs to do.*"

"*Are we game, team?*" Matteo looked to hear some noise and a lot of enthusiasm – he got both. We were excited and fired up.

"*One word about self-defense, guys. We are here on a visit. Not to conquer! So unless it is a real threat to your life and to our mission, we are NOT going to use AFF4. If we are stepping out as a team, only one person may wield an F4 in the group, and he may not use it unless the rules of engagement for F4 arises. So in most circumstances, we will instead use conventional guns for protection.*

This is not a new knowledge, we have been given this instruction in our training. I thought it would be a good time to refresh our minds." Matteo made his mind clear.

"So, if we face any danger, we look to our right, and to our left, and we run? Okay got it! Just kidding, Matt!" Vladimir chuckled.

"Eyep! We run!"

AFF4 stands for Automated Force Field version - 4[†]. † *(Detailed in the list of Inventory toward the end of this book.)*

A RAVEN is a small, nuclear-powered flying machine designed in the hybrid pattern of a B2 stealth bomber and a Stingray. More like the latter. The similarity with a stingray comes from the fact that the body of the craft is made up of a flexible, rubbery material so that it can warp and bend as a real stingray does. In terms of its size, it can be comfortably landed on an area as small as a tennis court with some room to spare. It takes four riders and a pilot. The craft is capable of rapid maneuvers and quick acceleration to shake off any flying hostiles chasing its tail.

Three of us boarded the RAVEN. Matteo took control, and Elea and I sat immediately behind him.

The **RAVENs** are docked under the triangular hull of the ship in an upside-down orientation. To board it, we need to come through a corridor that runs like a tunnel inside the ship.

We were soon airborne and in a few minutes, we were over the mainland. The spread of life in the prairie-like landscape down below was somewhat sparse as compared to the island, judging by the color of things.

There were signs of higher-order life forms down there. We saw herds of something and herds of some other things. Hard to say what they exactly looked like from this far up going at the speed that we are. Besides, this quick mission is about mapping the lay of the land, not cataloging native life, not yet. Dr. Bennet will do that in the near future.

The land below is full of characters, deep wide gorges, narrow precipices, big waterfalls, lakes and rivers, impossible overhangs, and snow-capped mountains - just like on Earth.

Suddenly, a dark cloud appeared far to our right. A large flock of some flying creatures.

"Commander, to our right and front, and coming straight toward us, a lot of them." I sounded the alarm.

It was kind of scary to see so many of them, like a spreading hurricane coming fast from the horizon.

"Okay, let's have a closer look at them," Matt said.

Matt actually turned the RAVEN toward the approaching cloud of somethings, instead of flying away, to have a direct look at them. He slowed down in midair using a maneuver similar to an F15 fighter jet and waited for the creatures to arrive within our visible range.

"Holy son of Jupiter, these are huge..." I said.

"And long too..." added Elea.

"Do I get the guns ready, Commander?" Elea wanted Matt to say yes.

"If they get too close, please do not hesitate to fire. I believe - offense is the best form of defense, Commander!" She pressed Matt again. The cloud approached us faster than we figured.

"Not if I can help it. Hold on! We are going up!" Matt was ready for the avoidance maneuver, swerving sideways and up. We held tight, anticipating a sudden acceleration.

Suddenly, the three leading creatures from the spearhead spewed some dark, thick liquid toward us, all at the same time! We did not expect such an offensive response!

Matt is known for his nerves of steel and quick reflexes. He was a test pilot in the Air Force before he became an Astronaut. As a test pilot, he had successfully tested some of the incredibly fast flying machines that Lock Heed Martin and Boeing had ever designed for the US Air force.

Matt quickly took the RAVEN up, much higher than the level at which these flock of *Astraean* equivalent of *Pterodactyl* was at that moment. Admittedly though, besides the fact that as large as these flying *Astraean Pterodactyls* are, the similarity with *Pterodactyls* ends right there. Although these are many times as large, they appeared very innocuous judging just from their looks. The best Earthly equivalent of their appearance will be something of a hybrid between a huge butterfly and a jellyfish. The jellyfish comparison comes from the fact that they had long loose tentacles dangling from their bodies. The differences are plenty too. These creatures have no wings, instead what might be construed as wings is their entire body that constantly changes its shape. They still propel forward at amazing speed nevertheless - just by contracting and expanding their bodies, and not by flapping wings as would a butterfly. My guess is they do that by compressing the air within their upper body and releasing it quickly behind them in a jet.

The dark liquid that the three front runners spat toward us had landed on our right-wing. It must be some kind of an extremely reactive compound because it peeled off a bit of the outer sheath of our flying machine. The dark ink was still sizzling even after the wind took most of it away. Must be a deadly venom of some kind that could burn most things on contact like that.

That was a close encounter!

"Did you guys at the main control get any of that?" Matt asked over the wireless to Slater, Saito, and Mirr. They can see everything we can, through the eight cameras that are located on this RAVEN.

"Yes, we did! That was too close. Please don't take such risks anymore Commander, even with your skills. We definitely need you all back in one piece." Saito responded from the mothership like an elderly statesman.

"I guess I will take that as an order prof. And I agree! Thanks!" That is yet another thing I admire about Matteo. He is willing to take responsibility for his own mistakes. It enhances his leadership on this team, I would say.

After an hour, Slater was in the air.

"Matt, the same creatures are coming our way, we see them in our radar now." Slater sounded the alarm.

"Please put the ship into the camouflage mode!" Matteo said. *"Also get ready to activate the force field on minimal intensity. We don't want those creatures to spit all over our ship!"*

"Yes, Commander!" Slater responded.

C-Mind **<I got this. Don't worry, I got this!>**

After some time Slater was online.

"Guess what Matt, the entire swarm dove into the sea and has not resurfaced yet! Must be amphibians!"

"Wow! Evolution here has put superpowers on this one species. They must be the dominant species here with all that versatility." Bennet was heard saying from the mothership.

"That is right in your domain, Bennet. How is your favorite 'evolution' so biased here?" Matteo asked.

"Still not as biased as it is on Earth and in our favor, sir! Evolution has given just one superpower to us – that of 'intelligence' and look where that has put us - in charge of everything on our planet. No power like brainpower!"

Bennet was right indeed.

"Could not agree more." Matt acknowledged.

As observed earlier, there were no signs of civilization as we understand it.

Maybe intelligent life forms like ours are much rarer, even on the scale of a galaxy. Maybe the evolution of complex life forms to intelligent life forms is not an inevitable path, even if we allow enough time for life to evolve. And *'intelligence'* could be one huge coincidence and even rarer. But hey, we have sampled only two planets in our lifetime yet. That is not large enough of a sample size to conclude on anything in a galaxy of 300 billion stars. It's like going to a sandy beach, looking at two grains of sand and saying – *"hey, there are no seashells on this beach!"*

Or maybe, just maybe, whatever intelligent life had evolved here, left the planet for a better paradise, just like we are trying to do.

But if any intelligent life had evolved here at all, it would have had a huge head-start compared to us. **Astraea** B is four billion years older than Earth is.

After several hours of flying over the mainland, we spotted a mountainous region. There were not many clouds in this part, so a large part of the mountains was visible for a long stretch into the northerly direction. Must be a super long mountain range.

"Hey Matt, can you just circle back? I think there was this nice expanse of plateau land in between the two ranges. And a lake and a waterfall too." Elea asked.

"Okay... going back..." Matteo responded.

This was indeed a beautiful place, besides, we needed a break and so we made our landing.

"O' lord in heaven! I could settle here for the rest of my life!" After we stepped out Elea was all over the place and gyrating with both hands stretched out like a ballerina.

"Look at the oxygen level here, it is around 24% here, 6% less than what is down there. Just about right for

our taste!" I read the atmospheric data display built into our suits.

"Not much Neon either! Just like we like it!"

"I can agree with that! With the lake and the waterfall and the river, we can generate a civilization here. And I assume those creatures do not fly this high." Matt joined in.

Meanwhile, closer to our starship our fellow crew members were engaged in other exploratory activities.

Ruskin and Greta were getting the *TALONs* ready to enter the Elysian forest on the island that they scouted from above yesterday.

This forest is right out of our fables. Big mushroom-like life forms, large Sea fungus-like outgrowths with skins painted in deep purple, and tall green seaweed look-like vegetation. The forest's appearance can be compared to what a snorkeler in the Caribbean would see when diving closer to the Coral reefs.

Greta and Ruskin were about to have the thrill of their lives, having taken control of the two *TALONs* and seeing everything that the two *TALONs* would see while inside the forest.

The first surprise did not take long in coming, at a bare seventy-meter incursion into the forest. What appeared like a static life at the first look, suddenly took to a quick flight on the approach of the *TALONS*. It appeared to look like a tall cacti with granite-like texture and stood as high as six feet.

"Did you see that, Russ?"

"I did!"

"How did it even run away? It did not look like it had legs!"

"Think of a snake or a worm in our world. They don't have legs either but move just as fast. They too must have some trade secrets that we don't know!"

"Thumbs! I can live with that explanation!" Greta liked Vladimir's explanation.

After many uneventful minutes, something like a tentacle suddenly appeared out of a garden of rocks in the middle of the forest.

"What was that?" Exclaimed Rus.

The tentacle was just that - a tentacle, without any body parts attached to it. It was swift and it took a swing at the *panther* and barely missed it.

Just when the *panther* barely recovered from the shock, another one, a lot darker in appearance than the first, appeared. This one got the *panther* wrapped in its crunching grip, like how a boa constrictor would do.

What ensued was an all claws out battle. It lasted a good three minutes with the cheetah helping on the side of the *panther*. It ended in the decimation of the *tentacle* in the hands of these two man-made mechanical beasts.

Greta and Russ orchestrated the combat remotely. That was the first hand to hand combat we had yet.

The *TALONs* resumed their incursion deep into the forest, the forest suddenly opened up into a large clearing, carpeted with the sea-weed like vegetation all over with patches of snow here and there. Apparently, the blades of these creatures were no fan of our mechanical beasts either. The blades kept on striking at their mechanical paws spitting out some kind of liquid in the act. Must be some poisonous substance. The two mechanical beasts built of human technology were a lot tougher than such bites.

The clearing would be about the size of a football field. Both *TALONs* took a pause here, turned, and looked around, 360 degrees around.

At the diagonally opposite corner of the field, something was definitely happening. There were signs of some rustling and stomping of the vegetation there. Something big and formidable. And then it began to take shape.

A big, shapeless hybrid of a large amoeba and something - I don't know what to fill in there! The thing had no shape at all. It kept on changing shapes, as big as a large adult African elephant at times, and at other times just as flat as a wide area rug. Suddenly, it dashed the *TALONs*, more like a wiggle of its body, squeezing and expanding like a worm but real fast.

"What do we do Russ? Fight or flight?" Greta asked worried and excited.

"Not sure! Looks pretty aggressive, that thing!" Russ was not sure.

*"I would say we branch out on either side of **Blobby**.*

Wait, not yet, wait for my signal, let it come a little closer!"

We were all connected wirelessly all the time so that everyone was on the same page on what was going on. As the big menacing-looking **Blobby** (*borrowing Greta's jargon for that thing*) approached closer and closer, Greta signaled Russ to begin the dash. They sprinted around the creature in circles and in opposite directions, totally confusing it. For some time it did not know which one of the two *TALONs* it should attack first. It surely had not 'seen' anything like a *TALON* ever either – assuming 'seeing' is something it does (even without a distinct pair of compound eyes).

Matteo came on the speaker.

"Guys! Avoid! We don't want to engage in trivial battles that do no service to our ultimate objective. Disengage from unnecessary risky combats- We don't want to risk losing a TALON."

"Got it, Commander!" Russ and Greta responded together.

But as soon as they said those words, **Blobby** swiftly elongated a part of its body that effectively functioned as a limb and wrapped *cheetah* all around in its grip. That tripped *cheetah*, making it roll on the ground a few times over as it was in a rapid motion. It could not wrest itself free from *Blobby's* grip. *Panther* joined the fight, drew its claws, which normally are retracted inside its mechanical paws, and took a few swashbuckling swipes at *Blobby's* elongated limb. The rapid strikes of the steely claws slashed *Blobby's* limb in half. The main body laid on one side and a severed slithering limb that still wrapped around *cheetah* but with a much weaker grip than before on the other side of the *panther*. With a bit of struggle, the *cheetah* freed itself and was back on its feet again.

"Guys – Russ and Greta, fall back, fall back, and leave the son of a bitch alone. Return to the mothership." Matteo saw all the actions.

"Got it. Heading back home, now." Ruskin replied.

"You guys are having a lot of fun, aren't you?" Saito took a little dig at Russ and Greta, just only in a jest.

Meanwhile, Bennet was exploring the shallow water of the sea, with the submarine drone. She recorded every little life form that looked of interest to her.

"The water here is full of life, just like it is in our oceans. The fluidity of water is what gives rise to life in the first place, so no surprise there!" Bennet was kind of speaking to no one in particular, but everyone.

"And you know what, I have been tracking this one for the last half hour, all along its entire body. I don't see its end yet. It is the same organism all this time – think of the Great Barrier Reef of Australia, except more mobile. I have easily traversed more than forty-five miles on it so far, yet it is the same living organism still. Wow! I bet we could have seen it from space if it ever came up to the surface." Some interesting titbits that Bennet shared with us. Who knows how many more such giants could be out there.

"Great job Bennet!" Matteo shouted out to Bennet.

Day four in paradise was really eventful. But it is no paradise out there.

We can make it a paradise, with our technology and our will.

A couple of hours later, we were back at the mothership. We docked the RAVEN under the hull. The *TALONs* took refuge into their designated cubbies inside a certain section of the ship. Both *TALONs* were somewhat bruised now. Some of the poisonous goo that they collected during the hand to hand combats were still stuck on them. The submarine drone that Bennet was driving will stay underwater for the night. It will be on a slow auto-pilot.

"By the way, the water sample that Rex collected yesterday contained thousands of tiny aquatic lives. We are still testing for the presence of DNA like complex molecules in them. Some of them could be dreadful pathogens for us, so I would be careful in taking a dip in the ocean yet. But here's the kicker. The oceans on this planet are not saline, not at all. It is all freshwater! Isn't that cool!" Bennet announced to everybody.

We congregated at the dining area to discuss the future course of action for the mission for the duration that we are on this planet.

It didn't turn out to be an easy discussion contrary to what I thought it would be.

Twenty - Division and Conflict in Paradise

That night we gathered at the dining area of the ship. An all-important meeting was about to ensue.

"Team, we are here, on this distant planet and we have survived day four, thanks to our technology and our determination. Honestly, I still cannot believe that we are here." Matteo started the conversation.

And he continued. *"The question that we need to discuss is for how many more days we should be on this planet. And where on this planet do we raise the barn first? What should we consider in choosing that place? Et Cetera."*

Saito approached the question from a different perspective –

"If you will pardon me, there is something that I must say to level-set any decision that we will make on that subject. First of all - the timeline. We have been on this journey for ten days, of which three days were spent in the higher dimensions. According to our calculation that actually translates to about 39.5 Earth years. That is just one way. If we returned the same way we came eighty years would have elapsed by the time we reach Earth."

That caused some murmur.

"That timeline is twice as much as we were briefed about before the mission. How come?" Matt said.

"Yes, Commander! Forty years, that is one way, as per the current calculation. I will come back to the timeline discrepancy question, but first, if I may I would like to present the other facts."

"The second fact to keep in mind is the need to maintain the system and all the machinery in a perfectly working condition. We see our main WARGER energy storage has drawn down by twenty percent in traversing through the other dimensions. Besides, we have nine additional WARGER packs left as reserves. Theoretically, that allows us to make three round trips to Earth and back with one pack to spare. When we started we had the MAM power reserve for 1 parsec or 19 trillion miles. In terms of light-years that is 3.24 light-years - one light-year shy of reaching Proxima from Earth on MAM power alone. We have expended around 47 million miles of that reserve in getting here. A related fact to consider is that the ship on a park mode still expends some energy daily. WARGER energy packs deteriorate over time, we all know that. So in one year of idling, we will lose about five percent of that

capacity. We have extrapolated that based on the fractional loss that occurred just in the last ten days."

"The third fact is about the force shield. We had 20,000 hours of force-shield capacity left, of which we lost 2 hours just yesterday. In another interstellar trip, we may have to use this for much longer than just a few hours, especially if we have to negotiate through a lot of planetary debris for a prolonged duration. Who knows how long such a situation can last?"

"In general there could be other accidents, blowouts, damages, or even attacks by alien beings that we may not have encountered yet."

"The bottom line is, whatever decision we take must consider all these factors."

Mirr and I were nodding, agreeing with the professor on everything he said.

"Thanks for the context professor! Yes, everything must be taken into account!" Matt agreed.

"I think we should dwell on the timeline thing a little more. Just as Matt mentioned we were told by the Mission Director that we will be back to Earth in forty years, which means twenty years one way. But what *you just calculated is twice as long. I don't get it, was he lying to us?"* Elea made a valid point.

"Yes, going back to the timeline discrepancy issue, I could not vouch for what Mission Director Dr. Amherst *spoke on that - if it was deliberate or just not accurately calculated. It is quite possible that this was a miscalculation. There are so many things still unknown in the science of inter-dimensional travel that he or anyone could be wrong on that timeline. Knowing Dr.* Amherst *so well, I would say it is more like an honest mistake."* Saito provided his explanation.

"Is there a way to cross-validate that timeline now by any other corroborative technique?" Matt asked.

"We have a clock that we had installed on Mars a few years ago. That clock is based on radioactive decay. It emits radio signals that we can receive from our ship if we were close to Mars to receive it any sooner. We used to tune in from the ISS (International Space Station) where I was stationed for a year. So, no, we could not do that from here –but on our return, we could tune into it." Slater said.

It took some time for us to digest that discrepancy in the time calculation.

"Team, I know how that feels but I would say, it is what it is. I hope that we are wrong and Dr. Amherst back home is right, instead. Since we cannot change time, let's get back to the topic of our discussion." Matt brought everyone back to the topic again.

"I would say, we should stay here for only a definite amount of time, no more than four to six months, and during that time do as many experiments as possible, collect as many specimens as we can, and leave for Earth." That was my instinctive response.

"My thoughts are along the same line, but I would leave sooner than later. Like in four months, maybe?" Elea spoke her mind.

"Slater?" asked Matteo.

"I would say we stay for a year and at the end of it, re-evaluate the situation to see where we are." Slater disclosed his opinion.

"Mirr?" Matteo asked next.

"I am more inclined to an under one-year time-line. We should go back at the end of it." Mirr opined.

"I agree with the under one-year timeline as well", Saito was in tune with Mirr on this.

"Bennet?"

"I would be willing to spend more than two years, maybe more like three years. I understand you may think I am speaking from the perspective of my fieldwork. Yes, I am, there is a treasure trove of gold nuggets in my field of work. But yes, I want to go back too. After all, we came here with a mission that I understand includes going back." Was Bennet's reply.

"I would like to go back by the end of four months. Why? Because I can't wait to ride my air-taxi again and resume my USTA tennis tournaments!" Greta responded

"Last but not least – Vladimir?"

"Well to your point first Ms. Thun! By the time we are back on Earth, eighty long years would have passed on Earth. Eighty long years, as the professor has just calculated. The people from your age group in USTA will be in their late nineties by that time or even dead. You will be playing with girls who would be your friends' granddaughters' age! (He paused and looked for the right pivot) ………sorry for saying so!

That would be fine except for the fact that there may not be any Earth left when we reach there after eighty

years. Wish I could call home and ask how they are coping with the mass extinction right now?"

Everybody was kind of stunned to hear Vladimir speak that way.

"Vladimir, what do you want to say exactly?" Matteo asked, looking straight at him.

"Well, just the facts, which you all are either in denial or are ignorant of."

*"You mean **Betelgeuse** bombarding Earth to bones?"*

"O' Yes! It's not like tribal knowledge anymore, right?"

"That is a theory. No one knew for certain. It could be in several centuries or may not happen at all." Mirr said.

"Well, that is the problem with you Americans. You only believe what comes in the news."

"Well, how are you privy to any special information that the rest of the world is not?"

*"A group called **'Open Information'** (OI) hacked! There is a vigilante public interest group who are good at hacking if that is any news to anyone!"*

"*Wait, what did they hack?*" I was curious too, so very curious, because I, more than any other person here know a bit of the story, from my dad of course!

"*I didn't do no hacking, just so you know! (He smirked). The OI nerds in Moscow did. They hacked IPNES, of course!*" exclaimed Ruskin shrugging his shoulders.

"*Impossible! IPNES kept all that information in its most secure vault.*" I was very straight on that.

"*Most secured?*" Ruskin scoffed. And he continued.

"*Well, even the most secured system has a back door! Let's just say some of the top scientists decided to free an important knowledge to the world, instead of keeping it locked in a secured vault forever that would do no good to anyone! Or let's say one of the scientists brought a copy of that 'secret knowledge home on his computer and did not take the necessary precaution to protect it from curious snoopers! I am just saying there are many possible ways that information could have leaked or stolen! I don't blame the scientist who might have made that inadvertent honest mistake and I don't blame the OI boys either.*

"*No!*"

*"If we are going to be eliminated, we at least deserve to know before we die, right? (Pause) But, hey, how do **you** know anything about it, if no one else does?"*

"Dr. J Song was the first recipient of that information. It is he who gave all that information to IPNES and the IPNES scientists in all their best wisdom decided to keep it secured. By the way, it is because of IPNES that we are here today. Is that a good enough answer for you?" I was demonstrably annoyed by his question.

"Well in that case your father must have broken his oath of confidentiality that he was not supposed to, right? He got tempted to share that little secret with his bloodline, huh?" Ruskin was really getting on my nerves now.

"He did not divulge anything to me! He gave a small note and all it said is this, word for word. It is in my pocket, I read it just this morning and it still is in my pocket."

"Let me read it for you –

If on your return, we are no longer there to receive you, be sure to look for my detailed message. I will keep it safe at an appropriate place inside the mission control chamber of the IDP complex. I will make sure you don't miss it.

I never told you anything about the glyphs, or how everything was connected to the glyphs. My detailed message will have everything, everything about your mission, about the future of mankind, everything that you need to know.

I happened to be the one to whom the twenty-three glyphs first arrived. I took the glyphs to IPNES.

IPNES decided to secure all the glyphs in a secret vault for the sensitive knowledge that they contained. I am oath-bound not to divulge anything beyond this point, at this time.

- Dad'. "

"That's all there is. He asked me not to open the message until after we reached **Astraea***. There is no mention of any end of the World, or* **Betelgeuse** *blasting Earth or anything. Do you want to see it yourself? Here!"* I was pretty straight with him, and I showed that note to him and to everyone.

"Well, in that case maybe the admission of that extinction is in the detailed message that your dad mentions in that note. But alas, we will never see that detailed message ever now because the Earth would not have survived just to safe-keep that one detailed

message" Ruskin sounded like he really believed what he knew.

"How can you be so feeling-less to talk about our Earth in such a nonchalant manner, Vladimir?" Elea joined in.

"Sorry about feelings, doc, but I am just speaking the truth in another way!"

At that point, the professor interjected with a solid point.

"Well, this is how I would reason. If the mass extinction event was known with certainty, all along, why would thousands of men and women work so hard to send just the nine of us on such an expensive trip? Would they not build an Ark instead, send thousands with us and be a passenger themselves, rather than sending only the nine of us?"

"Well, Professor, you got a good point there. I don't know the answer to that. But I trust my OI sources. I could not speak on behalf of the scientists why they would send just the nine of us and not build an Ark instead. There could be some valid reason – I just don't know. Hacking collects information in trickles if you know. But I trust my source!" Vladimir seemed pretty invested in his belief.

"*You probably got a corrupted version of that story from the person you knew, the person who knew the hacker who hacked some secret IPNES info, possible? An information chain that long could easily get corrupted from the original facts. You know that! Besides, the OI boys probably added their own cheese on top to make it more believable to the gullible, to make some money out of the sensation, no?*" I did not hold back some of my feistiness, not at that moment.

"*I also believe that they would not send us on an eighty-year long trip if the extinction event was known to have happened sooner!*" Mirr joined the conversation as well.

"*Well, I would say Vladimir may have a valid point here. His perspective deserves a consideration, just to be fair!*" Slater seemed sold to Vladimir's story.

"*All right, all right! Guys!*" Matteo intervened now, sensing the issue was getting escalated. "*Let's cool it down here!*"

There was a long awkward silence.

"*All right, a question for you Vladimir,*" Matteo asked.

"Just for once, assume that you did not have this prior knowledge from your sources. Would you still go back or would you not?"

Vladimir made some faces, his eyes and lips twisted and he came up with an answer –

"I still won't! I am sorry! I won't! I will not go back!"

"And why is that?" Matt insisted.

"First, we have this unique chance to start a whole new human civilization on a whole new planet. Such a chance comes once in the life of a civilization! We are very lucky!

Second, let's say we did get back to Earth and eighty-some years have passed. Who do you think will be alive from our time? No one!

Besides, Commander, if you will excuse me for saying this - you are missing a very important point. The deeper objective of this mission, I am afraid, is not just to visit some distant planet and to plant our flag there.... and...and..and come back home to report where no one you know is there to appreciate your hard work... and you go to another planet next, put another flag and.... repeat.

What is the real objective of this mission? To me, the real objective of this mission is to settle down and colonize a planet. The next mission after us will colonize some other planet and the next... you see... Besides, this planet looks just fine to me! It has water, oxygen, good climate...

We are not postmen, we are scientists and engineers who build something – this is a good place to build something!"

"*We heard you!*" Matteo then had a question for me too.

"*And Rex, were you privy to any knowledge that you are not sharing with us?*"

"*Commander, I have told you whatever I know. If dad had already told me anything in detail, he wouldn't leave such a sketchy note for me, would he?*

If you ask me, I personally believe that the chances of **Betelgeuse** *happening to us is a very low probability event.*"

I felt like I was defending myself for something. Not sure how convincing I sounded there. But that was what it was – the facts and my belief.

The group descended into a solemn retrospective mood. I have to admit that it was not like Vladimir Ruskin did not have a good reason for his stand, but I felt that he was hiding something there - something more than he talked about. It is not just the hacked information that he founded his belief entirely, but it seemed that he had something more there. But in a way, I sensed that Vladimir succeeded in seeding doubt in everyone's mind.

More importantly, our mission's objective is clearly to come back. We have the moral obligation to honor that objective.

Matt gave his executive decision.

"Okay team, my opinion is that six months is a good middle ground. I guess that should be some time for Bennet to do her research and for the rest of us to do some of our own experiments. I am not contradicting Bennet on the three years' timeline that she needs, but we have to juggle all the pins at the same time and keep all the objectives of this mission in perspective. We have already proven the science of WARGER, and in six months we will have proven the habitability question on an exoplanet. Which is our overarching goal, as we were briefed and so I believe, and firmly."

Matt meant six Earth months, which is about a year on this planet.

This planet makes one orbit around the barycenter of the binary stars in the time that Earth makes half an orbit around the Sun.

Matt continued -

"We found a location that looks perfect. It should be more like our taste.

Tomorrow we will go there and begin building an outpost for future explorers to take a break before continuing their journey.

We leave at the end of six months. So, here let me mark it on the ship's calendar. Number of Earth days until we return – 182."

The decision has been made.

Twenty One – We are not Alone!

I know it will be a difficult night to sleep, like every night so far. Our biological circadian rhythms have gone berserk. Can't complain, it is in our job description. We signed up for this voluntarily.

I tried my best to sleep, but the note that dad left me was bothering me. Especially after the perspective that came from Vladimir. What if his information is correct? I was afraid to think that my parents' days and the days of everyone I knew were so numbered. He has always been right on what he had told me on things that mattered to me. I just don't want him to be right on his doomsday prediction where he is helpless to do anything to save mom and himself. Knowing dad for most of my last twenty-one years of being alive, he would rather save another person than himself if that was the choice posed to him.

As I think about it now, partly incepted by Russ's perspective, I suspect there was a subtle implication of doomsday in dad's note.

We take power naps; seven of us sleep while two keep watch on the main control panel. It will be Mirr and I watching over the entire ship tonight, beginning the next hour. That is not like keeping a watch for any intruders as a building security personnel does. It is that and much more. Monitoring each important parameter of the ship to make sure that everything is working as normal is one important routine task during the shift.

The most important inventory on this ship, of course, are the three different engines – The **WARGER** engine being the most important of the three. If the **WARGER** system fails for any reason we are pretty much stuck on this planet forever. The **WARGER** packs need to stay a little warm, above 20 degrees Celsius because at anything lower than that, the reserve degrades quicker. To keep it warm we use fusion power, which means a small quantity of fusion fuel must always be expended during the night to keep the temperature from dropping twenty below zero. Besides, a ship as big as this needs some energy just to stay a little warm too.

Then there is the Anti-Matter reserve to keep a watch on. It is the most dangerous form of energy to tame - the matter and antimatter separation requires keeping one of the two large electromagnetic cores hot all the time. Any failure to do so could result in an explosion bigger than the explosion in Hiroshima. There of course are safeguards - multiple stages of protection are built into the design. But we still need to monitor it so one failure does not cascade into a domino.

There is the Fusion engine itself that needs to be maintained in a perfect working condition.

A few of the experiments that need to run continuously also require monitoring throughout the night as well.

If you ever thought space faring is all adrenaline and no work, you could not be more wrong.

You would think, what about **Cygnus**? Why is it not its job? Yes, **Cygnus** is there to safeguard and monitor the ship. But **Cygnus** does not care if we have nine **WARGER** packs or just one left. It does not care what specific experiments we conduct and need to watch over. Those things matter to us, not to **Cygnus**. To **Cygnus**, the notion of the ship's safety has a different connotation. **Cygnus** does not have all that baked into its algorithms. So...

Halfway into our shift, Mirr and I noticed that our mobile heat sensors in the **A** section of the ship were reporting some anomaly. The **A** section is where we store all kinds of foods and supplies needed for our survival.

Periodically, we run the automaton robot scanners to look into every nook and corner of the inside of the ship, besides, the starship has nerves running all over its body. There are known blind spots too, and we know that.

It is in one of these routine runs that our sensors detected some anomalies. It detected a few warm bodies inside one small zone in section **A** where there should be none. The heat signatures were that of a typical human body- distinctly four such - two adults and two younger ones.

"*See those?*" I pointed to the monitor displaying the transmissions from the rolling scanners.

"*Holy Molly... that looks like the heat signatures of four humans!*" Mirr exclaimed.

"*Yes, they are! Look at this!*"

"*Should we wake up Matteo yet?*" Mirr asked.

"*No, not yet, let's first get a visual. Okay, activating all eyes in that section to get a better visual,*" Mirr dispatched a few more baseball-sized robots to take a closer look in the area.

There were actually four humans - looked like an entire family.

"*How on Earth did they hitch-hike into the ship?*" I could not just believe what we just saw!

"*So what do we do?*" Asked Mirr.

"*We have to arrest them. Those warm bodies clearly pose a potential threat to this mission and to all of us.*" I knew what should be done in such a situation.

I dispatched two RS armed androids to the site to arrest them and bring them back here.

In a short while, without much resistance, the four were rounded up and brought into the central lounge.

I went to Matt's chamber -

"*Matt, urgent stuff. Sorry, I had to wake you up this way!*"

"*What is it?*" A visibly surprised Matt asked.

"*We have a problem! Apparently, there are people in this ship other than the nine of us! Stowaways. Hiding in the food shelves all along, after hitching a ride with us!*"

"**What the heck?**" Matt got up in one swift motion. "*Where are they now?*"

"*The main lounge!*"

There they were, the four of them, long-faced and appeared to have surrendered to their fate judging from their facial expressions! The man would be in his late thirties and the woman, likely his wife, in her mid-thirties.

"How on Earth did you freaks get into this ship? Who are you? Who let you in?!"

Matt was not even sure where to begin with them.

"Okay speak now… who wants to go first? I presume you are all one family?"

After a pause, the man replied softly.

"Yes!" the man started to speak.

"I worked for a company called Libra machinery and supplies. We provide a lot of the pneumatic and electrical machinery needed for the ship. I am the supervisor for a team of seven technicians, and I have the security clearance to get in."

"Okay, go on…"

"I know one corner in the food section has the dried meat section. I figured out that the roller robots can't distinguish between the dry cold meat and a human in

the mix. So I hid there with my family. (He took some pause and continued) We just wanted to live."

"*Elaborate please?"* Matt ordered.

"I heard the news from a source that the Earth will blow up and that it could happen in a century or even within a few months. I trusted him all my life."

*"And how did you get **them** in? They surely do not have clearance!"* Matt was referring to the three others.

"This is my family! You would agree that our world is biased in favor of the meritorious. It is always the smart and gifted who get all the privileges -all the good stuff. People like us? We are just people – never entitled for anything good. We are just people."

Matt was undeterred and was actually getting angrier by the minute.

*"**Not interested! I did not design the world, and I don't care how it came to be what it is! Just answer my question. How did they get in?** You could not have done that all by yourself! Who among the crew helped you to sneak in bag and baggage? **Who??"*** Matt was visibly mad, it was evident from the rising decibel of his voice.

The man did not answer the question.

"Okay, so you think we can't find that out ourselves... **Cygnus***, go back to the beginning of the mis* Cygnus.

<Yes Commander!>

The video search and match began and **Cygnus** presented a few short clips when the man got in followed by the other members of his family. There was the fifth person in the clip who seemed to be with them and helping them to get in.

Cygnus zoomed on his face.

After the face was clearly revealed, Matt turned around in a swift motion and the man seemed alarmed and spoke after him-

"It is my fault. I pleaded to Ruskin to help my family get in. And he agreed. Not for money or anything. He risked it for us! He is a God!"

Matt was not there waiting to hear it all, he was already gone to Ruskin's chamber. He overrode Ruskin's door code to get in, pulled Vladimir Ruskin up by his collars, and dragged him out of his chamber all the way to the control chamber. He pressed Ruskin hard against the wall and literally roughshod him with a few bangs against the wall with his big powerful arms.

"Playing God, are you? You son of a bitch!" Matt laid him on the floor face down. He was about to land a big blow on his face but stopped short of it. Instead, held him by the collar and dragged him to the lounge. We were still mesmerized at the quick turn of the events. Matt is a big and strong man, not always does he lose his cool that way.

"Is this your God?" Matt pointed to the humiliated Ruskin, still on the floor.

The man was visibly upset at how Matt treated Ruskin.

"It is not his fault. I pleaded to him. It is my fault.." The man said, in a very subdued voice.

"Well, hear this Mr., I got pleaded too, by a lot of people, some of them were my friends. They too were afraid-believing in the rumors floating around about the end of days. I am sure each of us got pleaded to by someone in private, for a ride on this ship.

There are scientists, engineers, soldiers, and medics who gave an entire decade of their life working to make this ship happen. They would have wanted to come on board too. They definitely did earn it as well.

Dr. J. Song, father of Rex, who is the reason why we are here today. He and the top IPNES scientists are the reason this mission was possible. They are the ones who built this ship from nothing. And the hundreds of scientists and engineers and workers who built the IDP port; they all would have been very willing to get a ticket to ride. But they didn't ask for one.

Dr. J Song could have said, 'I want Matt out - replace him with me instead' and I would have been dropped out of this team, just like that.

But instead, these nine of us were chosen, for some superior reasons based on some collective wisdom. Why?

Because this trip is designed for just nine, because it is an experimental trip because we are the test pilots to prove that the amazing idea of interdimensional travel works. So that this mission could be successful, so we can come back to tell the story and bring more people in the next Ark.

This is a human experiment! Not a rescue mission for people of anyone's choosing."

There was total silence.

By this time all the others were in the lounge, trying to make sense of what just transpired. I was worried about Matt's safety as much as his fury. What if he gets attacked by Ruskin under this circumstance? These four are obviously going to side with him, and what if they then begin to control the ship at a gunpoint!

I control the RS armed androids besides Matt and I will be willing to give any command to save Matt if I have to, even if it means to shoot.

Matt turned back to Vladimir who was now standing by the wall, his head hung from his shoulder in disgrace.

"Why did you choose these people and not anybody else? Why?" Matt asked.

"No one else had requested me for such help. I reasoned that when it comes to life how am I to judge who gets to live and who does not. There is no good criteria for that. I just ended up helping him for no vested interest as such. It was like he asked for it, he was there first to do it and I extended my help….he was just lucky." Vladimir responded, rather feebly.

Matt continued his justifiable rant of fury.

"Each of us has prepared our entire life to be here. Each of us has undergone rigorous training. Each of us has gone through all kinds of medical tests and procedures so that this ship is not contaminated by pathogens that could become superbugs in the conditions of space. We have earned our ticket to this mission among millions who applied for it, through sheer hard-work!

*These people have done nothing to earn it. **You have to earn it**! They do not have any training, nor have they undergone any medical procedure to hygiene themselves. They have put this ship, this mission at risk. And this idiot is playing God for random people just for asking?"* He pointed to Vladimir as he said that.

And Matt continued. *"If we all played God, all people on Earth would be here! Do you understand?"*

The woman and the girl were all misty-eyed at this point. The boy looking down as was the man, in guilt and shame.

Matt was still not done. He kind of whispered these words – near their faces.

"All these people are specialists in something, something that is of use and of importance to this mission. What the hell are you guys good at, huh?" Matt

233

asked the man looking straight to his eyes. The man was looking down in acceptance of guilt.

There was some silence as the question got reverberated in their minds.

"*Teach us, please.... tell us what to do, we will give everything for it.*" The misty-eyed woman said in a fearful voice. The nine-year-old girl was sobbing now and nodded her head in agreement with her mother.

That was kind of moving for me and anyone watching. It might have affected Matt too. He became somewhat quiet. Mirr and I approached him from either side, showing our solidarity with whatever decision he might take, as tough as that decision might be.

Russ got himself together, shaken by the suddenness of the events that put him in the eye of the storm for which he solely was responsible.

"*All right Commander......... I am sorry. I am sorry. I really am. I admit. I cheated and they cheated. ....I am sorry!*" Vladimir Ruskin was not running away from his responsibility.

There was nothing we could do here than to accept the four as one of us.

"The only reason I am not throwing you all in a cage right now is because I don't have an extra person to watch over you. We have better things to do than to police you! You, you and you too - you are all going to serve some long sentences after we get back home at the end of this mission. Even if there is no one back home I will put in a jail and make sure you all serve your sentences. Do you understand? You all have violated many laws!"

Matt hinted Slater to come close to him into a corner, apparently to decide in consultation with him - his deputy.

"Yes, Matt!" Slater stepped in. He was mostly quiet all this time. He probably did not feel like interrupting in the middle of his rage.

Matt looked at him, they conferred something between them. I did not get any of what they talked about.

"All right Commander, I will take care of the situation from here. Please go and take your rest for the rest of the night." I heard Slater assuring Matt.

After Matt left, we all stayed frozen for a while, trying to organize our thoughts. The man and his family were totally resigned to their fate, their heads down and shoulders drooped.

Slater was in charge now, and he said -

"Get these four examined medically, and lock them up in the D zone. Ruskin too. It's Matt's direct order."

Dr. Elea and I stepped forward and took them to the medical examination room with their hands still tied. There they will undergo a few medical tests before they can be admitted to the living quarters for the crew of this ship.

As Mirr and I escorted them, I asked how they survived the last extreme acceleration phase of the ship when the ship was on **MAM** drive.

They told us that they were warned about it by Ruskin even before the launch. Russ briefed them of a special chamber around that location for emergencies.

The man told his name as Angelo. The woman, his wife is Rubbia. Daughter - Mariam and son- Leo; ten and thirteen years of age respectively.

Angelo told me this as I walked him and the family to the Q-chamber in the medical section -

"I am good at all kinds of mechanical repairs as well as in building houses. I have this knack for troubleshooting things. I will not let this mission down!"

Later, as Mirr showed Rubbia her cubicle – she said something along the same line.

"I can cook any cuisine from many cultures. I am good with preparing food. I have a degree in culinary arts."

The kids pretty much said the same thing –*"I can learn!"* and *"I will help, with anything you guys ask me to!"*

It was kind of plaintive.

But we have to carry out a direct order. Two RS android robots grabbed Vladimir and the man by their arms. Mirr and I followed behind them

After the medicals, they all will go to the designated detention area of the ship.

Soon after we put them in the secured zone, I searched up in the ship's knowledge-based system to know some more detail about Angelo.

He had a clean record, no criminal background of any kind. He was of mixed race - White, Hispanic, and even some Asian blood in his ancestry – not that any of these matters. Rubbia – like her husband was part Caucasian part Middle Eastern. She did have a culinary degree as she said. I was relieved to know that they are normal people, and not criminals, which is a good start.

Whether we like it or not they are all humans - like us. But an important question of justice remained unresolved - Should we abandon the rule of law in favor of compassion even if they were guilty? That is a difficult subject with good arguments on both sides. A lot will depend on what Matt thinks on that.

Twenty Two – The Settlement

We are all set to lay the foundation for the very first human settlement on an exoplanet.

Astraea-B is different, even when it is somewhat like our Earth. Being different is good for our experiment. If we can terraform a small part of this alien world, as a proof of concept, we can gain confidence that we can terraform any planet that is somewhat like our own.

So, we set our flight path to that chosen region where we shall begin our first settlement. It is actually quite audacious to be flying this way in the broad **Astraeaian** daylight, not caring if native lives in this world see us. I just can't help thinking what kind of an impact such a view would have on Earth should a huge alien spaceship of our size fly above our heads in our skies. We are being audacious because we assumed that there is no intelligent native life on this planet. The fact is we just don't know if that is the case, yet.

Our destination was this flatland spread over an area large enough for our ship to park. This is a high altitude plateau that I had mentioned to you about - a stretch of plain land of an area comparable to a city in size, with its own lake, a river with rapids and a waterfall. The atmospheric composition here is in the right proportion for us. The area being located in the equatorial region compensated for what could have been an otherwise extreme cold climate. The lake was partly icy and patches of snow scattered all over the plateau as well.

We coined a name for this place – '*Pamir*', after the mountainous area in the *Gorno-Badakshan* area of Tajikistan, which was considered as the most inaccessible region on Earth. *Pamir*, if you did not know already stands for the phrase '*The Roof of the World*' - in the local lingo.

The name '*Pamir*' - stuck.

North of this *Pamir* is bounded by the tall snow-capped mountainous ranges that run for a thousand miles to the east from here. The south of *Pamir* begins after a deep gorge, followed by several ranges of lower hills that gradually get flattened until the valleys after which it is all flat- land to the south for the rest of the continent. Beyond the mountains in the North, lies the major part of the continent. It's a vast region of undulating contours interspersed by some stretches of flatland all the way up to its Arctic circle. There could not have been a better location than this for us to begin a settlement from.

The objective is to *terraform* this area with the means and the tools to jumpstart a small settlement, quickly.

Vladimir and the family of four have been under arrest for the last forty-eight hours.

At the end of it, they were released although not exonerated, because of the exceptional circumstance that we were in forced us to do so over the rule of law.

Except for the young daughter, the three of them each have to wear a metallic ankle band at all times. The bands are controlled by Matt and by **Cygnus**. I never asked Matt what that band was supposed to do. I supposed that it keeps them under watch all the time. Ruskin was spared from that requirement as an exception for his otherwise good reputation. Hope he learned his lessons. The man – Angelo, his wife Rubbia, and son Leo gladly accepted that humiliation as a redemption for their unlawful act.

It is time to focus on what we came here for.

First, we would need to solve the energy problem. Any civilization would need a source of energy to power it. We have an adequate number of sets of water turbines, generators, and cables to start a mini-hydropower generating station that could power a neighborhood of two hundred average households. We also have solar panels, chargers, and battery banks and we have two complete kits for two medium-sized wind turbines as well.

While we set it all up, we had some help here – on the energy front. There were at least two geo-thermal veins beyond the rapid. We could definitely make use of those.

I could see ourselves do some nice cook outs next to those, using the power of the boiling water holes, to boil some eggs or cook up some soup.

We successfully set up a mini hydro-electric generating plant in that small river. The machinery and the equipment that we brought along - especially the wearable Exo-Skeletons that we called *SKEL* enabled us to set it up sooner. *SKEL*s are different from the *TALON*s. A human operator actually has to wear the *SKEL* over his body to orchestrate its every move, just like a crane operator operates a crane's every move. The point of it is to enable a person to lift a weight that is eight times heavier than we normally can. The mechanical strength comes from a powerful engine that powers the two mechanical arms. In its appearance it could roughly be compared to the 'Transformers' of DC comics except a *SKEL* needs to be driven by a real human from within.

Within a week's time we set up some dwellings made of prefabricated materials enough to house the twelve of us comfortably in which Angelo played a major role. True to his words, Angelo has been very useful in such works. Rubbia prepared decent meals for all of us three times a day while the rest of us got busy with our scientific works.

Dr. Bennet was totally consumed in her own work of collecting samples of different kinds of organisms, mobile and static, cataloging them, looking deep inside them at the molecular level. She is an extremely passionate person when it comes to her work.

Elea has been taking care of our health, monitoring us for any potential health issues, besides helping in other areas.

I am responsible for the **WARGER** system, primarily. Mirr and I are the two experts on the **MAM** propulsion system. Besides being the ship's mathematician, Mirr also is the Fusion propulsion system backup for Vladimir. Professor Saito is our father figure, a true polymath, who has the most rational explanation for many difficult problems spanning across several domains. He knows the theoretical details of all three propulsion systems. Professor Saito is going to set up his own experiments designed to prove some important theories of Physics in his primary domain.

Vladimir is the go-to guy when it comes to things related to the Fusion propulsion system- its operation and maintenance. Greta is the resident expert in the maintenance of the auxiliary crafts and the other semi-automaton machinery such as the *TALONs*.

Greta will also help mechanize some of the terraforming work.

Ten-year-old Mariam is helping Dr. Bennet, like her assistant. They are morphing into one solid, two-person team already.

Matt is our Commander, our principal security officer, and our leader. For now, he will lead the terraforming work on *Pamir*. He and Leo will cultivate crops and plant lots of trees. Our kind of trees, trees to support Earthly kind of life. It will be interesting to see if our plant-life thrives here on this alien land. Will our plants grow to become the new super invasive species on this new planet or will they just succumb to the local life and never rise from the soil. Time will tell. We can only render our effort and take care of things, the result is not in our hands.

Matt and Slater are mechanical engineers through education and training. They both know a lot about machines that support the working of the ship, including the cooling, the air-conditioning, and the pneumatic systems.

All these might look like ordinary daily work that we used to take for granted on Earth. But that is the point, can we replicate the same easiness with which we make all that happen on an alien planet? Considering it's a different Sun, a different Earth, and a different ambiance – everything here is so different. Can we prove our ability to be a multi-planetary species by replicating our civilization on this alien planet?

Into our third week at *Pamir*, Dr. Bennet revealed something, something very insightful.

"I have looked at a lot of the samples of local static life here. Guess what all life forms here are at the deepest level?" Bennet drew our attention.

"Tell us...," Matt asked.

"*They have the opposite chirality to ours. Meaning, at the molecular level things here spin in the opposite direction to the things on Earth.*"

"*Okay, which means what to us?*"

"*Which means, nothing here is edible for us! Nothing! Even if we eat a whole truckload of them for lunch, they will not convert to any energy for our needs.*

Another way to say this, there is no native food for us here."

"*Wow - that is deep!*"

"*It sure is, Commander!*"

Good that we are planting our own food now!

As days and weeks rolled on, the grain and vegetables that we planted were beginning to sprout. That actually is so very amazing when you think about it. It proves to some extent the commonality of the ingredients necessary for life across the galaxy. The same ninety-one elements that are everywhere, of which the most abundant of all are Hydrogen and Oxygen. We need these two separately and in combination and we need all other elements to sustain life.

Our little dwellings have been extended and by now they are beginning to look like a real settlement.

Our days thus passed in Pamir - the days turned into weeks and the weeks to months. Three months are already past us.

In the middle of the total length of our stay at Pamir, Professor Saito suggested that it might be a good time for us to make a visit to the continent on the other side of the planet. Saito made the schedule for an excursion to that other continent. I thought this should be an exciting time for everyone.

However, Ruskin, Bennet, Angelo, and Rubbia opted to stay back. Each for a different reason I guess. Angelo and Rubbia did not have any particular interest in the other continent. They were just happy to be at *Pamir.* Ruskin had his own reasons, probably. Bennet on the other hand is too engrossed in her current work and would not want to be distracted.

So on the scheduled day, the six of us left with the mother ship for continent-2. We left one large **RAVEN** for the folks that stayed back, just in case.

Besides the fact that continent-2 was mostly all snow covered, whatever life thrived inside its caverns and glaciers was very much different from that of continent-1. Not surprisingly, because the two landmasses are totally unconnected, life evolved almost entirely independently in the two continents.

We collected a lot of samples in those four days of the field trip.

After we were back Bennet told us that the sample from continent -2 had opposing chirality with that of continent-1. That was a further evidence of our initial belief that life must have evolved completely independently on each of these two continents and that they do not share a common ancestor.

What an interesting fact that is if you think about the commonality of all life on Earth across continents.

Life in our little colony on planet Astraea B is going good, very good.

Twenty Three – The Last Days in Astraea

I get hit hard, once in a while. Migraine, a unique kind of a painless migraine. Tonight happened to be one of those terrible nights that I could not sleep due to this migraine. When that happens and for a good hour I experience a *kaleidoscopic* vision and my peripheral vision gets distorted. It is a very rare condition. It does bother me when that happens.

I looked away from my bed, through the window. We all have great views from our cabins, mine looks over the plantations and the lake beyond the plantation. The lake is at a slightly higher elevation than the plantation area and therefore is always visible over the plantation with the sheet of ice on the surface like a silvery plate. The two other planets were shining like two huge crescent moons in the night sky.

It must be midnight by local time. Suddenly I felt that I saw two things in the open space between two rows of plantations. Whatever they were, they did not have any shape – they were more like two completely transparent spheres, causing a clear lensing effect of the lake behind them so that the water surface seemed distorted around the edges of these shapes. I rubbed my eyes to make sure. They were still there. Is it my painless migraine acting up or just my overactive imaginations - I was not sure either way.

I did not want to wake anyone up and decided to take a closer look at them myself. So, I stepped out quietly. But there was nothing there when I went out in the open.

The visual stayed in my mind ever since. I was not sure if I should broach the topic the next morning or at another time. Wild ideas were playing in my mind that I know I cannot support by any logic or evidence. I was thinking what if these are the original intelligent species of this planet capable of total invisibility? Maybe they are just checking on their former habitat. Maybe they are so advanced compared to us that they now exist in some kind of amorphous, bodiless, and immortal state. Maybe they are just checking on us! Maybe they are so advanced compared to us that we do not excite them at all so they are not speculating on making any contact.

By the way, I might have forgotten to tell you, Matt opened the ankle bands from Angelo, Rubbia, and Leo long back - just a week after they wore them the first time.

After our return from the Continent-2, I could not help notice that Vladimir and Bennet have developed a great bond between them ever since. That is not unusual by any measure. When two people spend more time together they get to know each other better, which in turn improves their relationship. This was not bonding in any romantic sense. They just agree with each other more now than they did before. That is a good thing.

Ruskin also surprised us with his knowledge of the human brain even though he was always a propulsion engineer by profession. He would say- what better ways to pass time while being drowned in a glass of Vodka during the cold of the Russian winter than to solve mind-bending puzzles. Those mind games drew his interest in understanding the human brain.

Vladimir was actually likable but a whole lot more mysterious than any other person among us. Sometimes it feels like he is up to something, but I could not figure out what it is. He is an excellent propulsion engineer, and what he happens to be besides is his choice.

The count down to the end of the 182 days will start in a day. So, just ten more days before we wind up our business here. We will be leaving behind plenty of evidence of our hard work and human ingenuity.

I felt that some of us were having mixed feelings about going back to this soon. I sensed they thought we could spend some more time here. I can see the sense of an 'unfinished work' but I believe it is incumbent on our part to go back, to tell our tales to the rest of humanity so that someday we can establish an actual interstellar highway between Earth and this planet.

To me, NOT going back is not an option. We are oath-bound and we are deeply obliged. We owe a lot to a lot of people back there to think otherwise. It does not matter if we liked it here or not. Besides, we can always come back if we need to.

This is the seventh day of the countdown to departure. And tonight we will settle the question of Go-or-NoGo. So, over an open-air dinner against the dramatic backdrop of the three other planets illuminating this night, Matteo took the time to address us on a more formal note.

"Team! We are just three days away from our departure now. I have to say, all this time we have bonded with each other like a true family. I thank each one of you for that. In this short time, we have achieved

a lot. We could not have fulfilled all our mission objectives in just six months, but we did what we could - far beyond our own expectations.

Tonight is probably a good time for us to recognize our own work.

So here is the list of specific things that my team did. My team includes – Slater, Greta, and Leo.

- We planted over five hundred trees – from red oak to pistachio to pine and many flowering plants as well.

-We grew tuber, corn, rice, wheat, tomato, bell pepper, mustard green, spinach, rosemary, thyme, and sugar cane.

-We farmed chicken.

-We developed a small vineyard and even set up our little brewery. How cool is that?

- We sodded and landscaped.

We terraformed our little Pamir with these few Earthly things.

Next, I will let Professor Saito state his reports." Matteo looked at the prof.

Saito stood up and began his address –

"What have we learned or understood from our cruise through the higher dimensions? I guess - a lot. We have tons of data as captured by the observatories in the ship. There is work here for generations of Scientists and Mathematicians here - to sift through all that data and make sense of it all.

We set up an experiment to observe the two red dwarfs from this close-up and we have captured valuable data about the nature of a binary red dwarf system.

We had a much better view of the SAG A star - the supermassive quasar in the center of the Milky Way from here than we ever had from Earth. We have collected valuable scientific data on that too. The sky here is so clear that it is like renting the Kepler Space Telescope full time all for ourselves. From here we have a different view of some of the constellations as seen from Earth that helped to correct many inconsistencies in our previous understanding.

Folks - that is a wealth of work done in just this short six months.

I think Rex and Mirr should talk about their work." Professor passed the baton.

Mirr signaled me to speak on behalf of both of us.

"Friends, we kept our eyes on the WARGER, the MAM, and the Fusion Systems. All three systems are working fine as they should. However, we were a bit concerned at the rapid drawdown in the WARGER reserve packs. It could be because of the very low night temperature at this altitude that the system had to endure. It has drawn down somewhat faster than we had expected. About 10% faster. Having said that, we still have enough to make three round trips home.

The Anti-matter- system has maintained its reserve well all this time – and we are glad to report that we fixed a major point of failure which could have spelled a major disaster en route. We found the root cause and addressed it. We are good on that front now. So, you can let that sigh out. Finding the root cause required a lot of number crunching, analytical deduction, and assumptions. Thanks to my friend Mirr, we teamed up pretty well on that..." I concluded our joint report.

Mirr wanted to add something to that, so he said.

'Friends, at this time I just remembered what my mentor Dr. Kobayashi had once said about interstellar challenge. Our main adversaries are not any alien life, but our own technologies. To keep our technologies working has been the true challenge. Rex, and I fully

lived through and appreciated that statement during the last six months that we were here."

Vladimir's turn was next. "*This is a joint report of Greta and mine. Commander Slater helped a lot as well whenever we needed any. Greta and I worked closely all the time. She is a real genius in all kinds of machine stuff!*

In a nutshell, we kept all mechanical components moving as they should. We followed a scheduled routine. We inspected every rotating blade and every moving part and kept everything well lubricated. This included all the RAVENs, SKELS, and TALONs - I mean both the dumb ones and the not so dumb ones. (Everyone laughed out). You know!

I put lubricants everywhere including the door hinges of our cabins so that they do not squeak. And I put a drop of lube in the bronze buckle of Commander Matteo's leather belt too. He does not know. It used to make a little sound, now no more (everyone looked at Matteo and laughed out loud, Matt chuckled as well).

Okay, I am done! What else do you want to know?" Vladimir ended. There were applauses all around on his closing remark. In response, Vladimir raised his glass of champagne!

I wondered if he was taking a dig at Matt with the buckle metaphor. Could be his way to settle the score with Matt after Matt roughshod him six months ago.

"Okay, let's hear Bennet and Elea now." Matteo invited them to do their honor.

"Okay...Thanks, Vladimir for such a humorous way to present a lot of difficult work. You have been a great companion in my stay here.

Thanks to all of you for making this mission so historical.

I have cataloged over five thousand species and built a hierarchical nomenclature just as Charles Darwin would have done. At the gene level, our DNA and the DNA we find here are different. In fact, so different that I am having trouble calling what I find here as DNA at all. It's altogether a different kind of molecular structure. For the same reason, I would argue that the microbial life form here is unable to cause any harm to us as we are just not compatible with it, it does not need us. But should some of them become pathogenic for us, I would say we are pretty much done. We will have no remedy.

Having said that, some of the larger organisms here have a single cell structure. So everything that is inside that organism is all housed in that one big cell. I still have no clue, how organisms as large as a soccer ball could have just one cell and still go with the business of living just fine! There is still tons more work to be done on this. Six months in my line of work is just not enough.

By the way, the samples collected from both Continent 1 and 2 differ from one another in a lot of other ways too. All my work is in detailed sketches, with photographs and I have uploaded everything to the ship's archive!

Mariam has been like a shadow to me in my work, without her keen interest and hard work, I could not have done even half as much as I did. Big applause for her please!"

With that, Dr. Bennet concluded her report. We all stood up for her and for young Mariam, who was rather shyly smiling away through her lost front teeth.

"Let's hear from Angelo, c'mon Angelo, fire away!" Matteo called up Angelo.

Angelo stepped up where he could be seen by everyone.

"My son Leo and I built most of the dwellings, the community kitchen, the lab room, the lounge, and twelve individual bedrooms. Hopefully, your stay was comfortable just on that front. (Everybody applauded). Rex and Mirr helped me in installing and commissioning of the turbines, the generators, and the panels, etc. From that point onward Deputy Commander Slater and I have maintained the entire system without any disruption. My family and I are ever grateful to you all for a chance to be part of this. We truly are! Thank you all!

I am still sorry, Commander Matt, and to everyone!" Angelo was rather emotional as he still had the guilt of sneaking into this amazing journey without a proper ticket.

Everyone applauded, some came up and patted Angelo on his shoulder.

"Rubbia - please", Matt invited Rubbia now.

Rubbia, like her daughter, was shy, shy in public. She presented the briefest speech of us all.

"All this time I cooked 2160 breakfasts, 2160 lunches, 2163 dinners, 820 quarts of wine, snacks, and 2003 cups of coffee, and 3000 glasses of juice. I hope you all liked my cooking!"

Everyone burst into applause!

"*How come there are three more dinners than lunches?*" Saito asked.

"*Matt, Angelo, and Leo ate two dinners each on that one night they worked super hard!*"

Rubbia said with her eyebrows raised and a wink to end it all.

"*Oh yeah, I remember that!*" Matt confirmed the figures. This received some more laughter.

"*Okay, who is going next, Slater or Elea? Let's do the good doctor first!*" Matteo showed his hand to Elea!

"*Hello everybody I kept a watch on your health and I conclude as Dr. Bennet had said - the microbial life form here is somehow incapable of causing harm to our organic structure. Our body defense seemed to have been enough for us to stay healthy. However, there were a few strange conditions that bothered me all the time. Our blood somehow gets thicker and tends to get clogged inside our arteries and veins at times. I have no explanation why.*

I had to keep all of you on a blood-thinning regime all the time. Probably gravity, gravity on this planet being somewhat stronger here than it is on our Earth, took a toll on our system. That kept me awake at night.

Besides all that, I disinfected the entire ship twice during the last six months, the last one being a week ago. Takes a full five days to do just once. We don't want to take off with any alien microbial life forms on our way back. They all want to see us healthy, wealthy, and wise. Nope, not wealthy... nope, no one expects us to be wealthy ..." She smiled as she ended her report. So did everyone.

"Well, that leaves only Deputy Commander Slater, the stage is all yours Slater!" Matteo asked.

"Well, I was the liaison man for all the sub-teams. I helped out as much as I could with the extra hand that each team needed at times! I kept note of the progress report of each team so that we were aware of our progress as a whole. Think about my role as a program manager or a facilitator. I tried to provide any kind of logistic support that any team wanted. And yeah, a big hand to all of you, each one of you!" Slater ended his report.

This was a night to remember. There won't be another one, ever, with these same folks, in the same settings on an alien planet. Who knows what future awaits us on our return.

Less than 72 hours to D day now!

D for Departure!

Twenty Four– Departure from Astraea

So the day of the departure arrived. It is tonight. The dwellings that Angelo, Matt, and Leo built will be left behind just as it is. We are not dismantling anything. These are our temporal signatures on this planet.

We are packing up everything, loading our lab equipment, folding back our experimental setups, everything, back to the designated places in the ship. We packed most of the samples and specimens that we could - all packed and sealed.

We also installed and commissioned a beaconing tower up on the rocks. The natural tower is a rocky outcrop that no one who happens to fly over can miss. It will beep radio signals into the cosmos. Eight hundred and forty-two years from now, we should be able to receive the signal from Earth if we point our antenna in its direction. It will emit a full message in radio waves. Any intelligent species who can intercept the stream of radio signals should be able to decipher the meaning in it.

On the face of the rock just below the natural tower formation where our beaconing device was, we curved out the galaxy and our position in the galaxy on the rock. We chiseled the spiral arm of the Milky Way and marked the region where the solar family is.

On the rock, we carved out the date of our arrival about a time frame based on the radioactive decay of Potassium to Argon. If any intelligent alien ever visits that place, they will be able to calculate the time based on the science of radioactive decay. We embossed a representation of the two Atoms (K & Ar) next to each other with an arrow showing the direction of the decay. The original quantity of Potassium was sealed in an air-tight glass container.

The time to check out from our grand-hotel *Pamir* is set at midnight tonight - *Pamir* local time.

"Okay, guys, this is it. We probably won't be coming back to this planet anytime soon or even ever again." Matteo concluded.

Then came the bombshell disclosure! And it came from a totally unexpected quarter.

"I am sorry to say this Commander, I think some of us will prefer to stay back!" It was Bennet who said that, a totally shocking disclosure for the rest of us. I did not expect Bennet to say those words. No one did.

That admission reverberated even in the silence.

"What?"

"Yes Commander, you heard right! I am staying back, to finish my unfinished work." Bennet said in a calm voice.

"What? What does that mean? *You got to be kidding me!"*

"I am serious Matt," Bennet repeated.

"Finish all the unfinished work? *...to what end, and for who? There will be no one who will receive that knowledge."*

"I guess you are right, Commander. I will archive all my work in a sealed box inside a safe if ever someone from Earth happens to visit this place again. I have uploaded everything that I know so far into the ship's archive!"

"This is insane, Bennet! You will go insane living here on this island all by yourself, it will feel like serving a life sentence in a solitary confinement. What are you saying?" Matteo just could not believe what he heard Dr. Bennet say.

"She won't be the only one, Commander. I choose to stay back as well!" That was Vladimir. Somehow I predicted to myself that he will too.

And then Angelo spoke slowly – *"My apology Commander, I choose to stay back as well, and my family too."*

"Anyone else?" Matteo was now not sure if he would have even half the crew going back with him.

And then the next bombshell revelation came, from none other than Slater, the Deputy Commander of the mission! He said.

"I am sorry Matt, I too am in favor of staying back as well. There is nothing out there anymore. I kind of agree with Vladimir and Bennet!"

I had a general sense that Slater was suppressing his renegade mind the entire time since the mission began, but I did not imagine he would go against Matt this way!

"What??" Matt and the rest of us five just could not believe hearing Slater says that!

"*Slater! You too!*" Matt wanted to make sure he heard right.

"*Yes, Matt!*" Was Slater's short reply.

No one else responded.

I kind of noticed Slater not addressing Matt as Commander, as he should under the circumstance!

"*Okay... so six of us are going back and seven staying? Is that how it is now?*" Matteo asked. The silence spoke back like that in fact was the answer.

"*You are wrong to go back, Matt. That is a very poor judgment on your part.*" Slater was rather rude!

"*Seriously! Deputy Commander Darius Slater!*" Matt did not hide his disappointment as Slater's framing of the sentence definitely irked him.

"*I am serious! And in case you have not noticed already, the majority is on our side too!*" Obviously, Slater's action was premeditated. They planned this together, ahead of time. Don't know when, but they did!

"*This is exactly what the architect of this mission foresaw could happen. The majority doing the wrong thing!*" Matt said.

"Define wrong?" Slater was feisty, too early. I sensed that something was going to happen, something bad!

*"Are you doubting my judgment? **This** is the mission's objective – to go back! All of us. We owe this to all the people of Earth at the least - to go back, so we can bring more, do you understand? You are sworn to this oath as well!"*

"The mission's objective has changed, in case you have not noticed. And the majority has decided, so!" Slater took his stand not to budge so easily.

"This is not something that is up for a vote! Both you and I know that this mission has a constitution. In case you read the constitution at all, a simple majority cannot change the objective. If you are so legal minded, where is your two-third majority needed to change the objective of this mission?" Matt asked the tough question.

"Don't need, don't care about the Constitution. It's an existential question for us now. Going back, risking another inter-dimensional trip, only to find the Earth or the people not there anymore - is naïve and stupid!"

"Well, I care about the mission's constitution. I care about the people we left there. Even if there was a one in a thousand chance that the Earth and its people still

exist, I will go back. It is my decision. Don't forget I am still your Commander!" Matt was pretty authoritative when he said that.

"You were. Not anymore. The constitution of this mission does not say anything about a two-thirds majority needed to vote out a commander. So we are voting you out by a simple majority. I am the new commander from this moment. Does anyone have any questions?" Slater's mutiny was turning into a *coup d'état.*

"Well, be the commander you want. I sensed that you always wanted to be one. But know this. You all may stay back and do whatever. We six are going back with the ship. The ship can't be divided. I'm pretty sure you understand that!" Matt responded appropriately.

"Well, in that case, we are keeping the ship! It is not going anywhere!" Slater was going head-on. He obviously knows he won't be much of a commander without a ship!

Matt gave a clear smirk to that response! Looked straight into Slater and said -

*"It is very unlikely that **Cygnus** will choose to stay back, you know how **Cygnus thinks** don't you? **Cygnus** is already programmed for the departure tomorrow! And no one can change that now! Not even me! **Cygnus** will follow the diktat of the two laws and which means **Cygnus** will leave in eight hours from now, whether or not any of us are in it!"* Matteo made it very clear.

"No Commander, I don't believe it. A Commander should be able to override everything!" It was Vladimir.

"Well, believe what you want. You just were not privy to that briefing. Slater knows! Nothing can change that program now, period!" Matt replied.

Slater pulled out a gun, I did not know he had one. He pointed it on Matt.

"Well, Matt, I know that there is a 3ʳᵈ law. Who is that 3ʳᵈ law?"

"Aha, great! Well, a gun was the only thing missing here, haan? Okay! Just so you know- there is no 3ʳᵈ law!"

"Lie! I am pretty sure there is! We both know, I was in the same briefing" Slater of course knew about it.

"*Then you must also know that I or any Commander has no authority to persuade the 3rd law on anything,*" Matt said.

"*A commander should have the authority to invoke it, don't lie!*" Slater was pretty rude now.

"*Obviously, you did not pay good attention to the pre-mission briefings, did you? A Commander can only propitiate the 3rd law but he cannot know who he or she is or persuade him or her to do anything against his or her judgment. Is that a good refresher? And yeah, you are the new Commander as you said! Why don't you invoke it?*" Matt asked him back.

"*You bet I will. Please hand me over the badge! The badge and the shoulder band. Now!*" Slater ordered Matt, cocking the gun.

"*You are making a big mistake Slater! Step down, Slater!*" Saito intervened for the first time.

"*Shut up, professor!*"

Slater forced the badge and the band from Matt.

"*All right, Professor, you are the Plato of this ship, correct? And you know how to configure this badge and the band to **recognize** me as the commander! So let's do it now, Plato!*" He pointed his gun on Saito now.

Matt looked at Saito, hinting him to reprogram the two devices as Slater has asked so that **C-Mind** will recognize Slater to be the new Commander.

Saito had to carry out the order, as he was suggested, he had no choice now that Matt was asking him to do. He took the badge and the band pressed some codes in there, which took about ten minutes. At the end of which the badge acknowledged the change by blinking green a few times.

Suddenly, the ship parked a quarter of a mile away from where we began to blink a few times in acknowledging the change. *C-Mind's* voice came over from the device loud and clear.

<Hello, Commander Slater!> C-Mind said.

"*Good! Cygnus, I am your new Commander!*"

<I understand!> C-Mind responded.

"*I command you to cancel the scheduled departure for tonight. Do you copy?*" Slater gave his order.

<Sorry Commander, I can't obey that order. I am locked for the lift-off tonight, in eight hours from now!>

"Cygnus, I am invoking the 3ʳᵈ law, now!" Slater ordered!

<Sorry Commander, you can't invoke the 3ʳᵈ law, you don't have the authority! >

"Who has? Does ex-commander Michael Matteo have?"

<I don't know the answer to that!>

"I need a name!"

<I don't know who! It is not in my program or knowledge base to know that. It's a secret. You can 'ask' the 3ʳᵈ law invocation procedure to be set in motion, but you cannot persuade the 3ʳᵈ law to obey you. The 3ʳᵈ law has to be willing to do it. Only the person who has the code to invoke the 3ʳᵈ law can invoke the 3ʳᵈ law! So, in a sense the person who knows the code for the 3ʳᵈ law and the 3ʳᵈ law itself are the same.>

"It is designed to be a secret, in case you have not paid attention to the pre-mission briefings well, you son of a bitch!" Matt did not hide his despise for Slater's actions. He was not afraid to say so even with a gun pointed on his head.

Slater thought for a moment.

"All right, it is simple. I get it. The person who has the right to invoke the third law has to be the one among the five of you. Professor, Mirr, Elea, Greta, and Rex. Whoever you are among the five of you, will step forward and invoke the damn 3rd law. (Pause)

Wait – it can't be Greta because she is too young or it can't be Elea because she is not on the Engineering side of this mission. So it must be one among the three of you.

Well, so who is that among the three of you? We don't have a whole lot of time. We have just five hours because we have to be inside the ship three hours ahead of departure!"

There was total silence.

"Are you all deaf? *Haven't you all heard me? We have just **five** hours left. Am I clear?"* Slater was yelling and eyeballing each of us three one at a time.

Dr. Bennet stepped in support of Slater's case – *"Please guys, there is no point in going back!"*

Vladimir stepped in as well and said.

"I am sorry guys, to force you all this way. This is an existential question not just for the seven of us but for

you six as well. Time is not on our side. Please. There is nothing out there!"

No one spoke for a tensed minute, but Slater was apparently getting impatient by the second for not being able to figure out a way to get the 3rd law to step up.

*"**What are you going to do now? Shoot them for not telling**?"* Matt sensed Slater's impatience.

*"Not something I **want** to do, yes it will be a hard decision! I will rather do that then let you six fly away with the ship."* Slater was still in his belligerent best. We were surprised that he hid this side of him from us all this time.

*"Here is the logic of this situation, Slater. If the one among us who has the authority to invoke the 3rd law invokes it on your asking, there is no guarantee that you will not shoot him after he invokes it, correct? But know this, if you accidentally kill the real 3rd law on your assumption of rolling a dice because she or he did not step up, you lose the ship anyway. Want to know why? **Cygnus** has been eavesdropping on all our conversations as it is supposed to. It already has figured out the situation. It has sensed violence and knows that you - the new commander are perpetuating that*

violence. If you now force anything on it, it will invoke the 1ˢᵗ law and bolt away. You know that.

There is no scenario here where you can win this ship.

Also, remember, if you kill any of us, you lose that expertise needed to fly this ship. Each of us is essential to this mission - essential to run this ship." I laid down the inevitable consequence of the current situation and the futility of Slater's attempt to control the ship.

Fortunately, **Cygnus** is rational and it is smart! And for once I am actually glad that it is largely autonomous - in this situation we needed it to be.

Looked like as if Slater and Vladimir got the picture now.

Slater lowered his gun.

*"If **Cygnus** bolts, we all lose. All the **RAVEN, TALONS,** and **SKELs** are docked inside it, everything else is packed in as well, and everything that we need to survive here is packed already. Without a craft, we are stranded on this rooftop of an alien planet. That will exactly be like serving a life sentence in a gulag Siberia."* Matt said, rather calmly, knowing that Slater had no leverage on the situation at all.

*"Time is not on our side folks. **Cygnus** will leave without us, if need be. Let's finish our work!"* Saito goaded us into action.

"Slater and Vladimir, even when I am holding myself hard from knocking your teeth out, I still urge you all to give up your wrong ideas and fly back with us," Matt spoke like a commander!

There was a long awkward silence. Matt spoke again.

"All right, we can't fix stupidity, can we? But we are not as mean as you are, we will leave behind enough inventory for you all to get by with your lives here.

*We will leave behind one large and one small **RAVEN**, two **SKELs**, one **TALON**, one nuclear power module, the mini-hydro gen-set stays, and a good supply of medicine and food. (He paused for some time and continued)*

Well, I get it! It is your right to choose the path of your own life, and you have the right to dissent.

You all have just one more hour to reconsider your decision."

By now we all sensed that there is no way to talk them out of their decision to stay back.

Led by Matt the six of us started walking to the ship. We are now running against the clock. It takes hours to get a journey such as this to be readied. All protocols must be followed. All checkpoints must be checked. And we need time to unload the inventory that Matt promised them. And especially now as we are reduced to less than half the team, unfortunately!

Before he turned his back on Slater, Matt said this –

"You may keep that badge and the shoulder band. I don't need those to be a Commander. **Cygnus** *will recognize me just the same. Good luck and goodbye, all of you!"*

It was quite an emotional moment for us all. We are breaking a bond that was forged in the common desire to survive and succeed, and so unfortunate that it happened in such an unsavory way imaginable.

Besides, unloading the things that Matt promised, we also gave them two powerful computers so that Bennet can continue her research.

Among more other things, we left them three RS android armed robots for their protection, one AFF4 gun, and a few conventional arms and ammunition as well.

Just before we boarded the ship, I saw those two things again. The two apparitions like things that created the same lensing effect just like the ones I saw earlier in the wee hours of the morning a few days ago, appear at a distance. This time just over the edge of the lake close to our settlement. I turned away just to make sure it was not my distorted peripheral vision from the migraine acting up again. When I looked back again, they were gone. I could not even point anything to anyone else to begin to share my experience.

Five hours later we managed to warm up the **WARGER** system to get ready for the launch. The system check routine started. At the end of the third hour from now, we leave **Astraea B**.

We secured ourselves to our designated seats. In a short two minutes, the sequence will start and in the next twenty-five minutes, after the *bubble* thickens to a necessary measure, we will be gone.

We looked from our main control through the viewer. There was the beautiful settlement that we built, three-quarters of a mile away, in direct view from our main control dashboard.

The starship is ready to sail now. It levitated a hundred and fifty feet into the air and the **WARGER** *bubble* formation routine initiated. The bubble began to get thickened by the minute, until and up to the critical measure needed. Just as before the fog began to form all around us.

And just like that, we were gone from the view of **Astraea**, as if we never were there, ever!

Before we knew it, we were back in the 4th dimension. The coordinates of the flight control panel are now configured to where the Earth is. *C-Mind* knows what to do. It is the same way back home, the way we came. We cruised through the 4th for a good length of time. Not sure how long that was, just as before our sense of time got numbed in the higher dimension in an unconceivable way. **Cygnus** alerted us that we just entered the 5th.

As we're cruising through the 5th, suddenly something incredible happened. A solid sphere that was colored in midnight-blue, with three streaks of thick and rugged lines parallel to its equatorial band, appeared out of nowhere. It was like three claw-marks of a large feral animal on a tree. The three lines glowed bright blue. On both the Polar Regions of that sphere were designs made of strange symbols etched on solid gold (*apparently*).

It slowly took a rotation around its own axis and displayed the exact same three indentation patterns on the other side. It then took a full orbit around our ship and disappeared from our view. By a rough estimation, its diameter could not be longer than the height of a street lamp.

"Holy ... I know that thing. I know that thing!" Mirr almost screamed, loud enough to draw all attention to him.

"What is it?" Saito asked, and we all were curious too. How did Mirr know anything from this dimension?

"This is what my dad saw as emerging out of the river when he was just a child. So did my grandfather before him. Those three parallel lines in the equatorial region, that looked like claw marks, the shape, the color and the size of it, the gilded design around the polar areas, everything just like he described to me!"

Mirr was definitely excited, and he continued.

"Is this really where these things come from? That was like a century ago! Remind me to tell you the story in full that my dad told me when we reached home."

"Is it also possible that that craft is just one of its kind, and that 5th dimension could be its native universe?" Saito added his thoughts.

And then the thing reappeared from nowhere, posed straight ahead of us just on the outside of the control chamber. It now covered most of our front view, as if trying to make contact with us. It stayed that way, locked in our forward view. Slowly some shape or form, very patchy and very amorphous, appeared to be forming on the outer surface of the sphere. The shape was anything except any clearer. There was nothing anthropomorphic about it either. What freaked us out was that a small part of that entity began to creep into the inside of this main control chamber as if the solid body of the ship did not exist at all. The portion that was inside the chamber, was constantly shifting its shape.

We all stepped away from it, in a fearful response, like we were possessed.

The object stayed that way as if struggling to get itself together and to say something to us. The communication did not happen. It was more like an attempt to say a '*Hello*' to us in its own style. Apparently, it quit on us. The portion that was inside slowly dissolved as the sphere receded away from us -

slowly at first, and then swiftly. The entire sphere then went right through the hull of our ship - through solid metal, as if this ship did not exist at all. As we saw on our monitors via the remote cameras it reappeared on the other side of the hull and was gone in the next instant.

"*Whoa! What was that?!*" Matt said.

It took a mild jolt of turbulence to get us back to our senses.

<We are experiencing some kind of turbulence, again!> Cygnus brought us to our senses.

The same turbulence jolted the ship, in irregular intensity from one to the next, just as before. Something about that dimension causes that turbulence and that needs some correction, we just don't know what it is, yet.

"**Cygnus**, do you know, why that happens while we are on the 5th?"

<Sorry Commander, my troubleshooting routines do not have an answer.>

Until **Cygnus** figures that out, we will just have to hold our nerves. **Cygnus** took us one more direction up.

For the brief period that we were in the 6th dimension, the turbulence was gone and we felt as if we were near some planetary system. We felt we are passing through some kind of an existential plane where there are beings. But everything is so fuzzy, it's like we are submerged deep in an ocean where the visibility is so very sketchy and the liquid around us so very viscous. We could feel that creatures and entities are passing by, not caring to stop by or to make any contact, as if starships like ours are a commonplace here. It may be that they cannot see us or make contact with us just as we can't with them. Some of these creatures appeared so huge that it was not possible to get our minds to wrap around its true size. All we saw were bits and pieces of it but still felt like they were parts of the same gigantic being. There were others that were much smaller and clearer roughly resembling a serpent, with very brightly colored scales, and none of them exuded any sort of intimidating behavior at all. Some had something like a pair of wings but then could be anything else too. It is all a collage of a thousand things, difficult to grasp where anything starts and where it ends.

Most of the journey was otherwise uneventful, except in the last leg of it when a disaster struck. The **bubble** began to evaporate earlier than it should. All disaster lights were blinking red and disaster alarms playing ominously, all so suddenly.

C-Mind <Warning, I detect thinning of the WARGER bubble ahead of time!>

"Yes, by the numbers showing on my monitor, the bubble is evaporating too early!" Professor added his concerns.

We were totally consumed in the sound of the alarms and red beeps.

That news has to be quite unnerving for anyone. If we fail to take corrective actions on time we are done. There will not be anything left of us or the ship, not even our atoms and molecules.

C-Mind <I can recoup it.>

"What do you say, Professor?" Matt asked Saito.

"We should not risk doing it. We should follow the tried and tested method now. This is not the time to experiment on this. We don't have time on our side, Commander! A minute and thirty seconds to total annihilation! Commander!" Saito was firm in his opinion.

*"Ok **Cygnus**, throttle down to the lower dimensions...*
Now...We will resume our journey after we regenerate
the bubble to the necessary measure." Matt stayed the
course of Saito's suggestion.

C-Mind < **No need to panic Commander, I can recoup**
the bubble while in the higher dimension>

Matteo already took his executive decision, as we all
wanted him to at that moment and began the
overriding protocols to bring the ship to the ***base-dim***.
Somehow, I trusted him more than *C-Mind* on this
specific issue.

Matteo initiated the protocols and logged the reason
for his doing this manual override under the
circumstance.

"All right, Rex, please initiate override on my direct
command!" He ordered.

"Yes Commander, on it" I overrode *C-Mind* and
initiated the action to bring the starship back to the
base-dim. The ship was brought back to the *base-dim*,
with just a little time to spare before the *bubble* would
have completely evaporated.

C-Mind <**We are back in the *base-dim*! Regenerating**
the bubble now!>

Within the expected time the **WARGER** *bubble* was boosted back to its original strength.

We re-entered the 4th dimension and ascended to the 5th, 6th, and 7th – in that order to resume the rest of the journey.

This time, however, the turbulence in the 5th did not happen. It just might be that the disturbance is what caused the bubble to thin out prematurely. Or was it the other way around? Maybe we did not build the bubble thick enough, to begin with when we started from **Astraea**.

Something to investigate when we get a chance.

In a short two days from now, we should be re-entering the *base-dim* again. This time it will be the last sixty or so million miles to home.

Hours after we resumed our fantastic journey and we got settled, Greta asked that innocent question that she was not supposed to –

"Who is the 3rd law among us?"

"We are not supposed to know who he or she is!" Matt replied with a smile!

And I was smiling in my mind too. Only I know the answer to that question and I cannot tell anyone about it. Yes, I am the designated 3rd law of this mission and only I have the right to override **Cygnus** if the commander 'asks' for it. Matt does not know that either and he could not have compelled me to invoke the 3rd law if I did not think it was the right thing to do.

*"Commander, would **Cygnus** have recognized Slater as the new commander?"* Greta asked. We needed to know that answer too.

*"Let's hear it from the horse's mouth. Can you answer that, **Cygnus**?"* Matt redirected it to C-Mind.

< I won't recognize him as the Commander, No! I have heard enough. He was unfit to be a Commander. I would have quit on all of you and returned back to Earth!>

Twenty Five – Return to Earth

Inside the main mission control of the starship, crackling of electric charges within a crystal ball like a hologram, presaged the activation of *C-Mind*.

C-Mind < **We are exiting 4th dimension in T-minus twenty seconds. As we enter *base-dim* you will feel somewhat heavier again. You've been through all that.** >

"Roger!" Matt acknowledged.

The countdown to re-entry has begun.

C- Mind <**Nineteen, Eighteen,.................Five, Four, Three, Two, One**>

Starship *Pegasus* materialized somewhere between the orbits of Mars and Earth. The rapidly changing display on the main dashboard showed the distance to Earth from here as about 62.4 million miles. Considering the distance between Earth and Mars at the closest point in their respective orbits is about 147 million miles – this is closer to home than it is to Mars.

But seconds after the starship materialized, *C-Mind* came crackling again. The starship began to shake at the same time as **Cygnus** began to speak.

C-Mind <Initiating force-shield, maximum intensity...starting... Now.>

"What is it, Cygnus?" Demanded a worried Matteo as the rest of us looked sharply toward the still crackling *C-Mind*.

As displayed on the big monitor a thick layer of sparking and sizzling force shield was rapidly forming all around the ship.

C-Mind <Imminent collision ahead, Commander! Deploying offensive maneuver!>

"Steer clear instead. I repeat, steer clear!" Matteo ordered.

<Sorry Commander, disregarding your order. Not enough distance to target for that. The target itself is approaching very fast towards us and is huge. Deploying LAFF4 guns to vaporize targets. Now!>

Suddenly a massive rock appeared on our forward monitor and it was headed straight for us for a direct head-on collision. In an instant, the eight *LAFF4* guns at the front of the ship fired their lethal shots at the same time, obliterating the massive target ahead with everyone watching the event in real-time. The activated force-shield continued to incinerate whatever debris that kept coming after the strike.

The starship drilled through the now empty space that would have been a huge ninety-mile wide space rock if it was not blustered into million pieces.

The aftermath is now behind us, the eight *LAFF4* ‡ guns retracted into their original docked position inside the ship and the force-shield deactivated.

"What was that, Cygnus?" asked Matteo.

‡ *[LAFF4- is an acronym for Large Automated Force Field Model 4 gun as detailed in the list of Inventory toward the end of this book. LAFF4 is the larger and a few hundred times more destructive version of the handheld AFF4.]*

C-Mind < **Commander, a huge ellipsoidal rock ninety miles long!**>

"Cygnus, that does not make sense! The asteroid belts are far behind us. No rock of that size should exist in this region!" Professor Saito wanted to know.

C-Mind <**You are right Professor, surprised me too. Wasn't in my pre-configured mind map.**>

That unexpected encounter will linger on in our minds for a while.

After some moments of internalizing what has just happened, Matt spoke again.

"Don't know why, but I guess we have jumped the gun here! Big time!"

And he asked,

*"**Cygnus,** confirm our location one more time, please?"* Matteo ordered.

C-Mind **<On it now, Commander>**

C-Mind initiated a routine to reconfirm the current position in relation to the known pulsars and constellations in our galactic neighborhood.

C-Mind **<All good, Commander!>**

The big old familiar Jupiter emerged as the dominant object on the rear monitors. We still need to locate Mars, which could be in any position in its orbit around the Sun at this moment.

If science fiction ever gave you the impression that it is easy to find your way back home in space, well, nothing can be farther from the truth.

Imagine yourself driving through an endless desert on a pitch dark night, with no roads visible ahead or behind, and all you have for navigation are the tiny glowing balls of fires that we call stars, and even those are far away and far in between. Occasionally, some icy objects might zoom by you. The solid rocks that we call inner planets in our solar system have no addresses written on them, just rocks that they are, invisible if not lit up by the Sun. This is just talking of things within our Earthly neighborhood. In deep interstellar space, you will have lots and lots of, well - nothing, pitch dark nothing! In that pitch darkness, outside the aura of any starlight, invisible objects of all sizes are moving in a frantic rush - faithfully following their endless itinerary to nowhere and doing so at unimaginable speeds such that any contact between one another is certain annihilation of both.

That is how it is - tens of millions of endless miles ahead and in all directions.

That is the reality of a journey through space.

The distance to Earth from here is somewhere in the vicinity of 62 million miles. From here we will be on **MAM** drive to generate the necessary acceleration to reach home in a good time. At the max speed of nearly 940,000 Kilometers per hour on **MAM** power, we should reach Earth in about five days considering that we will need to slow down toward the end of the journey so that we do not overshoot. To reach that max speed, we will first need to accelerate at a very rapid rate and do that for several hours. We have been through all that before.

Jupiter was still in our rearview and will be for a long while. What an amazing planet for a view. I remember watching Jupiter through a field telescope of an observatory when dad took me there with all my astronomy enthusiast friends. Looking through that field telescope, it appeared no bigger than a marble then. This is that same Jupiter, now behind us, in full view, covering a fourth of the screen area in one of the aux monitors.

Elea directed a possible scenario question to Cygnus-

"Could we have emerged inside of Jupiter instead? Or even in the middle of the asteroid belt and possibly be colliding against a dozen asteroids now?"

C-Mind <No Elea, I would not make that mistake. Jupiter and the Asteroid belt are pre-configured in my mind map>

"... Guys, there is Earth on the forward monitor." Professor Saito said, pointing to the blue dot on the

monitor. The first clear view of our home after a long time.

"....wow, home sweet home!" Greta was excited as we were too.

"Okay, beaming our arrival message home now...so about 2.14 minutes for the message to reach Earth and the same amount of time to get a response back?" I said.

"From where we are right now? Yes, about that time frame!" Saito validated.

The radio signal announcing our arrival in five days was transmitted to earth.

Home is not too far now. Maybe like a quarter of an Astronomical unit away.

"We need to calculate the actual number of years that we were gone, taking into account the effect of time dilation." Professor Saito said.

Mirr and Saito got busy doing just that. After recalculating a few times, rechecking, and re-validating a few more times, they were still getting the same unexpected result. Mirr breaks the news -

"You guys ready for this?"

"What...?"

Everyone was waiting with bated breaths sensing something unusual, again!

"Ninety-five years have passed since we left Earth!" Mirr breaks the bad news first.

C-Mind <Yes - **that is about correct, by my calculation as well.**>

"That is about fifteen years more than we calculated while we were at **Astraea***! How come – so much discrepancy?"* Matt was curious.

"I am afraid we may still have to cross-validate what we just calculated from another independent source. Remember, we have been wrong on the time calculation before.

*If you guys still remember, we have a radioactive decay clock on Mons Olympus of Mars, which is designed to beam out time readings in radio frequencies. How about using that for a cross-reference? Mars should be within range from here. Chances are **that the clock** is still beaconing and there's a good chance that we are on the right side of it at this hour."* I made a point.

"You are damn right. Mirr, would you tune into it, please." Saito almost forgot about the Mars clock.

It did not take much time for Mirr to tune our receiver to the radio wave beaconing clock on Mars. The clock runs on the energy of cosmic radiations. It should be working even after all these years.

And it was.

After we received the transmitted time from the clock stationed on Olympus Mons of Mars, Mirr showed the reading as received to Saito.

The way they looked at each other in shock and confusion caused me to be alarmed as well!

"*Do it again, Mirr!*" Saito asked Mirr to revalidate the readings from the beaconing signal from Olympus Mons.

Mirr did. Same results! Something was fundamentally off!

The professor still would not settle for this, so he ordered -

"*Galileo! Please calculate the sidereal time based on the current location of all the known constellations as of this moment!*" Saito invoked a special program that does such astronomical calculations. The position of the zodiac changes every few thousand years, which is what **Galileo's** algorithm is based on. **Galileo** is the

alias of an auxiliary, knowledge-based system –
separate from the ship's main navigational intelligent
system – the *C-Mind*.

<Yes, professor! Doing now> *Galileo* responded. In
less than a few seconds, it announced its findings.

<*By the position of the constellations from this
location - five thousand, six hundred and thirty-four
solar years have passed since we first left Earth!*>
Galileo confirmed, to our absolute shock!

"What?" We almost screamed together.

The figure that *Galileo* calculated did agree with that
of the reading from the clock on Mars.

*"Five thousand, six hundred, and thirty-four solar
years!!! Which means we are in the year 7680 AD!"*
Professor Saito slowly spelled the shocking revelation.

We were so frozen that it was as if our faces were
covered with icicles. We just stood there staring at
each other, like some mind-less terracotta figurines.

*"7680 AD!! Can we even get our minds around how
huge that timespan is? How is that even possible?"* Matt
wanted Saito's opinion on this.

"Beats me, totally. This is beyond anything we ever knew and understood. Maybe that is what the higher dimensions do to our timeline. They twist it hard, so very painfully hard!" That was the best response that even professor Saito could come up with.

There was very long radio silence in the chamber now.

C-Mind weighted in after that long spell of silence.

C-Mind < **Time is relative!**>

"To you. You are a machine and time has no meaning to you. But for us humans - time is everything!" Greta quipped back to Cygnus.

C-Mind < **Everything is a machine, just of a different kind!**>

"Humans are not machines and you can't even begin to understand what we are!" Elea said.

The emotion in the air was so thick that one could cut a slice of it. I could see eyes becoming misty. We knew we were gone for a very long time, but not this long. We were prepared to accept forty years of absence, but five thousand and six hundred years- that's a real stretch. We were even looking forward to a reunion meet with people we might still know back home, as old as they might be.

We did not sign up for such a large order of time dilation. We were still in denial -how could we not!

"We are just drifters in the ocean of time now. I am sure the world has lost interest in us by a long shot. There will be no one out there within any number of generations from ours. We are probably just some names in some historical archives to them now. Okay, it is what it is. Nothing much we can do now than to get used to it, guys. (He paused.) *But remember we still have each other."* Matt reminded us to accept the truth and tried to infuse some optimism into our minds.

"Who knows what kind of beings humans have evolved into in such a long time!? Or whether our kind of humans even exist anymore out there!" Greta said.

"In terms of evolutionary time scale, not that much for humans to be something else, speaking in the physiological sense, unless they mastered evolution itself. We'll know in five days from now," Saito responded to that.

"All right, in another thirty seconds, we should be able to hear back from Earth." Mirr got everyone back to reality, igniting some hope that at the passage of the thirty more seconds we might hear something humanely.

Thirty seconds gave away to five minutes, there was no response from the earth.

"Looks like no one cared to say 'welcome back'. Let's beam another dispatch again...Cygnus," Matt addressed this to C-Mind.

<Yes, Commander> Cygnus responded.

A repeat *hello* message was dispatched again.

After the dispatch, *C-Mind* flashed out its warning -

<Sorry to interrupt the thread but it is time to power MAM drive full throttle now. Everyone, please secure yourself in the G-chamber.>

Just like before, we did what we should. We knew the drill and we followed accordingly. Matt pressed the green button after ensuring everyone was fully secured in the G-Chamber.

C-Mind **<Initiating MAM drive now, in T minus thirty seconds>**

The ship at the moment was already going at an incredible traction of 85,000 kilometers an hour and will accelerate for another two and a half hours up to the max speed of 940,000 kilometers per hour on MAM. That is some monstrous speed!

To think that even that speed is less than one-tenth of a percent of the speed of light, makes you realize how far away even the nearest star to our Sun is!

Two and half hours of accelerations later we are now at the cruising speed of 940,000 km per hour, which is the max velocity that we can practically achieve on **MAM** power. The **MAM** drive *per se* can accelerate much more given enough time, but the other constraints such as the mass of the ship and the material of the ship come into play to put a limit on the achievable system velocity as a whole.

We are out of our G-Chambers now. We will stay at this constant speed for the next four days until we slow down beginning the fifth day.

A good three hours have passed, no one from Earth has responded.

"Where is everybody ... someone's got to be there?" Greta, like us, was expecting a response from home.

I just announced my thoughts out loud - *"Going by the non-response to our dispatches, something big probably has happened there. Five thousand is a very long time. Hopefully, it is not some planet of another kind now!"* It could be that the possibility of the

apocalypse was subconsciously playing in my mind
after the argument we had in **Astraea B.**

Twenty Six – The Non-Welcome

The Earth is in the full view of our front monitor now. The same old blue planet, the only one – and the one so beautiful! It did-not look like anything that could be wrong with it judging from this far.

But the moon was beaten out of shape. Totally! Shattered and spread out like a comet with a tail of pebbles and rocks. Something hit it hard, so very hard that it has not got itself back together since.

Even when it is so badly bruised it still orbits its big sister – Earth, ever so faithfully.

"Oh my!" Another shocking view for everyone it was.

So many things are happening against our expectations.

After a long pause, while still trying to make some sense of it all, I said –

"We should circle the Earth first, just to take a look all around it."

"Agreed"- Matt

We were in for more strangeness. It was not just the moon that got out of shape, something else had happened too. There were a lot of small icy bodies orbiting around our very own Earth, giving it its own Saturn-like ring, except not as prominent.

We made seventeen orbits around the Earth, just like the International Space Station used to in one twenty-four-hour session, in the good old days.

We mapped as much of mother Earth as we could. Here again, surprise did not leave us far behind. The Earth down there didn't quite look like the Earth we used to know. Africa drifted apart, and it is its own landmass in the middle of the Atlantic now. It still looked a lot like the Africa of the old. North and South America are now naturally separated because what was the Panama Canal is now a narrow sea between the Caribbean Sea and the Pacific. The subcontinent of India does not exist anymore, the Himalayas begin right next to the shores of the Indian Ocean. Taiwan no longer exists in this new world.

But for a lot of sporadic dimly lit spots, most of the landmass other than the deserts is just one huge deep green forest. Must be very beautiful down there.

"Even five thousand years is not enough a time for such massive geological changes to happen. Something else definitely happened after we left that caused the

tectonic plates to reshuffle so much." Professor said to no one in particular, looking at the view ahead of him.

"Wonder, if anyone could possibly survive that much reshuffles!" Mirr said.

"There were eight billions of us when we left! Somebody got to have survived!" Elea made a wishful point.

"Looking at those many odd bright spots, some people could still be down there! It's possible that the civilization as we knew has regressed to the point that we are back to the pre-industrial era now!" Professor Saito reasoned.

"What do you say, team? Do we look for the same IDP port location that we left Earth from, or do we just find some suitable flat land and make our landing?" Matt invited opinions.

< I recommend sending a RAVEN (shuttle) down first before landing the entire ship, Commander. What if there are hostile beings out there that we don't want to engage in a conflict right away?> Cygnus asked.

"You have a point there, but I would say we should land, whole hawk! We have enough firepower if we are attacked. Where else do we go anyway? This is our final destination, this is it, our home." - Matt said

I added a piece of my mind - *"It is our home. We go in. Defend ourselves, if need be."*

"I would say that we should land in the general vicinity of IDP if there is a suitable place," Saito asked.

"Agree - somewhere on the Colorado Plateau, closer to where the IDP port was or is. Cygnus, is that still like it used to be?"

Matt made his decision known.

<Mostly, it is!> Cygnus confirmed based on the fresh data collected over the last few swipes around the globe.

*"All right **Cygnus**, set the coordinates for the Colorado Plateau region near the border between that desert and the forest toward North."* Matt pointed to a location on the monitor showing a closed up view of the region.

C-Mind **<On it, Commander!>**

I felt sad to be back home in such an altered circumstance, a home where there is no one to welcome us, where the neighborhood had changed so much that it does not feel like home anymore. I don't have to guess, I know others feel the same.

Twenty Seven - Home that Wasn't

We made a smooth landing at the northern edge of the Colorado Plateau, closer to the former state of Colorado. The lush green forest begins a short mile from here.

The sequence for powering down the ship was initiated.

It will still be a day or two before we can get out of the ship. We will spend that time in the acclimatizing section of the ship - a special chamber in Section C. Like all astronauts had to undergo in our times, we too will need to get used to our planet now. It will have to be some days of inactivity and getting used to before we could get out there.

The automated health scans for each of us came back as normal as could be - that was comforting.

As per the tests done, we have not lost a whole lot of bone density or muscle, but it will still take us some time to get used to Earth's natural gravity as opposed to the artificial gravity inside the ship. I'm not sure if the fantastic voyage we just returned from has altered us from within.

I just hope that this journey did not alter us so much that we could not adapt to our own planet now.

I want to stay human, no more, no less.

This is the fifth day since our return.

We are feeling good. We can't wait to smell the air outside, walk the walk, and feel alive on our own planet once again.

It was a glorious day, not too warm, just perfect. About 9 AM.

C-Mind popped up again.

C-Mind <**I have checked the air outside. It is safe to breath. No pathogenic microbial airborne life form or any allergens detected in the sample that I analyzed**>

"That's perfect, Cygnus!" Elea liked what she heard **Cygnus** say.

C-Mind <**I would still warn you against putting your bare feet on the ground.**>

"Don't worry Cygnus! We will be fine. This is home!" I lightened up *C-Mind*. *C-Mind* is always serious about everything.

"Can you ever joke, Cygnus?" Greta asked.

<I actually can, I will laugh at my joke but you will not. My tickle bones are different from yours.>

"Don't lie, you can't laugh like we do! Cygnus!" Greta replied, giggling away.

There was a sense of elation in all of us. Deep inside us this special feeling of anticipation that we will be able to touch our own home once again, brewing.

As soon as we got out of the ship, we opened our shoes, kicked them up in the air, and dropped our clothes until we were clad to a bare minimum. Our clothes - strewn everywhere on the hard ground.

We were actually feeling the Earth on our bare feet now. Never thought that touch will feel so very special!

The immediate feeling was our knees twisting and buckling under our weight like how a heavily intoxicated person would feel.

With some real struggle, we made it to the edge of the desert, and from where the forest begins. It was probably the longest mile that we ever walked.

The zero-gravity condition of interstellar travel does take a toll on the human body.

We stopped short of going into the forest. We won't go in today, not in this condition, not this very first day out. Besides, not knowing what might lurk within, would be taking a big risk.

We stood at the edge of the forest. The forest begins here, surrounding this side of the desert, as far as the eye can see. Just in this vicinity, a lot of the trees seemed taller than the tallest of all giant Red Oaks of the Redwood forest of our time, competing with its neighbors to be the first one to reach the sky.

We need to begin somewhere. Exploring the forest is a good place to start. But not now, not yet.

As we looked back from where we were, our beautiful starship was visible in its entirety against the backdrop of the desert to the south. It was the dominant presence in that direction. As huge as that man-made machine is, one has to be as far as we were to be able to see all of it at once. Such an amazing beauty that we sometimes tended to take for granted. It's our home, our noble stead, our past, present and the future.

Any deeper excursion into the forest will have to wait until tomorrow.

Several hours later we were back at the ship waiting for C-Mind to open the main air-lock entry for us.

"*Cygnus, please open the door!*" Matt asked *C-Mind* after putting his hand on the biometric pad.

C-Mind <Sorry Commander, I cannot open the main entrance. Please proceed into the Auxiliary airlock entry instead. The aux entry leads to the decontamination chamber – where you all should undress and get fully decontaminated before getting yourself admitted into the ship.>

"*C'mon Cygnus, it is not like we had been to a pandemic zone or something. We will leave our suits within the DMZ area of this main entrance. That should be good enough.*" Matt tried to talk *C-Mind* into opening the main airlock door.

C-Mind <Sorry Commander, the safety of this ship is my priority. Please proceed to the aux entry and follow the procedure, the right way.>

"*Huh!*"

It felt a bit weird to find *C-Mind* behaving so strict on the Commander. But it's okay, it is doing what it is supposed to, which is for our good, I reasoned. I had this uncomfortable feeling that *C-Mind's* near-total degree of autonomy in a certain situation might prove disastrous for us. If *C-Mind's* creator team ever saw this I bet they would have changed a few things in its program - altering the **1ˢᵗ law** will be one of them, to begin with.

The plan is to go back to the forest on the aerial bikes, and explore it from within while staying at least twenty feet above the ground.

That is slated for tomorrow.

Twenty Eight – A Glimpse into the Forest

The early next morning we were airborne, sharing rides in pairs on three aerial bikes. Fast as these machines were, in less than a minute later we were inside the forest.

The forest floor is thick with undergrowth everywhere. Apparently, the Sun barely shines through the forest's dense foliage. But as we went in and stayed hovered twenty feet off the ground, we found the forest nicely illuminated from within. The illumination was mostly due to the light emitted by the trees of a certain kind. These glowing flying insects that looked somewhat like butterflies added to that luminescence. With all that luminescence we could see everything with our naked eyes even when not much sunlight penetrates the forest canopy.

There were swarms of things besides the glowing insects here and there, many things, and species not from our time. The forest was teeming with life, life with colors of all hues and shapes. At sporadic spots in the forest, another kind of a translucent tree was emitting light from its entire body, brighter than the others that we saw yet, illuminating their surroundings even more. Each of these brighter trees was like how we decorated a tree with a garland of lights in our front yard during the holiday seasons leading all the way to the New Year's Eve. It was as if the whole forest was in some kind of a celebration.

We scouted the forest for several hours and we saw the same endless arboreal expanse in every direction and repeat of the brighter neighborhoods at irregular intervals. We did not see any animal at all. No wild horses, no buffaloes, no grizzlies, no arboreal monkeys or squirrels, and no bucks. It seemed like there was not enough time for any such higher life forms to evolve. If there are so many insects around there should be the carnivorous plants as well, the kinds that feast on the insects. Wonder, where are the other players of the ecological game of balance –the participating teams in the food chain? If our ancient past is any guide there got to be a food chain. But in the altered Earth, I wouldn't be surprised if insects were on top of that food chain. Is the Earth now the planet of the insects?

In our stop and go explorations of the forest we found this one lake deep inside the forest, a mid-sized one, like a quarter of a mile across in all directions. We screeched to a halt in mid-air to have a good look at it. The lake was about a mile in all directions. A portion of the Rockies starts from the opposite end of the lake. As we hovered over the lake, we had a clear line of sight to the snowcapped Rockies. What a fulfilling sight that was!

Suddenly, a swarm of small flying fish emerged from the lake and disappeared into the forests only to come back several minutes later. They wasted no time and dove straight back into the water. Hard to tell if these were the same schools or were just another batch.

We have had a long eight hours of exploration, enough for once, and enough for today.

Then Greta noticed something first, underneath the clear water of the lake.

"Isn't that a big ship down there?"

"Oh my God! It is!" Elea was as shocked as we all were.

"It actually is a destroyer!"

"How on Earth is such a thing doing under a lake in the middle of nowhere?"

"Whoa! What could land a destroyer from the seas to this far into the mainland?"

"Beats me!"

"Obviously the same event that caused the Earth to change so much.."

Took us a while to get out of that eerie sight.

"I guess we will have to leave the ship alone for now, until we know better."

Time to go back to the mothership, go back to the drawing board, and decide how we would restart our lives on our planet.

By sundown, we were all back inside our ship, through the same auxiliary entry as **Cygnus** insisted us to do.

Twenty Nine – Geological Forensic

An hour after we came back to the mothership, we were still internalizing the experience we had from the scouting trip. For once, we could not help feel like aliens on our planet.

"What do you guys think of everything that we saw so far?" asked Matt.

We were exploring our minds to come up with an appropriate response.

"First, we need to know what exactly caused the planet-wide reset of life and the rearrangement of the continents. For that, we will need to collect a few soil samples from the forest. The soil should tell a story." Saito suggested.

Matt agreed with two quick nods and said.

"How much I wish that Bennet was here with us now!"

"I agree!" Elea.

"If we knew what really happened, we might have a clue for where to look for any survivors. It is possible that a few did survive, even if civilization as a whole regressed." Saito continued.

"Is it possible that people might have become subterranean or even aquatic?" Greta asked.

"Subterranean - possibly ...aquatic - hmm much more unlikely - I guess" Saito replied.

We kept dwelling on that subject until late that night.

Let me fast forward to tomorrow.

Elea and I were inside the forest the next day and we chose a spot to dig for soil samples hoping to dig up the crystal ball that will tell the story of what happened and will happen.

By late afternoon, we will have collected a few twenty-foot long soil samples in steel tubes, from different locations.

The samples revealed that at every one thousand and nine hundred years, starting near our timeline, there were distinct layers of dark soil depositions followed by lighter deposits.

The proportion of carbon isotopes in the sample at the darker layers revealed the evidence of extremely high temperatures prevailing during that period. Something had happened at those specific timelines that incinerated everything on Earth. The Earth probably was one angry fire raging planet during those times. The fiery conditions stayed that way for months - probably years, enveloping the planet in a planet-wide carbon-di-oxide cover, fogging everything, warming the planet to a hellish condition. This was followed by a planet-wide freeze due to blocking of the Sun's insolation for a prolonged duration. At the end of both of these periods, the planet slowly healed itself into the Holocene condition that is seen now. Clearly, the same pattern happened twice already, if the smoking gun equivalence of the soil samples were to be believed.

Twice!

And if that pattern holds the third one is not too far away!

So, all those rumors that we heard before we left Earth five thousand six hundred years ago of an oncoming global extinction event were real after all. Or was it something else that caused this? Something else altogether? We have the forensic evidence of its impact, but to determine the real agent of that cataclysm will be another kind of an investigation.

If the soil deposition pattern is correct, the next extinction event is coming in less than a century, and the precursors to that could be much sooner. There will never be enough time for a species as complex as we to evolve, let alone a civilization like ours be developed ever again. During the short intervening Holocene periods between the apocalypses, this planet will be the planet of the insects - at most.

Going back into the past from our time, we had five known mass extinction events that had wiped out most species of those times. But those were far apart from one another, separated by *epochs* and *eons*. This is back to back, a separation of fewer than two thousand years!

In every sense, this Earth is a completely different planet now. Amazingly, we could still breathe the air now as we did back then, the atmosphere could very well have been composed of anything except oxygen.

We barely made it back home, and it may be time to check out soon, could be much sooner than we imagined.

But if some humans did survive, where are they? Where do we even begin to look for them?

Where is everybody?

Thirty - The Restart

Here we are, back in our planet of birth, our origin, our true home - except there is no home here anymore. Two global-extinction events had happened in a short span of five thousand years, and if that pattern holds, the next one will come again, and another after that -that much is now certain from the soil samples that we analyzed. Even if we reboot a new civilization, our tenancy on Earth has a short and a hard end of lease date, which at most could be a few hundred years at most.

This is the third week since we arrived. The main **WARGER** storage has been drawn down by half and the standby reserves we now have seven **WARGER** packs out of the nine left. As I had mentioned before, the storage and the reserves leak away with time. We can recharge all that if we find the lost IDP port in a revivable condition and reboot it back to life. Hopefully, it is still out there where we think it should be, and if we are lucky, the subterranean part of the IDP could be intact.

But first, we need to settle down, start some sort of a stable life, and go from there. We need to eat some authentic, freshly grown earthly food. It's been a while and we are dying to put our teeth on some good food.

We are a crew of just six now, after whatever happened at **Astraea**. Add four RAVENs, two robots, five SKELs, five **TALONs**, sixteen RS android armed robots, and five aerial bikes - still, a tiny army if we are to reboot anything in the size of a civilization[‡].

Over dinner, all of us were huddled around the table, and Matt asked - *"Team, based on what we know now about the fate of Earth, we need to decide whether we want to settle here for the time being or we don't. Time being in this context could be in the range of a year or even a decade or two, alternatively, we could just fly away to somewhere else and start there from scratch."*

*"My thought would be more along this direction - our first objective should be to find and revive the **IDP** – whatever it takes. If we can revive IDP we can recoup our lost energy reserves and that will enable us to make a better decision in terms of which next planet do we aim for. As such it is almost given that the Earth is no longer the paradise that we could settle down for long."* I presented my opinion on the table.

*"I would second that assuming we did find the **IDP** in a revivable condition. This will not be a small task, but worth an attempt."* Mirr said.

"In either case, we will need to settle down for some time at least - say a year or two. We need three people to engage for the IDP reboot work - full time. Let's call it the IDP team. This team could use four semi-automaton SKELs for the heavy lifting, two TALONs, one RAVEN‡ to assist them in their work, and two RS robots for security. They get whatever they need, first and foremost, this work is the top priority." Matt began to structure teams.

"We'll need to develop a secondary settlement. We'll build some dwellings, do some agriculture and farming as well. It will not be on the scale of what we did at Astraea. We are not proving anything anymore, just surviving until we revive IDP to working. So, we will need two people to be engaged full time on that– for some time. Once they get freed up, they will join the IDP team."

‡ *(Please look at Extra - A Catalogue of Pegasus' Inventory at the end of the book to know these abbreviations)*

"That leaves only one. That person could be engaged in exploration work - explore places for any sign of survivors, including looking in the subterranean caverns or inside the buildings and subways of the lost cities. If we find any survivors from the last two apocalypses, we recruit them as fast as we can."

The last line of course was meant to be a joke and it drew a chuckle as intended.

"The three teams will gather in person once every week. What say, everybody?"

"Makes sense!" Elea said.

Matt continued - *"Our goal – to revive IDP. Friends, we are all leaders and our mantra in achieving our goal would be - automatic individual responsibility. No one holds on to any information privy – we will be in constant communication with each other. We all are specialists in our respective fields and we shall work toward the same goal."*

"Absolutely, Commander!" Saito expressed his unequivocal consent to what Matt laid out.

"So in that spirit, please don't call me Commander from here on. Just my first name – Matteo or just Matt."

I likened our situation to one that probably happened a million years ago to our ancestors of the long past.

Once upon a time, probably a million years ago, a handful of nomadic Homo sapiens crossed the Great Rift Valley of Africa, leaving behind their cousins, to migrate to Eurasia. Over time they gave birth to the entire species of mankind outside of continental Africa. They were probably confronted with much of the same existential questions that we are facing now. They did not codify their thoughts at that time, they did not know how to codify anything. I likened our situation to what that one lonely band of humans must have faced, then.

This is our second chance. Honestly, we are much better equipped to reboot humanity than that lonely band of proto-humans from millions of years ago ever was. We have a fully equipped starship, with technologies needed to reboot a civilization from the very start. And we have us, the six of us, maybe the last six standing from the entire human race, a group of people specialized in multiple fields. We've just got to ensure that we don't lose anyone from among us.

We are the priceless cargo of our own mission now.

If a band of nomadic proto-humans from a few million years ago, possessing no science and confronted with very many extenuating circumstances could do it, we certainly can.

If we fail - shame on us!

Time is not on our side - we are on the clock again. The difference this time is we don't know what deadline to write on the wall. *As soon as and as best as we can* is the best we could do. If the apocalypse is cyclical, which most likely it is, then the next one coming is not too far away. Secondly, we know that all systems deteriorate over time. So will our ship and the machinery in there, and the degradation of stored WARGER energy is another thing to be factored into our calculation. We have none of the support system and supply chain anymore. To revive the **IDP** port, our biggest challenge will be to find a way to generate the necessary amount of power, in the order of GigaWatt Hour, to recharge our **WARGER** packs.

So, the only path forward for us is to build a huge solar farm near the site of the **IDP** to generate that kind of energy. But where do we find so many solar panels, in a twice beaten post-apocalyptic world? We have only a few hundred in our stockpile. If we have to get more we will need to build a mini-factory of some sort, to begin with, which in turn will need us to build more upstream factories. It easily gets more complicated from there.

We need to get innovative and summon all our collective creative powers at once.

Solving the power equation is just one part of it. It assumes that the main subterranean understructure of the **IDP** – the **WARGER** system generator still exists. It is reasonable to expect that it does as shielded by ninety feet of solid rock over it. We knew it was designed to survive the most catastrophic events above-ground.

Without much difficulty, we found it – the **IDP**. As big as it was we could not have missed it. It was the same legendary **IDP** complex that we started our journey from. It still exists. It indeed was shielded from destruction by the layers of solid rock – just as we hoped it would. The inside of the subterranean structures was still intact, just like we had found the pyramids intact even after several thousand years of disuse. It was not quite the way we left it, but still more than good enough. We can work to make it usable from this point up.

It still was such an awe-inspiring sight to see the size and scale of this gigantic and elaborate underground complex once again. It appeared much enhanced than we remembered it to be.

"Wow, isn't this a beauty?"

"Wow!"

"We took it for granted then, never looked at it with much appreciation. But look at this! Hard to believe that people just like us had once built it."

The first time we entered the subterranean complex those were the words that we came up with to express our feelings. We just marveled at this awesome creation of our own that was built so deep into the rock and so very intricately, sprawling in all directions inside the network of tunnels. What a genius of an architecture and design that it had to be to have survived two planet busting apocalyptic events! This gigantic structure tops all the *Wonders of the World* from all ages, hands down!

Hard to believe that it was less than eight months ago, from our perspective of time-span that is, that we were here when we left for our maiden voyage. Yet over five and half thousand years have passed over this land. It was a strange feeling to see something of this beauty and size left dilapidated in that short period of less than a year –speaking from our perspective of time again. It was as if fast-forwarding reality and waking into a bad dream.

This also means a lot of work will need to be invested to revive this mega machine complex, the principal challenge being to solve the hard problem of energy generation. No energy - no nothing! And we need a lot of it, in the order of two GigaWatt hours and in a controllable form. That is equivalent to the capacity of a major captive-power plant capable of powering a mid sized city.

How can we, a band of six people, achieve that kind of a feat? Such a project needs an army of skilled people and resources.

How innovative can we be?

That sounds like what despair is – this vexing problem refuses to reveal any solution to us.

But, somehow, when despair is at its darkest, something always comes up for us. In serendipity, Mirr and Saito stumbled on a solution. A solution that was always there, we just never looked hard enough.

It happened to us during one of our casual walks into the same primeval forest, on the same trail that we created by frequenting that area as many times.

We were at the foot of one of the luminescent trees. The sheer verticality of these very tall trees could hurt anyone's neck when looking up for any length of time. Through the gaps between the large thick leaves, I could see bits of the blue skies as well. The beams of light that percolated through the gaps in the canopy and merged with the lights emitted by the luminescent trees created a kind of a surreal backdrop in all directions.

Then, at that moment, Mirr asked the most important question.

"Obviously, there is a connection between the luminescence of this tree and the Sun. I suspect a very direct one. I actually am beginning to wonder if this is an example of nature's own form of a solar panel. And I wonder if somehow we could use these abundant, natural solar panels?"

That statement as if caused all our collective neurons to fire all at once. We exchanged a long pondering gaze at each other.

"During the night, the direction of flow of energy gets reversed, which is from the roots to the leaves, which in turn creates the bright luminescence we see during nights." And Mirr continued.

"For the glow to last the whole night, there must be some kind of a huge energy storage down under.... And I suspect that the roots of these luminescent trees form a network and somehow draw power from that underground reservoir in some ways!"

"It could be as if the network of roots tap into some energy veins that tap into a reservoir deeper down. That reservoir could be an ocean of a massive underground ion bank...!" Saito paraphrased what Mirr said.

"To your point, if that is the case the network of those veins running down under must be dense enough so that none of these arboreal growths miss tapping into one, even when at times the trees above ground are so widely spaced." I intended to refine that line of thinking.

"There is only one way to find out – we stop-digging-around-the-bush and start digging around the tree instead!" Mirr suggested.

"Sure, let's do it!" I concurred.

We had our digging machinery in the camp that we set up at the edge of the forest, which we used for digging for soil samples earlier. Time to roll up the sleeves and get our hands dirty.

A short hour later we had our equipment set up.

The next thing we knew, we were digging.

"This seemed to be one of the primary roots. Let's follow this." I pointed to a root that appeared to be spread out far and seemed to be the longest one of that chosen tree. Fifty feet further out it was still the same root running and not too deep beneath the soil, so we could follow it. The next luminescent tree was about another twenty feet away from that point, yet this particular root was still running strong. Then at a very close proximity to the trunk of that other luminescent tree, the root that we were following dives into the soil.

Now, this will take some real digging.

For the next two hours, we dug and dug to confirm where that root of interest might be heading towards.

And then it revealed!

"Whoa...Holy son of Jupiter!" I screamed.

"What!? The root of that tree runs this far only to become a root of this other tree?! Whoa! So, does it mean that these two trees share this one root between them? In other words, these two are the same tree, conjoined at the roots, even though they look clearly of two different species! How does that work? Whoa!" I exclaimed!

"Let's follow another root on the other side!" Prof suggested.

"Okay, let's do that!" Mirr agreed!

We picked another root and followed it to its other end, up to the next neighboring tree, just like we did with the first one!

And the same story repeats here too!

And we picked yet another one, to establish this theory beyond any doubt!

The rest of that afternoon we dug and we dug.

No matter which root we had selected it seemed to run into the next tree and become the root of that tree!

And the pattern was repeated for the next to the next tree.

All the roots of all neighboring trees are connected, even when the trees apparently belonged to a different species!

And we all came to the inexorable conclusion that all the trees in this forest are all connected down there, which the professor gave an acronym for - rhyming with the World Wide Web -

"It is a Forest Wide Web of roots! FWW!" Saito just coined the perfect term for it.

Whether or not a tree had any ostensible bio-luminescence property, it still participated in the critical task of connectivity, making the forest a true web of fully connected roots. It does not matter what species a tree belonged to –every tree was part of that web. It almost was like the entire forest was one huge living organism, in a real physical sense.

"So, it looks like it conforms to the theory in general! All the roots are connected in a network and the network, in turn, connects to the sub-strata below which is an ion bed - an ocean of charged particles – a vast reservoir of energy. It may also be that the network of roots itself

holds the energy within it – it is the reservoir." Mirr said.

"If we can tap all that energy- we have an auto-replenishing source of energy to power the WARGER packs, right here and everywhere." An anticipation of a breakthrough showed through our eyes when Mirr said it.

"Not just WARGER - anything! We can power anything with it!" I just put a bold font to what Mirr said.

"And this is really no different from how we used to use fossil fuel in our past, except here we do not need to combust anything to release the trapped solar energy in it," Professor added another perspective to this.

Fossil fuel of our time was nothing but the trapped energy of the Sun from the long past converted into a biochemical or organic state of matter! Energy to mass conversion principles and the law of the conservation of energy held well during our time and will hold well now. It's just that the form of that energy is different this time.

Post-apocalyptic evolution has created the plant kingdom of Earth so much different from that of our times.

During the day the thick foliage dines on the burst of energy from the generous Sun in the form of billions of packets of photons. The magic of photosynthesis then works inside these leaves - just like it always did. However, the difference this time is - a bulk of those free photons also get passed through the millions of capillaries down into the roots. As the photons pass down the trunk they trigger some bio-chemicals in the trunk and that causes it to light itself up and the neighborhood. Think of an optic fiber strand that has microscopic holes at irregular distances along the sheath causing some lights to leak – just for an analogy and not in actuality.

In the night, the reverse flow happens - the excess energy that is stored in the network of the forest-wide web of roots in some ionic-bio-chemical forms travels back to the leaves. The leaves have a bio-mechanism to convert it back to the beautiful glow that we saw spread out as bright spots all over the globe, much more in some regions than in others. We first prematurely assumed these to be some kind of an algae bloom like bioluminescence phenomenon.

"I suspect that the total energy yield from this forest should be in the order of a mini star. A mini star at our

*disposal, **think about that.** If we knew how to tap it!"* Mirr said.

*"Which means all we need to do is to connect the main power switch of the **WARGER** system with the primary root of the nearest big tree, somehow,"* I added my thoughts.

"To establish that connectivity we will need to develop the Root to Cable interface, a joint between - a biological endpoint to a metallic endpoint of copper and steel". Professor said.

"Correct! I suspect that the energy of the forest is either in a chemical or in an ionic state. If it is in the ionic state, even more expedient it is for us." I summarized the energy conversion process.

We did the necessary calculations that night. We also recognized that the side effects of that massive drain of power from the **FWW** (*Forest Wide Web*) may adversely impact the forest too, such as the **FWW** (*Forest Wide Web*) itself may get dipped in deep drawdown, but that should be only temporary in nature. Nature is resilient and robust - the next day's rising Sun will re-invigorate the forest back to its previous state. It's just that the forest will be feasting on sunlight a bit more vociferously.

We are going to run with this idea, all the way!

This should work! We hope!

Thirty One - The First Contact

Matt and Greta made over fifteen trips around the North American Continent, in turns. They were all over the map – literally! The objective was to find any human or animal survivor from the last apocalypse and also to map the landmass below from a thousand feet above the ground.

The plate tectonic movement of the African continent and the expansion of the landmass of Antarctica northward caused the creation of a new ocean. The old Atlantic still exists between the now drifted Africa and the rest of the Eurasian landmass. The new portion west of Africa and East of the Americas now qualified to be a new ocean with its own name. We gave it a name – the *Humanity* Ocean, even if it is just the six of us who would ever call it as such from now on. This was a fitting commemoration of the legacy that we humans once were on this planet, a small tribute to our lost civilization at the least.

In the locations where the cities once were, the ruins of the landmark skyscrapers of yore were still there. The twin world trade center towers, the space needle in Seattle, the happening cities of Dallas, Houston, San Francisco, and Los Angeles were all there just all buried, dilapidated and covered with thick arboreal overgrowth. In the former Middle East, the *Burj Khalifa* still rose high above the desert sand, even though only four stories of it stood defiantly above the ground, refusing to be cowed down by the ravages of time. Some reminiscence of the Eiffel tower was still above ground, but all bent and melted from the intense heat of the cataclysmic event -just like the melting clocks in a Salvador Dali work. So were the many other iconic structures elsewhere - at Singapore, Shanghai, Beijing, and Tokyo.

One of the shocking sights was the pictures of the International Space Station that lay scattered in dismantled condition that Matt shared with the team as he flew over the Australian outback. It must have been knocked out of its orbit during the apocalypse.

Another shocking find was that the part of a huge building that looked like the Empire state lay in the location where the Niagara Falls once ran. A huge space rock must have knocked off the upper part of the Empire State and the enormous force of cosmic gale carried it this far landed it there. That is a distance of about 380 miles! It somehow managed to land with its head up. There must be a lot of such chaotic relocations in many more places than just this.

Everything everywhere was in ruins, charred or defaced, but still bearing the unmistakable proof of our once-great global civilization.

If we did have the leisure to do so, we should one day dig up the lost city *of Las Vegas* from under the dunes that it is buried under. It couldn't be too far from where our now parked mother ship was.

There still could be some lives out there under the necropolis of the former megacities. The lives there may not necessarily be like that of any human type. We would be willing to accept even a rodent as one of our own at this point.

However, exploring these underworld cities is not something we planned to do any time soon. We've got a much bigger fish to fry. We need to revive the **IDP** back to a workable condition, to its former glory!

Meanwhile, the rest of us congregated under the same luminescent tree that we dug up the roots of – raking our brains out to find the best way to build that interface between the **FWW** and the **WARGER** system – to tap the vast energy from the forest. We pitched two tents there and set up our machinery and equipment closer to the area where we made our discovery. This is not too far into the forest and we could easily see our mother ship from this point.

Days passed. A few days, several days actually –with not much luck.

And then it happened.

It was Elea who first registered the familiar whirring sound and she exclaimed!

"Something is happening to our ship!"

We all looked towards our starship *Pegasus* - our noble steed, as it started whirring and the lights all over it started blinking rapidly. Then it took off and hovered at around five hundred feet up in the air. The low-intensity mode of the force shield appeared to have been activated and the four mid-sized AFF4 guns raised. The ship tilted itself at 45 degrees aiming to shoot at something it anticipated as coming from the south-eastern azimuth. Everything was happening autonomously - *C-Mind* was on its own.

Suddenly we spotted two crafts that appeared high up in the sky, south-eastward. Then the aerial shootout began - the attacking crafts drew first blood. In a very intense aerial battle that was unfolding right in front of our eyes, one of the alien crafts got vaporized by a lethal AFF4 shot that landed its load on it. The other disappeared fast into the blue as it realized that the battle was lost.

When the threat was over, our victorious starship retracted the guns, deactivated the force shield, and landed back on its location.

But, who did **Cygnus** really fight against?

Thirty Two - The Relocation

Back at the control room.

"*Cygnus, explain what happened?*" asked Matt

C-Mind <This location is no longer safe for us>

"*Who were they?*"

C-Mind <No clue, Commander>

"*Thank you for your timely maneuver. If this ship went down, it would have been all over for us!*" Matt acknowledged.

C-Mind <Don't worry Commander, I know how to protect myself >

We were still reeling from the shock of that hostile close encounter.

Here we were, we traveled through the higher dimensions, over a thousand light-years in the base-dim and we did not encounter any confrontation from any aliens of any kind. And yet we are getting attacked by some unknown entities, right here in our own home!

This does not make any sense, why would anyone or anything attack us, here! Who were they?

"*It appears the attackers came precisely for us. Are they the new natives of this planet now? Maybe the Earth has a new tenant now. If so, they are perfectly right to consider us as the intruders.*" Professor made a valid point.

C-Mind <**I think they are not native to Earth. Based on their trajectories, they definitely came from beyond the Van Allen belt.**>

"*Have we sustained any damage, Cygnus?*" I asked C-Mind.

C-Mind < **None at all, Zero!**>

"*Looked like we definitely had the technological superiority over them for once. But, again, that was just round one.*" Surely others will agree with me on this and feel relieved and concerned at the same time.

C-Mind <**My intuition says we will be attacked again, soon. We have to relocate.**>

"*The more reason for us to bring the IDP back to full operation as soon as we can if we have to defend ourselves against more such attacks in the future,*" Matt said.

Much of our continued superiority depends on our ability to recoup the energy that we lost. We are betting all our chips on the **FWW** for that. Hopefully, nature will bail us out one more time, even if it is a pain for her to do so. Mother nature has always sacrificed for us.

Matt cut his crisscrossing world trips short and told us his decision to move the ship over to the **IDP** port, and to camouflage it with the invisibility cloak (*not like a tarp on the top kind, but by distorting light and making light bend around instead of reflecting back, and thus appear invisible*) so that the starship gets blended with the environment.

Until we are ready to take off on a full tank of **WARGER** storage and reserves, we will have to reside somewhere inside the many chambers in the subterranean part of the **IDP** complex.

There should be no problem in finding some suitable living space in that enormous complex of a mini-city. Besides, the subterranean shelter will also give us the needed cover.

We followed that plan to execution.

We packed up the tent and flew the starship to the **IDP** harbor, put it in full camouflage, and idled it in a low power mode.

First things first - we need to continue working on developing the interface built, more desperately than ever, the interface that will connect **FWW** with the **WARGER** system mains of **IDP**. That is the most important milestone to complete in the critical project path to reviving the **IDP**. In addition to the primary objective of charging the packs, we need the energy to light up the **IDP's** subterranean infrastructure and do so without compromising our location to anyone looking to hunt us down after what had happened. We have to assume that the attackers will be hunting for us in greater numbers now, wounded as they were. We also have to assume that what we saw was only an encounter with a small casual advanced patrol of their full Army, a fraction of their full capability. They could be lurking in some corners, biding their time, waiting for us to get complacent and come out in the open.

"To defeat thy enemy you gotta know thy enemy" – as Sun Tzu once wrote in his book - The *Art of War!*

Unfortunately, we just have no information about who they were. Surely they have something of a vested interest on this planet and our presence here is not in line with that interest somehow.

They demonstrated that they are willing to shoot from the hip - shoot first, and ask no questions.

According to our plan, we will be mostly working inside the tunnel.

So, we set up our workshop inside one of the two miles long horizontal tunnels in the subterranean part of the **IDP** complex taking residence beneath ninety feet of solid rock, while starship *Pegasus* stayed fully camouflaged and parked above us.

There is this inexplicable feeling to this whole horizontal tunnel thing that begins from the steep vertical south façade of the plateau and goes deep into the interior of the mountain for more than a mile, running parallel to the surface above, as a part of the **IDP's** massive subterranean complex. If you ever stood at the gaping mouth of the tunnel beginning at the vertical southern façade of this plateau and you happened to look down into the valley below from the edge of a sudden three hundred feet drop, you could lose your mind to a severe vertigo.

The slanting rays of the afternoon Sun make their ways into the tunnels and light up a fraction of the underground volume for as long as they do. For one short hour, the Sunlight reaches up to the **WARGER** mains chamber. That is the farthest reach of natural light into the complex. That actually is encouraging -

we can use some of that daylight inside the tunnel for our work.

Several weeks of hard work finally paid off. Mirr, Saito, and I worked on engineering a solution to this hard problem of FWW to the system mains interface, but we hit a wall at one point. We hit a dead-end using our line of thinking. It was Greta, her unique approach to problem-solving that did the magic for us. This young lady did earn her admission to this mission for a solid good reason.

Toeing along Greta's suggestion and after expending five days of sweats we finally solved the problem of the interface. We are now almost ready to test the last connectivity between **FWW** and the **WARGER** main - the all-important last hundred yards connecting nature with technology.

Tonight is the night that we will test our work. In a short hour from now as the night sets in, we will throw the main switch down to test our work up to this point.

Over five thousand years of disuse has rendered the entire electrical system dysfunctional. All that web of electrical wirings must have faults at several places. There were more hurdles that we had to overcome to get the power flowing up to the **WARGER** system mains.

As expected, the first throw of the switch caused a lot of *sparks* at many locations, but we were screaming with joy exactly because of that. The *spark* was the reason for that joy. That means the **FWW** as a power source is a sound theory. There indeed was power coming in from the forest through the interface that we had built.

Within the next few days, we got the power in up to the **WARGER** system main. We also got a lot of bulbs to glow in different sections of the underground chambers.

From here on, we will inspect and revive each system component that makes up the **WARGER** complex. It will be mostly Mirr, Professor, and I who will be working on it every hour of the day and well into the night. Matt, Elea, and Greta will engage in exploring the chambers and the lab facilities that are located further into the massive interior. They will venture into the darker depth of the complex where no natural light ever illuminates.

As we brought in light into the subterranean complex, we also discovered the horrific side of it. There were a large number of human skeletons in almost all the chambers that we lit up to this point - skeletons of people desperate to find a safe haven as the Earth was scorching in the hellish conditions from the apocalypse, above. They probably died of asphyxiation than of anything else, as there were no charred bones found inside any of these chambers. The heat might not have reached this deep underground but the toxic air did.

Who knows, some of those bones could be of people we knew depending on when that apocalypse had happened. One of them could even be my dad who used to frequent this facility as one of the key persons of the programs.

After the hellish conditions subsided and the atmosphere detoxified itself, termites and other microbes gnawed away most of the biodegradable remains including any wooden structures that once existed.

After a few days of such daily visuals of human remains inside this necropolis we almost became desensitized.

But it was not just the skeletons that we found, we found more - a treasure trove of time capsules - from our time.

Thirty Three - The Time Capsules

It's been weeks now and we've gotten to the point where things are really looking good for us. We are making progress. Hopefully, we will be able to do a complete regression test of the **WARGER** system soon – the end to end test that is.

We discovered the main mission control chamber from where the launches were orchestrated. The huge chamber has survived the ravage of time, largely. It looked much improved and enhanced than we last remembered it to be. This means several more launches probably had happened after ours. Bigger missions and bigger ships that needed more enhancements to these facilities. The chairs with worn-out upholstery over steel frames sat lay strewn everywhere. On the desks were the name tags cut on steel plates, thrown in total disarray. The hall seems large enough to fit up to eight-hundred team members at once.

This must be it – the place where I sensed I should find some relics connected to my dad. If my dad, and the other contemporary and prominent scientists whom I knew personally had lived until the time of the apocalypse, they each must have had their name tags among the disarray of things lying around.

And then I stumbled upon a name-tag on the concrete floor. It bore the three words - *Dr. J Song.* On the back of it and cut on steel was this – *Chief Scientist, Program Zulu, Andromeda.* That probably was the last program that dad led from this chamber.

Tears rolled down my eyes – and I whispered – *"Dad!"* as I ran my fingers over his name.

I felt Matteo's large hand of comfort on my shoulder. I also felt Greta hugging me from behind.

There was professor Saito, holding on to two name tags, of people that he knew very closely. He too was in tears like I was.

There were other names who I knew through dad, the other colleagues of his.

The founding **IPNES** scientists I knew through dad probably did not live to the doomsdays. They were much older than dad was.

Still, their names have to be somewhere here considering their immense contributions to the program!

We went to the next chamber, which was four times as large. There was no furniture here, just arrays of glass-covered stainless steel coffins – a thousand such, stacked along the walls. In them lay skeletons of men, women, and children. The coffins with a pair of skeletons inside were the most common ones. Many of the coffins had an entire family inside. All these unnamed and untagged coffins must belong to the people who ever worked in the IDP complex or were connected with the programs in some way. All of them at one time gathered here and quietly accepted their fate, within hours or minutes of each other. Inside each of the steely coffins was a tiny bottle, something to poison oneself with to a quicker end rather than to suffer death through painful asphyxiation, I suppose.

One of those couples would be my mom and my dad, I guess, no way to tell which one.

Still, the dead here are a lot more fortunate compared to those hapless people who perished outside this chamber at random places in the random locations.

The high walls opposite the RIP rows were engraved with the names of all scientists from all disciplines, from all nations and from all ages until the year 2091. That wall of fame featured the names of Dr. Steinberg, Dr. Tao, Dr. Kobayashi, Dr. Chandra, and Dr. Amherst.

On the wall opposite to the 'Wall of Fame', engraved on granite and repeated just below it on stainless steel, was this –

"Please look inside, here"

There was a lever next to that caption. When I pulled it a heavy steely door opened into a vault. Inside that vault was a library of some sort, divided into different sections based on the subject matter. All subjects from Music to Poetry to Physics to the many other fields that human ingenuity ever produced were there. There were three versions of each resource. One, in printed material, another - engraved on special sheets of metal like cuneiform tablets and the third - a digital record housed inside an airtight container. On the wall of the **Physics** section, all the great equations ever discovered by humans were engraved.

Within this section was a sub-section titled – THE **WARGER SYSTEM.**

The probable idea behind keeping the three versions of the same information was this - if it ever happens that some solar flare or electro-magnetic pulse wipes out the digital media, the other versions should survive.

In another corner of the large chamber were several specially designed personal computers. They were designed to be functional over a long period. Some pictorial instructions were engraved on the granite nearby, depicting a technique to build an electrochemical battery from ordinary household materials.

Inside the **WARGER SYSTEM** section was a small glass-covered metallic box with a name embossed on it –

Dr. J. Song.

I instinctively lifted the box, showed it to the others and bagged it in my backpack.

I will go back to the ship and open it tonight.

Thirty Four –Dad's Message

I told my fellow crew members that I will use the evening to view dad's message.

So, back in the privacy of my chamber, I connected the digital version of dad's message to the computer system. It gave me two options that said –

[If you are Rex Song please click this, otherwise click this.]

I clicked the first option. He appeared as lifelike as can be but looked much older than I knew him to be, and he spoke directly to me.

He recorded the video like a direct conversation between me and he, like it was in the old times of our days at the beach. It was a *smart* recording in the sense that I don't have to watch it linearly from the beginning to the end. I can actually pose my questions at any point during the run and the *natural language processing* built into the program can take me to that point in the recording where dad addresses that specific question.

The conversation with my dad from the long past thus began.

"Rex, my son! I know that as per your mission objective, one day you will come back. We also precluded that your traveling through time makes it impossible for us to ever meet in person again.

Hopefully, this message survives the apocalypse and finds you, which it has because you are watching this now.

This is the year 2091, which happens to be also the last year for most life on earth. I am ninety one today." He began.

"Happy Birth Day, dad!" I found myself saying.

"Thank you, Rex!" He responded.

He actually said that, as if he was right there in front of me. I don't know how, but he made the recording interactive and smart.

I will listen to him in the sequence that he wanted me to listen to.

"Rex, let me start off by saying how proud mom and I are of you. You made it to the first Inter-Dimensional Interstellar manned mission ever undertaken by humans. This is equivalent to being among the likes of Neil Armstrong, Buzz Aldrin, Mike Collins, Yuri

Gagarin, and Valentina Tereshkova. Congratulations son and congratulations to your crew."

"Thank you, dad!" I said again!

"You are welcome!"

"You might be wondering how I am responding back to you like I am a real person in your present? We have to thank the **glyphs** for that. The **glyphs** taught us how to create a time-independent exchange of information so that I can change my response based on your question. The **glyphs** showed us how to communicate at the rawest level that the brain understands. Being able to communicate at the rawest level is foundational to our ability to build a clean, and a perfect civilization. This is not a video recording, although you may experience this as such in your perception. It is a program. I am actually talking directly to your mind. We are communicating via a very different method of communication."

"Dad, I don't remember you mentioning any such programs to me." I was curious.

"You are right! I hid it from you because I was under oath at that time. Besides, the program was locked away in the secured vault of IPNES." He answered.

"In that case, are you not breaking your oath by telling me this now?" I asked.

"No, not now, not anymore, the statutory period of that oath will have long expired by the time you would view this."

*"Sorry to interrupt, what's a **glyph**, dad?"*

"There is another recording in this archive that explains it all. It would not be such a bad idea to watch that first. I can wait. We can resume after you've done watching that recording!"

Yes, I followed his suggestion and watched the 'other' recording so I could understand the sequence of events and that is how I could narrate everything to you up to this point, even those events that happened before my birth. Took me a while to go through the other recordings. I could not view all of them as there were too many, but I have viewed enough to understand what had happened.

I pressed 'Continue' on the second recording and dad resumed.

"Okay, you are back. I assume you had viewed the first recording already. If not, for now just understand that someone - a totally unknown someone, not of human

origin, sent us some **glyphs** that contained some very extraordinary knowledge for us so we can save as many of us from an impending global extinction event.

By the end of this year of 2091, no life form on Earth that we know, will have survived. The gamma blast from **Betelgeuse** will take everything out.

They implied that in the 19th **glyph,** although not in very certain terms or with any specific end date. So, we knew about the coming gamma blast even before we saw the nebula the very first time. We knew since 2034 that we were on the clock."

"So sad to hear that, dad," I said.

"Okay, about the **glyphs** again ... The information conveyed in the glyph was more than a bombshell revelation for humanity and letting it loose on the public domain could land the world into a chaos like never before. So our first reaction was to keep everything confidential until we figured out how to deal with the issue of dissipating the knowledge in a world divided into adversarial nations, divided societies, and asymmetric power structures. The difficult task for us was to decide who do we dissipate that knowledge to and by what modus operandi? We reasoned that – if 'they' wished they could have revealed the glyphs to every person or groups in the world all at once, they could have given it to someone in the government instead, or to the well-known media. But they didn't, instead, they chose IPNES, through me, as the keeper of that enormous knowledge. And they took it away from Liu, not sure why – 'need to know' basis I guess. We kept deliberating on this issue for a year as we could not arrive at an unequivocal conclusion.

But we, at IPNES, were aware that sealing that information forever in that vault is equivalent to trashing that enormously powerful knowledge into oblivion. We argued that even when we democratized that knowledge among the right kind of people to begin with, we also have to make sure that even if powers that be interfered subsequently, the outcome is not reversible.

In short, we had to devise a way by which most people could be benefited from the enormous knowledge in the glyphs – not just a few who might use it to subjugate the large majority into something less than a human. This required us to equalize the playing field first. But we are scientists, not political leaders with any authority to bring about that kind of a social change, surely not in such a short time. We don't have that time. Time was running away from us, fast.

Also, keeping any secret this big is not easy, if anyone might think otherwise. Especially this kind of a secret.

So we had to act fast and act on many fronts at once. We argued that just telling the world about it wouldn't help in anyways. What would the common people do even if they knew, besides protesting to the governments via street demonstrations? Chaos certainly is not good for anything, definitely not for the mission such as ours. We need tranquility and stability to convert the suggestions and recommendations in the glyphs to a material solution that can actually save as many of us as possible – if not all.

Besides, we still had a long way to go before we could even prove WARGER science itself. We needed a proof of concept, a working prototype, before we could tell-all.

Your mission was that prototype and you all were the test pilots.

After the presumed 'success' of the first manned mission that you are a part of, we decided that the technology was proven, and now is the time to democratize the knowledge in phases to as many people as we can. This would not be like appearing on CNN and doing a town-hall. We decided that we will create a global society of 'good' and 'able' people. Recruit as many as possible and carefully dissipate that knowledge in stages without causing consternation. We have to prepare the members of that society (that is yet to be formed) to be able to absorb that knowledge and to be useful in the whole scheme of things to rehab as many humans on another planet as we possibly can. The society would educate its members to inculcate an altruistic mindset knowing fully well that not everyone can be rescued. We will need to find the best among us to populate our species within and beyond the galaxy in the next phase, a totally new phase of the human experiment.

The process for the democratization of that knowledge began at the same time as our scientific work of building the next Ark continued on a massive scale.

We planned to democratize the knowledge through a secret society we formed called WARY"

"*I see*" I was actively listening.

"*We decided to develop WARY - a society of trustworthy and incorruptible people recruited from all corners of the world, to whom we could then dissipate that knowledge. Whoever qualified to earn a membership we made her or him to be sworn into secrecy, first. The* *public face of WARY was a bigger society, it was started as a movement, a movement called **Science for Humanity (SoH)**. Membership to SoH was open to anyone who had any interest in Science. Whoever showed interest in SoH became our potential recruit for WARY. So, WARY recruited from within the ranks of SoH. WARY was the rational mind. SoH the face."*

"But how would you judge who is 'good' who is not, who is trustworthy and incorruptible, and who is not?" I asked.

"Yes, that remains a difficult task. The age-old argument of 'Nature vs Nurture' is the essence of that task. Is 'goodness' a genetically predisposed condition or is it an outcome of the environment in which one finds oneself? There was no easy or straight answer to that argument, both sides of that argument had valid and rational justifications. So we took a holistic view of an individual. One's interest in SoH was definitely a good start to know if an individual had any interest and drive at all. But we went beyond SoH should someone be left out of consideration just because he or she missed out on SoH. We shortlisted a long list of individuals who popped up in our search as someone who made some worthwhile contribution to their society in any field, whatever contribution that might

have been. The person was also expected to have a good general reputation among his community or in his society. The word 'contribution' does not necessarily mean monetary contributions but extends to include acts of bringing in positive changes. We relied on algorithms to cluster people based on their online profile on several psychological aspects to see who is out there for a cause of real value to the society. Then we approached him or her through our grass-root volunteers and we tried to understand their minds – using the science of the '*glyphs*'!

We then kept a watch on the shortlisted until we were confident that he or she earned it – the badge of trust, a life membership of WARY. One can be a SoH member without being a member of WARY.

WARY is the core - the true badge.

Until this point, WARY has ninety-five thousand members worldwide, of people that we deemed trustworthy and incorruptible. WARY works under the auspice of IPNES, of course. Through WARY we began to democratize the knowledge in the glyph.``

"Okay."

"Yours was the experimental prototype and the first manned one. Your crew are the test pilots of the fastest ship for interstellar travel ever conceived by humans up to that time. After your mission, all subsequent missions will have a declared goal of adopting a chosen planet – to start a new civilization there, at the destination, wherever that might be.

Humans already have become a true multi-planetary species as a result of these efforts. We made an all-out effort to make human 2.0 be a much better group than we ever were.

We know your ship has left the harbor and is not coming back within our lifetime or even in a thousand years.

We deliberately introduced an error in your ship's navigational system so that any calculation of time will regress toward a range between forty to fifty years so that you would have a valid reason to come back if you wanted to. We wanted you to come back to see the post-apocalyptic world and decide for yourself if you would want to reboot a new human civilization on Earth!

That decision is for you all to make.

The fact is that '**time**' is just an illusion. It is the way we humans think of our existence. Whoever sent us those **glyphs** made us realize the futility of thinking in terms of small, relative '**time**'. When it comes to true any *interstellar journey – 'time' as we understand is just meaningless. If we have to explore the cosmos we have to be timeless too. Professor Einstein had already figured that out for all of us, over a century ago.*

*Whoever they were who sent us those **glyphs**, they themselves must exist beyond our kind of 'time' frame. They must themselves be eternal or must exist for a very long time at the least."*

"Which is why Mirr and Saito never got that math of calculating the time correctly! They were not wrong! They were set up to be wrong! And for a good reason! I understand now!" I remarked.

"Sorry Rex, I don't know how to answer that question. It must have a future context that I could not have anticipated." Of course, dad could not have anticipated that specific question about Saito and Mirr, while he made that recording, in the past.

"Never mind dad, please go on!" I said.

*"Great! We gave your mission the choice, to come back or to stay and adopt **Astraea B** as the planet where we make our debut as a multi-planetary species. Either decision would have been acceptable to us."*

"We did both, dad. We divided ourselves and half of us stayed and the other half of us are back." I responded.

There was another spell of radio silence on that comment. Dad could not have anticipated that comment either. It was not a question nor an answer to a question that I posed to him, so dad in that recording did not *'know'* how to respond to it, instead he just continued.

"Your mission was the model for all ten missions that followed except each of them were designed to be an Ark. Those launches carried many more people than yours did. All these launches were equipped with the necessary infrastructure-building machinery and tools to begin the civilization-building process quickly at whatever destination they eventually arrived at."

"Dad, was there a plan B, of another kind of a program in case these launches failed?" I asked.

There was a glitch in the message at that very point. Dad went silent. I asked again, but he did not address that specific question.

He continued on his own.

"I have to tell you a side story here. Just a side story."

"Sure, dad!"

"Remember Dr. Roy Wallace?"

"Yes dad, I remember you telling me about him a couple of times. What about him?"

"Yes, just like that, one day, a few years before you had left, someone knocked on my door. The gentleman at the door looked a bit Middle Easterner and had some Asian facial features as well.

He introduced himself as 'Usman Ghulam', and said he was from Iran and that he needed to talk to me, he said. It was about something of extreme importance, he said."

"Okay," I was curious.

"This 'Usman Ghulam' guy –says he wanted to talk to me in private. He told me not to be shocked at what he is about to reveal to me. So, I invited him to my home office. He opened his laptop and activated a program to read his own biometrics. His eye biometric perfectly matched everything that the FBI had on Roy Wallace.

The voice however matched only somewhat but the fingerprints did not match at all. In fact, the gentleman sitting in front of me had no fingerprints at all.

He told me that he is Wallace, that the Feds were after him, and that he was among the top ten most wanted in the world. He took the identity of another person while still retaining his own – he said. To convince me further, he recalled everything we did together, in my study from several years ago - such as some of the specific discussions on the 12th **glyph** that I had with him that only he could have recalled.

But how could someone look so different, sound so different, and behave so different, I asked. He told me he did some plastic surgery to look different and got rid of his fingerprints by some dermatological procedure, and he literally took the personality of one gentleman from Iran who once was his patient. He devised a way of using the same **back door technique** that we used to view the glyphs together from years back, and he used that to assume a partial personality of 'Usman Ghulam', side by side his own self. The theory behind it was detailed in the 12th glyph he said.

I have explained some of that in detail in the other recording that you should watch if you have not already. It takes time to watch everything, I know - maybe even weeks. He now has a dual personality, one superimposed over the other – kind of an acquired bi-polar condition. But he still had the consciousness of his original personality as his primary self.

He had to do all that just to avoid getting identified and incarcerated by the Feds."

He continued.

"To be fair to Wallace, I raised the issue of offering him the membership of WARY, at one of the governing body meetings. The collective wisdom was NOT to take him in. He had several flaws in his resume, which could be disastrous for WARY and for its overall objective.

I don't know whether he assumed another identity or simply met with his death afterward, but someone sent me a detailed work on the subject of 'The neural connectedness of all living entities –the rawest level' via postal mail, someone anonymous. Had to be him, of course. I have disclosed that paper to IPNES and to the WARY governing body. The work was not fully completed, he probably wanted to send more. But there was no more. My guess was he probably died before he could complete it. He probably sensed a danger to his life which is why he sent a partially completed work hoping some other scholar will pick up from where he left.

I have suggested IPNES to give Roy Wallace the credit for that paper.

The name Roy Wallace being in the hit list of the most wanted, IPNES decided not to use his name, lest IPNES be held 'complicit' to the 'presumed' wrongdoing associated with the name 'Roy Wallace'. Instead, IPNES decided to put his authorship credit in a cryptic puzzle within the body of that writing, hoping someone in the future will decipher it, and give him the necessary credit for his work."

Poor Wallace, how he was so misunderstood all along, I thought to myself.

"One last question, Dad! Did the senders of the glyphs ever reveal to us any time?"

"No Rex! They never did, as yet! Although our suspicion all along was that they have visited us or have been living with us long enough to know us – and have decided to help us in their good judgment."

"Okay. On our return through the 5th dimension, we saw some spherical crafts like what Dr. Denzing had witnessed as a child a very long time back. One of them tried to make some contact with us too. More like dropping by to see how we were doing. Could they be the ones, dad?" I asked.

"I could not answer that question from my current context, Rex!"

"Of course, I understand, dad. They probably did not want to reveal to us or contact us yet, for if they wanted they easily could. They instead just teased us a bit. Maybe we are not up to them yet. Maybe they will, in the future." I said.

"I could not understand that either, Rex!"

My conversations with my dad from the past continued, most of which were personal and emotional for me.

Not something of any relevance to anyone else, so I will not dwell on it here.

Thirty Five – Prisoners of the Future

Having viewed the time capsules that dad left us, we now know a lot. We know that our mission was born of a threat and that the apocalypse had actually happened. We also know that the apocalypse happened not once but twice, already. That is something that no one from dad's time could have even imagined. We also know it will happen again and again.

Earth is a cursed place now. It had its joy of hosting our kind of life once. No more. It is done with that responsibility. On Earth, we ourselves were a major factor of disruption to the balance of nature in many ways. Nature got rid of us and every other species from our time, in a sense, and in a strange way.

All my fellow crew members, the last humans standing as far as we know, are all on the same page now.

I cannot describe how strange it is to realize that we six are all that is left of the entire human race, that's it. It's not exactly a sigh of relief of having escaped death.

No! Not one bit!

It is a feeling of emptiness, a deep sense of loneliness, and a depressing sadness that could easily gnaw our minds subconsciously, from within – if we let it.

It will be months and years before we can come to terms with all that we learned through these time capsules. I'm not sure who we should even mourn for! I guess even mourning is a luxury that we can no longer afford, we have to use every bit of time at our disposal to get IDP working and to survive for the continuity of our species! Reviving the IDP is really taking a toll on us, it is taking all the juice out of our lives.

"Vladimir Ruskin was not wrong after all, I have to admit." I was not ashamed to say so.

"He was not!" Matt agreed with me. *"I am kind of ashamed of how I treated him that one time. I feel guilty. But Slater, no! He was a snake."*

I did not know Matt actually had been carrying it all along! The guilt I mean.

"It wasn't your fault, Matt! He did wrong, whatever he did. He knew that even if we found out about Angelo and his family, we had no choice but to take them into our fold. He took advantage of a probable outcome where we had no options. Your response at that time

was exactly how anyone in that situation would have responded." Saito explained it to him.

"Maybe you're right. Hindsight is a strange thing, it changes the original justification."

At that point, Mirr said something that did not occur to us this entire time.

"But do you guys even realize, by the time we landed here on Earth over two thousand four hundred solar years have passed on **Astraea-B** too?

Which means - Vladimir, Bennet, Angelo, Mariam, Leo, and Rubbia are all dead already! And by a long shot!"

We were in total silence in that sudden realization!

"You are so right, Mirr! How come we did not even think about it!" I said.

We had another shock to add to our list of shocks now.

"I wonder what became of their descendants after all these years!? Have they successfully built any civilization so that Astraea B is now a planet of Humans?"

"They made a big mistake. A very big mistake. They should have been with us. They would have been alive." Saito said.

"How strange this thing called 'time' is, isn't it? It ticks differently for different space-times!" Greta joined in the conversation.

"If we get a line of sight to Astraea, we might be able to receive the radio signals that we installed there. It must be beaming us messages since the last one thousand six hundred years considering it takes only 342 years for a signal to reach us!" I said.

"Yes, you are right!" Saito agreed.

It will be a while before we can tune into **Astraea-B** to know if Vladimir and all had been able to build a civilization at all. It is not as easy as tuning into a radio channel. It will need a lot of searching first, depending on at what point in its orbit it is at this moment- the blockages in the line of sight by all kinds of celestial objects in between and such! Of course, we cannot just start communicating even if we received any message now, there will be around 342 years of lag in between two responses!

We have work to do, we still haven't reached the summit, especially being under the threat of some unknown threat vectors that we are under. I am talking about that close fiery encounter that we had. We don't even know what they are or who they are, but we know that they are very trigger happy.

"We have not watched most of the time capsules yet. There must be a lot of information in there that we can use. But it will be a while before we can go through all of it." Saito.

*"I would rather use all the time we have to get **IDP** to a working condition. Once we are done with the **IDP**, we will have the bandwidth to re-engage in the time capsules."* Matt said.

"Is it possible that those that could not make it in any of those missions, could have re-colonized Mars instead?" Greta posed a valid point.

*"We can actually verify that by going to Mars and finding that out for ourselves, once we get the **IDP** fully working,"* I said.

*"Agree, getting this **IDP** working is our mission for now. If we get it right, we can explore the universes, go wherever we hitched our wagon to!"* Matt added to my statement.

It was late into the night, past 1 AM. We need to get rested well to fight another day, tomorrow.

We were gaining confidence in our ability to revive the **WARGER** system. It should be just a couple weeks from now if everything goes well.

The next morning as we were getting ready to go back inside the tunnel and resume from where we left our work from yesterday, *C-Mind* came crackling again.

<Good Morning Folks!>

*"Good morning! Any words of wisdom that you want to share, **Cygnus**?"* Matt asked.

<I have detected some unknown aerial flyovers last night. Does not look like they can see us through the invisibility camouflage yet, but I could not be too certain either.>

"Okay....!."

Something to worry about for sure.

<From the frequencies of the flyovers, they might be having a general suspicion of our location. I detected several columns of light beaming downward from some of those flyovers, far away from here.>

"Hmmm..."

*"What do you suggest, **Cygnus**?"*

C-Mind <Do wear your full combat gear and be fully armed. As for me, don't worry. If I sense any immediate threat, I have enough firepower to protect myself.>

"*Okay, but we don't want you to activate the Force-Shield here. Not while we're docked on the harbor,* **Cygnus***. It might destroy part of the foundation and destroy our chance to be able to revive the* **WARGER** *system.*" Matt gave **Cygnus** a clear order.

<Yes, Commander. I will use the low-intensity EMP field instead, should they try to breach their way in. Alternatively, I could just fly off faster than they can catch. I will keep the ship ready today, just in case, to be able to respond instantly.>

"*Good!*" Matt then briefed us –

"*We are going to be in combat-ready mode. Greta and Elea will be riding the* **SKELs***. Each of us will wield a conventional gun. Greta and Elea will carry two - one AFF4 mini and a conventional weapon, just in case. We are not going to use AFF4 except in the extremely emergent situation. Is that clear, everyone?*"

Matt made his instructions clear.

"Yes, Commander!" we responded in one voice as soldiers do.

In our combat-ready suits, we looked like aliens ourselves, the movie kind of aliens. Admittedly, the suit makes us feel empowered, invincible and gives us some kind of adrenaline rush - just by wearing it. It is kind of inconvenient to work with the gears on, but defense surely is more important than convenience.

We have decided that we will not turn on the lights while we work today, we would rather use our suit headlights only, even when it is kind of dark inside the tunnels at this time.

Necessary precautions, while we work in the sketchy ambiance of the underground tunnel complex, so that the unknown enemy does not detect us easily before we detect them first.

Matt and Greta will mostly stand guard about a quarter-mile inside the tunnel from its mouth while we finish the last remaining work. The work today involves fixing the last circuit breaker that was giving us some trouble. We planned to retire for the day as soon as we complete this one last work.

It is late afternoon now.

Just when the last beam of light swept past the tunnel, something in the shape of two thick rings, a smaller ring on top of a bigger one, physically unconnected from one another, appeared at the mouth. It posed a distinct silhouette against the bright southern sky with two deep magenta lights blinking from the middle of the top ring. And suddenly a few more like it appeared by its side. They slowly began to move toward us, sticking themselves all around the circumference of the tunnel, some standing at impossible angles and some even upside down - defying gravity.

The two-ring entities now began to move, rolling on their bases. Slow at first and then they started to speed up toward us from the sunny end of the tunnel. There were a dozen of them, beaming tracking lasers at us at the same time as they were closing the distance between us and them. That was the panic point for us.

Matt gave his order –

"Open fire!"

Matt and Greta began shooting at the entities and we all joined in the shootout. The entities were too quick for us and they deftly dodged our bullets. One of them slipped past Matt and Greta and headed toward us rolling upside down from the ceiling of the tunnel.

"Retreat to the ship! Move, move, move!" Matt ordered.

"Mirr, go ahead of us and prepare the auxiliary entry to the ship. Hold the entry open as long as you can while we shake them off and join you." Matt continued.

"Yes, Commander!" Mirr hustled, followed by Saito.

A stairway leads up to the ground level where the *Pegasus* is parked. Matt, Elea, Greta , and I continued to provide the cover fire as Mirr and Saito hurried up via the spiral stairs that lead to one of the auxiliary entrances to the ship.

Mirr and Saito made it to the auxiliary entry door in a hurry, Mirr a few steps ahead of Saito and he put his hand on the biometric lock system and whispered as clearly as he could.

"Cygnus, Cygnus.... open the air-locked auxiliary entry B5, now!" Mirr ordered C-Mind.

<Sorry Mirr, I can't open it under the current condition. They are closing in fast and there is not enough time for you all to be in without exposing

this entry for them to get in as well. So I have to fly away on my own, now. I have to save the ship first! I apologize!> *C-Mind* gave us the shock of our life.

*"What the heck, **Cygnus**. We command you to open the damn air-locked door! **Now!**"*

<As per my judgment, I still can't conform to that command, sir!"

"Screw your damn judgment, open the damn door now..."

<Please stand down the ramp sir, I am about to fold now, initiating defensive maneuver shortly...>

C-Mind defied and betrayed us, totally.

It began to make that familiar whirring sound, in preparation for it to fly off.

Mirr and Saito had to rush down the aux ramp as starship *Pegasus* began to retract that ramp on them.

And just like that, this starship, our very own ship quietly took off into the night sky and fast - without us.

Unbelievable!

As **Cygnus** bolted on us we were left defending ourselves in the open ground of the **IDP** harbor now. The question now was – for how long?

Slowly we got surrounded from all sides by dozens of those two-ring entities that appeared all around us. They had no weapons on their body.

Suddenly, four humanoid-like figures appeared at a distance from where we stood in a circle. Their silhouettes are clearly visible against the evening sky. They all seemed armed and were levitating in mid-air, literally.

"Asking your permission to fire F4 now, Commander!" Elea whispered! She had the AFF4 trained at those levitating humanoid figures at about two hundred feet away.

"No..!" Matt whispered back.

"Commander! Requesting permission again!" Elea insisted again, in a whisper!

"No..." Matt was firmer this time in his response.

"Have you noticed that besides the tracking beams they have not fired a single shot at us yet? If they wanted to kill us, they would already have done so. Besides, we have been shooting at them for so long and not a single

one of them is down. I guess it is best to wait, watch and see what they want! Shooting F4 could destroy a portion of the port as well, so, hold off! I will give the order to shoot F4 at the right time if the situation so presents." Matt gave his reason for not giving the order to use F4.

We were now all huddled in an ever tighter circle, back to back, our guns pointing to the approaching entities that were zeroing on us from either side.

Dusk was giving way to a dark star-lit night now!

The four levitating humanoid figures began gliding towards us, fast in the beginning and then more cautiously as they began to close in on us. Then they stopped - some fifty feet from us.

And one of the four tall figures shot something at us.

The next thing we knew our hands felt numb, our weapons loosened from our grips, our lower bodies paralyzed. We were all cold feet, literally!

One of the two-ring entities came closer and positioned itself just twenty feet apart from Matt, facing him. Matt asked –

"Who the heck are you?"

The slowly rotating two-ring spoke back in a language we have never heard of.

¿Ωηο τηε ηεχκ αρε ψου?"~~

We looked at each other. Not understanding anything it said.

Matt spoke again - *"We are humans. The crew of starship Pegasus, the first Inter-Dimensional Interstellar flight from five thousand six hundred years ago."*

Suddenly, the thing rolled back all the way up to where the four other humanoids like figures stood. They conferred among themselves and the two-ring thing came back and apparently had something more to say.

It spoke to Matt in the same pitch and tone as Matt did, just repeating every word Matt said, and just as he said it, a moment earlier – as if mimicking him!

~~ *"Who* are you,' we are humans, the crew of starship Pegasus, the first interdimensional interstellar flight from five thousand six hundred years ago" ~ ~

What!??

The four levitating humanoids, all stood some seven feet tall, did not have a face as we think of a face. Levitating a foot up from the ground, they stood even taller than they were, and quite intimidating too - just from their appearance. They apparently are some mechanical beings – without a head. None of these strange entities looked anything like any biological life form. One of them slowly gilded towards us. There was a blinking light on its chest.

Two small crafts appeared behind the four headless humanoids from somewhere and slowly started gliding towards us. The crafts had the shape of a hard-shelled tortoise except more elongated. The longer axis of each should be no more than thirty feet in length.

As we stood paralyzed in our combat suits, the seven feet tall mechanical entities grabbed us one at a time as easily as lifting a flower vase. The craft that we were taken into was still levitating four feet above the ground. Its retractable roof got fully opened and each of us was secured on a seat. They had some trouble getting Elea and Greta out of the **SKEL**.

Our minds were active but our bodies - still paralyzed. We have been shot with some kind of a Taser gun - some sort of nerve paralyzer.

It was too dark now to make out anything around us, only the silhouette of the forest all around the IDP port was visible against the night sky.

There were several other crafts, much bigger than the two we were on, still circling over the IDP area looking for *Pegasus* and still figuring out what was there down below and is not there now.

Pegasus made a clean getaway. *Pegasus* is indeed good at dodging - with or without us!

The elongated tortoise shaped craft that we were imprisoned in began to ascend rapidly.

Thirty Six-*Nuevo Earth*

The craft that we boarded gained altitude rapidly and in less than thirty seconds we were in space. It was amazingly quiet and it flew as smoothly as a maglev train.

The headless mechanical humanoid-like figure piloting the craft was quiet all along, focused only on the electronic kind of display in front of it. We were quiet too mostly because we were experiencing intense awe, anxiety, and wonder while most of our bodies were still numb.

We have a clear view of the entire Earth now. The Earth receded farther and farther away from us as we began to gain acceleration.

And suddenly I started to feel dizzy, things panning out slowly around me, blurry and I blanked out.

I cannot tell you what I don't remember being in that state from that moment.

When I regained my consciousness, we were descending for landing, somewhere on a small world down there - small because we could see the curvature of the horizon even from this low altitude. Seemed like a watery world with islands, big and small interspersed at random locations on the watery surface. The surface of the water was glistening against a pavilion of starlight above.

Others too were awake by now.

We were descending upon one of the bigger islands it appeared. It was one very beautiful vista down there - indescribable in words. Several towering structures were huddled in clusters with arboreal and green landscapes in between. There were flying vehicles of all descriptions that appeared out of the gaps between the towers and disappeared behind the next.

We descended on some kind of a landing port. The next thing we knew, we were on the ground - of a new world, an impossible world that we could not have imagined exists. The landing was not exactly at the ground level for we could see trees further down from our level. It is as if we landed on a very large rooftop of some tall building. From this vantage point, several transparent tubes ran divergently, like jet-ways, connecting all other buildings around us. Not all such tubes ran straight. Some curved and meandered through the tall trees and disappeared behind the cover of trees and towers and only to reappear on the other side. Some of the buildings appeared to be made of crystal, some looked like a tower of solid granite, and still others presented a chrome-plated silvery metallic finish. Some painted in matt-finished soft colors from light pink to midnight blue, some appeared transparent.

The feeling of numbness was gone, I could feel all of myself now. We disembarked and sat our foot on the floor close to a jet-walk. As we began walking, a path indicator symbol appeared in midair in front of each of us. Without any effort, we began to experience ourselves moving forward through the transparent jet-walk – like gliding through nothing. The path indicators were small puffs of clouds moving at the same speed as us and ahead of us. It was probably the other way – we were just semi-consciously doing a *Monkeys see Monkey do* in following the puffs. We could see everything above and below us through the ceiling and the floor of the transparent tube that we were in, and we could see the movements of many flying vehicles below and above us. We continued to press ahead for some more time and until we stopped inside a circular area just before the entry into the huge crystal tower that we were headed towards. Some large dragonfly-like drones appeared over each of us and began scanning our bodies. They examined us from every side and in a quick action inserted a tiny needle through our suits and drew out blood samples. After they were done they flew away as quickly and disappeared into the ceiling.

Ahead of us was a two-ring robot and behind us were two headless bi-pedal mechanical humanoids wielding a weapon each. In the forward direction and into the building, another kind of an entrance opened up that leads into the huge building in front of us, one that was much bigger in cross-section than the jet-walk that we came from. The jet-walk that we came through ends right here.

The direction indicator puff of cloud appeared again and just like before we started to move again, without any effort, like standing on an escalator except there was no escalator.

After escalating for a short while we entered through a huge door into a large round hall. The high ceiling was a see-through dome, exposing the clear sky above it.

We were led to some kind of a lounge. The headless humanoids and the two-ring robots left us there and vanished through another door.

I couldn't help feeling that we were some kind of a prisoner in this exotic facility. There was nothing much to do other than to wait and watch.

Thirty Seven NErth-5

When I woke up on a bed inside a very cozy looking suit all by myself I had no recollection beyond the point where they left us at the lounge. Felt like I had a good night's sleep and was well-rested. I don't remember how I got in here or at what point I dozed off or if I was sleep-induced. I was not in my combat suit either. Hard to tell if it is in the morning or evening. I hoped others must also be housed somewhere near.

There was a restroom just like any restroom next to my bed, except much more gorgeous than we are used to seeing. A wardrobe full of clothes.

A digital like the display on the wall showed a number, 40. It began to count down with each passage of a minute. I instinctively knew that I was expected to get ready before it reached zero.

Three minutes to the end of the countdown I was ready. Dressed up with a new pair of dresses from the closet. It fitted snugly on my body, like a skin.

A minute before the end of the countdown, the *puff of cloud* appeared again, in mid-air. I instinctively followed it and found myself outside my suit and in a long corridor. At about the same time my fellow crew members and friends were out of their suits too, just like I was and just as surprised as I was seeing them that way. Matt, Saito, Elea were on my right, and Greta and Mirr were to my left. We were definitely happy to see each other. The *puff of cloud* hinted us to follow it and we did. After some walk, we were inside an oval chamber with rows of chairs in a semi-circular arrangement facing a raised platform on one end of the chamber. Some kind of a de-briefing room - it appeared to be.

There was a huge semi-circular table that was curved away from us like an elongated C, placed firmly in the center of the raised platform, about thirty-some feet apart from us. On the other side of the curved table, facing us were three large empty chairs.

We were just totally consumed by everything and were sub-consciously roving our eyes all around. The ceiling of the dome displayed the slowly shifting band of the Milky Way. The alignment of the Milky Way did not quite match up along the diameter of the dome. Hard to tell if this was just some make-believe or if it was real.

As we were still satisfying our curiosity about the extra-ordinary surrounding that we found ourselves in, we suddenly became aware that three figures had now occupied the three big empty chairs and were looking toward us. Not sure when they came in or if they materialized from down under.

 Unknowingly we stood up to have a better look at the three seated figures, -curiosity, and concern filled our minds.

They looked human, period! Their countenance appeared to be that of a young high scholar, tanned and closer to a shade of light brown. Each of them had bigger eyes, a smaller nose, and a fuller pair of lips. Overall their facial area appeared proportionately smaller than the size of their cranium.

Figure one in the middle raised his right hand in a gesture that we interpreted as asking us to take our seats.

"Welcome to Planetoid Nuevo Earth-1- also called planet Ellis! One of the planetoids in the system of seven planetoids together called the Nuevo Earth System"

We heard the person in the middle speak in a clear voice but it did not seem like he moved his lips at all.

"Thank you!" we said almost in one voice, surprised as hell to hear some strange looking figure speak, and in English!

"I am Drax Maz! On my left is Rox Rymh and to my right is Droon Zoy. Rox and I are the port officers of planet Ellis. Droon is an independent citizen observer."

"Soon after you were captured and for the duration of your trip from old Earth to here, we have collected some information about you. We now know that you are the crew of the first-ever inter-dimensional and interstellar mission launched thousands of years ago in the ancient times. Is that correct?"

"Yes, that is true!" Matt replied on our behalf.

"Welcome back! It is incredible to see someone like yourselves from that long ago in flesh and blood!" The person said, still without any lip movement.

"Who is your Commander?" the entity who called himself Drax asked.

Matt stood up and raised his right hand.

"I am."

"Okay, Commander, before we ask any further questions we would like you to answer this important

question. *Why did you decide to destroy one of our planetoids?"* Drax appeared firmer this time and looked hard at Matt for an answer.

We looked at each other, confused. Our minds raced to process the context of this strange question.

Is it about the big rock that we encountered and destroyed as soon as we emerged into the *base-dim* on our way back home?

That must be it. I guess everyone was thinking what I was thinking.

After a few exchanges of looks among us, Matteo explained the circumstance leading to that collision, in detail. He explained how that decision was made by *C-Mind* autonomously to avoid an imminent collision that would otherwise have destroyed our ship completely.

There was some silence as the three of them looked at each other and Drax started to 'speak' again-

"Okay, that seems to make sense. Your explanation is noted. Until after we apprehended you, we assumed that you are some aliens from another planet and have come with a belligerent purpose. We have been trying

to track you ever since and had determined that your ship had landed on old Earth.

The rock that you mentioned is a planetoid that we were developing – and would have been the newest addition to our system of planetoids, a place to accommodate our growing population. We were just beginning the terraforming phase. What you did has completely undone the project. We lost an entire planetoid, besides the loss of all the machinery and plants stationed there. It pushed us back by almost a decade and it almost killed two of our engineers who were working there at that time. They are fighting for their lives as we speak, in an Intensive Care Unit."

We were stunned to hear all that. After some pause trying to process what we heard Matt spoke -

"We are very sorry for what happened. We are deeply sorry for the two engineers that our action had harmed. We really wish they would recover. We're sorry for the setback to your planetoid program. We really are." Matt represented our apologies.

"Know this -that incident caused a massive scare in our world. I hope it is not difficult for you to understand why? We were arming ourselves to the teeth to defend

ourselves from a serious alien invasion and since been searching to destroy your ship on sight if we found it.

You have managed to hide it well." Drax said.

I really felt sorry for that accident, every time he said that. I am sure each of us has felt likewise. It was sad and shocking for us to have done such a huge damage, even if it was in an inadvertent act.

"By the laws of Nuevo Earth, such an action would be culpable and punishable up to two decades of hard labor," Drax concluded.

He and the two of his other officials conferred something among themselves at that point.

"I think we will leave judgment to the governing council. I could not promise you at this point, how they will judge you based on evidence that we will be collecting on the event and the statement that you just made!" Drax concluded.

"Would you mind introducing yourselves?" asked the man on the left of the center. Rox would be his name I guess.

And we introduced ourselves, one at a time. After the intro was over, Matt took his time to brief them all about our mission. They listened intently all along, without batting an eye-lid, like they were frozen, like statues.

It was our turn to satisfy our curiosity about them. Who they might be?

Drax began thus -

*"We are the products of **Project Atlantis** that was initiated five thousand six hundred forty years ago. Twenty years before the first extinction event that wiped out nearly all life on Earth. The program **Project Atlantis** was conceived soon after 2045, after you all had left, which is why you had no knowledge of this project.*

*The thought behind **Project Atlantis** was the realization that we in fact are the prisoners of the Sun. There is no practical way to find another home for humans outside of the Sun's influence, that is - should the interdimensional missions fail. We were not sure if any of the inter-dimensional missions had failed or if they succeeded. No one came back before 2091 to tell their tale, which is why **Project Atlantis** became the beacon of hope - the other alternative. Even if all the missions that left Earth succeeded without us knowing they did, we still needed this alternative. At the same time as **WARGER** missions were still carried on, one* *launch after another, **Project Atlantis** was moving forward in parallel. The will of an entire species was invested on this project as our lives depended on it.*

*The know-how on **Project Atlantis** was provided in the **glyphs**. The 20th and 21st **glyphs** contained the science of developing a planetoid by coalescing stray celestial objects such as asteroids and comets. The **glyphs** gave us the technology to fuse rocks to form bigger rocks, to fill it with water from comets and icy bodies, to create an artificial gravity capable of holding that water and an atmosphere, and to place the planetoid in the desired orbit around the Sun.*

***Project Atlantis** started with the goal of building two small planetoids out of the foundational raw materials harnessed from the Asteroid belts.*

*The **European Space Agency** was the first to land an unmanned mission on an asteroid – that was even before your time. So we knew something about the asteroids already. We used that success to land an army of worker robots on few chosen asteroids as a proof of technology.*

*From that point on, using the science learnt from the **glyphs** we carried on **Project Atlantis** in phases. We successfully placed the first planetoid in the desired* *orbit around the Sun and at the correct inclination from the solar plane such that the Gamma blast from **Betelgeuse** would miss it by a few million miles at the least.*

Even with all the know-hows if you thought developing a planetoid was any easy – it was not.

*We are the neo-humans born of **Project Atlantis**. In a true sense **Project Atlantis** never ended, we continue to fuse more and more rocks to build new planetoids. Besides those who left Earth in thousands after yours, we are the descendants of the other survivors of the Global Extinction event. We are the progeny of **Project Atlantis**. We are your descendants too, in that sense. On this date, we are about three millions in population that is all of the seven planetoids combined.*

It is extraordinary that you all have come back from that long a past to be here today, in full physical presence."

Drax explained it all as I quoted him here – what a story! It took us some time to process what we just heard! He spoke in the same lipless, mouth-less mode of communication. That explanation cleared a lot of things for us.

Now we know!

"How do you speak English? Is English the language of the Nuevo Earth System, after all these years?" Saito asked.

*"No, we are **not** speaking in English. Although the three of us here can speak in seventeen different languages from your time, English being just one of them. Our own language is totally unlike any language of your time. We created a perfect language instead, much more efficient and much more capable of describing any feeling, any experience, and any idea that germinates in the human mind."* The man seated to the right spoke.

"If you are not speaking in English, then what are you speaking in? And how are we hearing you in English?" We all had the same curiosity as Elea.

"You are not hearing it through your ears in the same way you are used to hearing and communicating with each other. We are communicating with you at a more fundamental level of communication, from one mind to another. It is in your mind that you are translating that back to your preferred language of use – English, in your case. We could do this same mode of conversation with someone who speaks a completely different language, and he will understand us just the same - in his own preferred language."

"I guess we are beginning to understand that concept." Professor Saito said.

"With this mode of communication, we can even talk to animals who cannot speak in any sound language but nevertheless they too have a language in their minds." Rox continued.

There was some silence, as we were trying to comprehend what we just heard. Drax spoke again.

"Switching topic – please know, until the governing council conveys their decision on the charges related to the destruction of the planetoid, I will have to restrict all your movements to just this detention facility. So, you all will stay here under house arrest until then."

"In the meantime, to help you get oriented to life on the Nuevo Earth system, Droon Zoy here has volunteered to be your attaché for the time being.

If you are found guilty we will have to take you to our permanent detention facility on planetoid XT. If found not guilty, you could choose your own destiny, whichever planetoid you may like to settle down at – we will help you in doing that.

This hearing is adjourned at this point." Drax concluded, and ended the meeting rather abruptly.

They disappeared into the floor as the three chairs got lowered, probably the same way they came to begin with.

I wondered what do we do now in our indefinite detention – play rock-paper-scissors?!

Thirty Eight- Droon Zoy

It's our third day of house arrest. We will have to stay that way pending some provisional judgment passed on our case. These three days have been a period of real concern for us - not knowing what our fate will be. What an irony - we roamed the universe in search of a future home for our species and our own future progenies have detained us here on a serious culpable charge. It was not our fault, but we can't blame them either. The destruction that we caused would be equivalent to a major act of terrorism during our time. Imagine someone destroying a whole city that was under construction, even if the action was inadvertent. The fact is we were the vectors of that destruction.

Their justice system is taking its time. We can perfectly appreciate that.

"We actually destroyed a whole planet. I can imagine the existential panic, anguish and concern that event must have caused them. Think about it - if someone inadvertently bombed a whole city in our time – how would we have treated him? I would perfectly understand if they had us shot dead by now. I mean shot me dead! I am responsible for it, not anyone!" Matt

was deeply guilt-stricken, he took it as his responsibility as it had happened under his watch.

"*Not your fault, Matt! Not anyone's*" Saito said.

"*Could **Cygnus** have avoided that collision, or was **Cygnus** too trigger happy? But can we even blame **Cygnus**? It could not have known that it was a man-made planetoid. It was just acting on the mission's interest just like it is supposed to do.*" I reasoned.

"*Absolutely!*" Greta concurred!

"*Hope those two people recover soon. Besides the fact that their lives are indeed as valuable as any of us, the outcome of this case would be heavily affected if they survived or did not.*" Saito said.

All along these days, Droon Zoy has kept us apprised of the development of the case. He had been also guiding us remotely on things that we should know to get by in our daily lives.

And at a certain time, a week after our detention, Droon Zoy appeared to us in person, unannounced.

We hoped that he had some good news for us.

And it was, he said – "*Good news! You have been provisionally exonerated, though the case is not fully dismissed yet, not officially. But you can roam free now."*

We were relieved in our minds.

"Thank you Droon! But will the two engineers live? Are they recovering?" Matt asked anxiously.

"They are not out of the woods yet, unfortunately!" He answered.

"We are really sorry! We really are!" Matt repeated.

He then continued on the subject.

"In the Nuevo Earth System, one cannot lie, because we can read minds. So although we could not confirm all aspects of the accident from your ship's logs because we could not yet find your ship, we read your minds, each of your minds. Based on that revelation the council has decided to provisionally exonerate and admit you into the Nuevo Earth System. You have your liberty now." Droon let us know in more detail.

It was still a feeling of relief to know that we are exonerated.

Droon left us to our thoughts at that time.

He was back the next day, in the same unannounced manner.

This time with a much friendlier face. After we exchanged some pleasantry, he said.

"I am your attaché in your orientation. I am here to help you ease the process of orientation on Nuevo Earth. You can ask me any question you like!"

Greta came up with the first question.

"I am just curious, do you have animals on Nuevo Earth?" Greta asked.

"Yes, we resurrected the animals from the DNA samples. Unlike in your time, we do not keep them in cages, or zoos. Instead two of the planetoids that we have here are equivalent to your national parks. We communicate with them directly in their language. But for a very few incidents of misunderstanding, most of the time they understand us and we understand them." Droon replied and continued,

"By the way, I am an expert on the pre-apocalyptic history of Earth going back to the Paleolithic age. I understand your culture and even your sense of humor- which is why I volunteered to be an independent citizen observer when I learned about you all. Please know our calendar starts from the first settlement day of planetoid -1. So, anything before January 1st, 2092 from your time is pre-history for us."

Droon is super tall at six feet and seven inches. It was difficult to guess his gender from his appearance. They all looked alike to our eyes. We will need to spend some time here to know one from the other I suppose.

"I will be your friend, philosopher and guide as you used to say in your time – until you get comfortable settling down in Nuevo Earth. Your settlement will probably be arranged on planetoid NEarth-5. I will take you there when the time comes.

So, how do you all like it here, so far?" Droon spoke with a smile.

"Super awesome!" Greta echoed our minds.

*"As Drax said, we will teach you the art of communication at the rawest level after you get comfortable here. That communication is no-hiding anything kind of communicating, just as one thinks. The **glyphs** taught us how to communicate without words - the **glyphs** from your time!*

*I guess you might also like to learn **Uukritt** – the perfect sound language that we had developed – that we use in public communications, in our plays, and in our entertainments!"*

I am thinking - wow, the **glyphs,** how deeply it is enshrined in our human history, heard it several times already! The **glyphs**!

*"You are right Rex Song Jr. It was your father Dr. J Song who first 'received' those **glyphs** in his machines and that is what ultimately saved so many of the human race."*

Droon surprised me, I did not say anything, I just thought about it! I need to get used to this new way of communication.

"Oh, I forgot you can read my thoughts!" I could not help saying it.

"Yes, I do. We injected a temporary procedure through the back of your skull when you first landed so we can understand you better. But you can block me from reading your mind, by simply doing this (he showed us a procedure). And if you want to go back to the default, you just have to do the same technique one more time.

To make this permanent, you would need to go through a minor surgical procedure, something that we all have gone through on Nuevo Earth as soon as we become adolescents. It is required here.

Trust me, with the passage of time you will not mind anyone reading your mind directly. In Nuevo Earth, the need to hide your thoughts is eradicated. There is no thought that anyone needs to be embarrassed about - not in Nuevo Earth.

In your time, being a homosexual used to be seen as weird and hence embarrassing for some, in some cultures, for example. Not here. In Nuevo Earth, we see every human thought outcomes and desires as nothing more than how the wiring and chemical reactions in the brain work, as governed by some specific gene. We now understand a great deal about the source of any thought, any behavior, or any action at the molecular level of the brain. There is nothing to be shy of or to be embarrassed about anything. There is no need to cover up on anything.

But you have the choice to keep your privacy if you wish to."

And he continued.

"All the credit for that science goes to two persons from your time - Dr. J Song and Dr. R Wallace."

"Dr. Roy Wallace? The NeuroSurgeon who disappeared from the face of the Earth without a trace? Was he ever

found, according to your records?" I was totally curious about what I just heard.

"Dr. Roy Wallace aka Usman Ghulam was found dead in a hotel in Bangkok, Thailand, a few years after your ship had left. This is all public knowledge and well archived, and which is how I know!"

And he continued.

*"Based on the revolutionary work of Dr. J Song and Dr. Wallace, a student in his Ph.D. dissertation formulated a practical way to converse in the rawest form of communication without expending words. That Ph.D. student was Dr. Phen Wen who survived the apocalypse to be one among the few thousands of us who escaped Earth to Nuevo Earth. His descendants are still among us. It is because of the continuity of that work that was started by your father and by Wallace, carried through by Wen and others that we owe the foundation of a noise-free communication between minds. Because such communication was possible all ideological barriers, misinformation, and prejudices have fallen wayside making it possible for us to build a clean and corruption-free civilization. Whoever sent your dad those **glyphs**, we owe our species' continuation! They chose to remain anonymous to us even to this day. We don't know who they are. We assume that they are*

some benevolent entities from some other dimension who wanted us to survive."

"We have noticed that we find you all look very much alike -is it how evolution has shaped humans in the last five thousand years?" Elea asked.

"No, we have not evolved into another species in the Darwinian sense. But we have mastered biological evolution to some extent.

The biological human body, like the ones you all have, was evolved in the plains of Africa to survive in the environment that existed at that time and stayed that way until much later. Specifically, to be able to run, walk, hunt, and keep the brain hydrated with blood and so to continue living. The ultimate purpose of that body was to keep the brain alive and to do that it needed all those supportive systems of organs – the heart, the lungs, the muscle, the liver, the digestive system, etc.

Our science of the day asked the question - what if we could keep the brain powered on without all these supportive organs, in the exact same sense. Besides, these supportive organs themselves need most of the energy that we intake from our surroundings just to be able to do their supportive functions with the ultimate objective of keeping you, the brain, alive. It is really the brain that is you. If you lose all your limbs it will still be you. If you lose your lung and replace it with an artificial lung, it will still be you, if you had a heart transplant or kidney transplant, you will still be you. But not if you had a brain transplant, the brain, therefore, is you – no –brainer of course. It is all pre-apocalyptic knowledge and who does not know, anyway?

By the end of our current century, we could successfully transplant or replace most of the natural organs with artificial ones, but we still needed these organs to be there. The theory of the nervous system and therefore the most complex system of all – the brain, eluded us all this time until twenty-five or so years ago, which is just before I was born. I am from the first generation of humans who were engineered at the fetus stage so that I could be developed into the first generation of 'directedly' evolved humans who could be powered to live on without the same arrangement of biological supportive organs. My sensory receptacles should work well with artificial organs just as well. Think of the prosthetic limbs and the pacemaker of your time – extend that.

We understand the functioning of the brain a great deal now. We understand how we can disengage all other organs and still power the brain with what it needs to stay alive. We still have to perfect all that, but we are on track for that.

So, theoretically, I can have an engineered body that I want and still have the same brain of mine, which is the real me. It could be a completely mechanical body as well. I could be a superhero of your time with the power of a hulk or an Iron man if I wanted to, theoretically."

"Are you?" Great asked.

He laughed and replied – *"No, I am not. I wouldn't need to be and will not wish for any superpower until everyone in Nuevo Earth has. We are still not there yet."*

"So how do the artificial organs supply blood into the brain?" Elea asked.

"Great question! The ultimate supplier of energy to the body is not blood. Blood simply is the transport system, like how the waterways were in the ancient city of Venice of your time. The real-life energy for the residents in Venice came from the fruit and vegetables carried on the Gondolas. Likewise, as long as we can supply the brain with what it exactly needs, we can keep it alive, without necessarily depending on the blood courier service. In the case of the brain, its

nutrition is some form of electro-chemical energy. I am
not an expert in that area, but if we can supply that
energy in the correct form and quantity, we can power
the brain on without blood.

And that is what our science has started to figure out
now.

If we figure out everything about this subject, our body
will be a very efficient engine powering an intelligent
life. It will use much less energy and will do much more
with much less." He took a pause, allowing what he
spoke to sink into our minds.

Professor asked the tough question at that point -

"Five thousand is a really long time considering that
even by the end of 2045 we were beginning to advance
at an exponential rate of progression. We were on the
hockey stick portion of the scientific breakthrough
graph.

In that sense, were there phases of regressions that
slowed down progress instead of speeding it up?"

"Great question professor. Yes, it was not always an
upwardly linear path of progress in rebuilding human
civilization. For a long time, our only business was to
keep clinging to life, somehow. We are talking about

adapting to a completely new life in a new world that was so much different from what we were used to.

Project Atlantis' blueprint included building two planetoids in the first phase - that was before the apocalypse. I hope you don't think that it was an easy task to build even one such. While engineering the very first planetoid we had a few disastrous starts that almost destroyed the proto-planetoid even before we could begin terraforming it. One such mishap actually put our program behind by five years. When the actual bombardment began the second planetoid had not started yet. We barely were done with the first one. Our focus then was - how to transport as many people from Earth to this new planetoid across a space of 62 million miles.

Our very first passenger space ship met with a fatal collision with a sizable space rock that came from nowhere - unleashed by the onset of the apocalypse. We lost all two thousand passengers in that tragedy.

Fast forward to the future, we could save only about three thousand people in our next two attempts through all the chaos of that time.

Only three thousand, from among how many? Eight billion people. Not all of these three thousand were tough enough to stand up to completely new living conditions in an artificially built planetoid.

Diseases, depressions, and challenges of adapting to the harsh conditions of the planetoid took out seventy percent of the three thousand.

It took generations before we could come back to the level of a basic science driven life. We did not have sufficient manpower to go on building another planetoid, until much later. The critical number of people needed to build anything was not there then.

Only centuries later we mastered some level of technological progress. We needed to re-invent everything, everything that we used to take for granted once upon a time- including a simple thing as a light bulb. A cell phone or an automobile had to wait another thousand years. We do not have fossil fuels on the planetoids, so we rely on the Sun alone for all our power needs. Nuclear power plants are far too complex to build in the small area of the planetoids. In the hustle of the space-exodus and the chaos that reigned supreme up until the doomsday year, we lost most of our collective knowledge of science and therefore lost the collective wisdom of our ancient civilization up to that point.

We had only two space ships, and they needed good care just to keep them in working conditions. It was not easy to maintain such a huge machine with no supporting infrastructure on the planetoid at that point of time.

If you were here during the mid-4000s, you would have found us pretty primitive compared to what we were up to the year 2045.

Even during the fifth millennium, which is between 5230 and 5310, when we barely were back on our feet as a technology-driven civilization, some other disasters had happened in which we lost two planetoids from the five that we had built up until that point.

So, to answer your question professor - no! Technology and progress do not always move in an upward curve with respect to time. Progress in our human experiment went through a rugged slope for a long time before it began to climb a sharp upward slope again - like what you had begun to experience and so had come to expect."

This was indeed too much for us to process all at once. There was much to internalize on what we just heard Droon say.

"It is a long relay race that started even before your time and was carried up to here. That marathon race is still going on. The nature of our challenges has changed but new challenges there still are - a plenty."

"Back to your current state of technology - you have mentioned that science today can replace all human organs. What about reproductive organs?" Dr. Elea Gruber had to ask this question, it is actually an important one. It is around this question that humanity's emotions and relationships are built on.

"So far we figured a lot of that out too. It's a lot less complicated than figuring out the brain, trust me. We have human baby nurseries where we can generate sperm and egg from the genetic code of two persons, no different in essence as fathering and conceiving a child. The conception, of course, happens outside of a human body, in a baby incubator. "

"What about the need for sexual union?" Elea asked in continuation.

"I thought this was a family-friendly audience?" Droon replied with a smile.

Everyone laughed.

When the laughter subsided, he responded.

"Trust me we figured all that out too, we mastered the nerves and the sensations. It is all okay, even better, no degradation of experience." More boisterous laughter followed this time, Greta quipped –

"I understand what all that means..."

Everyone laughed the third time.

"I love this audience... " Droon cracked!

Elea then asked a direct question -

"If you do not mind my asking, are you a male or a female, sir?"

He seemed amused at the question, and quipped –

"This cannot be a family-friendly audience for sure."

Everyone burst out laughing, again.

"I will talk about my gender on another day, another time. You guys are not going anywhere anytime soon!"

We are fortunate to have a personal guru in Droon in our adaptation to a new life on a new Earth.

We already liked him – a lot.

We would later learn that Droon is a transgender and is so by choice. And above all, Droon has a great sense of humor once he caught up with our culture.

Thirty Nine – Life in the *Nuevo Earth* system

This is our eight-month on *Nuevo Earth*. We are still learning the *what's what* of this new life. A good part of adapting to a new life is participating in the cultural and sporting events of that life – the stuff that enriches our lives and makes a civilization worthwhile. Droon is still showing us our way whenever we need him. He arranged for us to experience a sporting event. A global event, like the ones we had in our times. A soccer match between the two best teams in the N E system.

There are seven planetoids in the *Nuevo Earth* system after we destroyed the last one that was in the making. One of the seven planetoids is exclusively built for major events in athletic sports and entertainment. Two are national parks - home for various species of animals, birds, and other wild lives. Each planetoid has about the same surface area as of a major city of the size of Washington DC.

Every planetoid is essentially built the same way -built to look like an ellipsoid, averaging ninety miles across. The smaller diameter of the ellipsoid is about fifty miles. These planetoids are not built in the shape of a sphere, for the obvious reason that a spherical planet of that size will have a very small curvature unlike what we are used to on our ancient Earth.

As our species is now spread out in seven planetoids revolving in orbit around the same Sun, our chances of survival have gone up a lot more than if we had built just one big one. Even if we lose one or two to another apocalypse, we should still have a place for our species to continue.

One thing we all wondered about was – whether our story on **Astraea B** has any audience here at all! Will anyone be interested to even hear that story?

No one has even bothered to ask, yet. Apparently, the appetite for interstellar travel is not there anymore. This branch of mankind seems to have found its gravitas, so to say, for now.

There are no natural day-night cycles on the *Nuevo Earth* system unlike we were used to on Earth. Just dimmed light to bright light as the ellipsoidal planetoid sways about fifty-five degrees in either way while orbiting the sun. There are no nights. Think of Alaska or Iceland during summer.

The windows and doors of the houses can be configured to go dark based on the owner's taste. The walls of the houses are made of transparent materials that can be programmed to any color of one's choosing and can even be used as a TV monitor. They can be programmed to be transparent such that one can see everything on the outside - like living in the open.

The non-load bearing inner walls can be rearranged to any geometrical orientation. The gravity being much less here, things weigh much less too – (*duh, is that any news for anyone, anyway?*).

The citizens of the planetoids cannot afford to be as inefficient and wasteful as we used to be back in our consumerist plastic civilization. Recycle and reuse is a necessity.

The kitchen area as a whole is a semi-autonomous system. The *Chef System* in the kitchen can cook any meal in its menu as per the owner's taste. All that is needed is feeding it with the raw ingredients. The system has its own cleaning routine to keep itself cleaned.

Life is good!

One of the planetoids was specifically created for farming purposes. Everything that we eat is grown on that one planetoid. Another planetoid is exclusively reserved as the seat of the governing councils, Museums, Archives, Cultural parks, Theme parks, etc.

With what they have achieved so far, mankind 2.0 can claim to have mastered the art of survival within the bounds of our Solar system. Ours was a far more wasteful culture and was unhelp to the lives of all other species to say the least – The *Nuevo Earth* System is truly life-friendly for all species.

During the last few months, we also learned a lot about our own time between 2045 until 2091, from the NE system archives.

We learnt that post 2085 the hunger for interstellar travel fizzled out and any further development of the **WARGER** system was discontinued. None of the interstellar travelers ever came back to make the case for more such trips, besides us. The proponents of **WARGER** technology just could not justify their case on a leap of faith alone, anymore.

Moreover, the **WARGER** launches were painfully exhausting to arrange even for a civilization as developed as were up to that point. It sucked out oxygen from so many other aspects of our lives.

On a side story, there was one time, back in the pre-apocalyptic year of 2089, just over a year ahead of the onset of the extinction event, a sizable group of scientists and religious leaders had a rare consensus on one thing – but for totally different reasons. While the scientists were concerned that inter-dimensional travel is just not compatible with our sense of the time dimension, the religious schools opined that higher dimensions are the realm of divinity so no one should mess with. The scientists also feared the enormous fall out from any meltdown in the **MAM** and the **WARGER** system. The common public threw their weight against the **WARGER** system in a majority uproar – as they viewed it as not capable of saving most people and therefore did not justify the expense and effort that it incurred.

After five thousand years of hindsight, however, the fact says otherwise – the majority was just plain wrong. **WARGER** missions saved many more thousands of humans than **Project Atlantis** did. The ten Arks that left on **WARGER** drive rescued and rehabilitated no less than eighty thousand humans in total, and delivered them to somewhere in this big universe, in some safe havens. These missions did make us a true multi-planetary species, possibly even a multi-galactic one. In that sense, our survivability increased by several times too.

Those people probably now have grown in numbers to millions, if the missions went as well as planned. That number would be thousands of times more than the number of people that ultimately survived and prospered in the *Nuevo Earth* system.

Unfortunately, the end of the straw for **WARGER** missions came when a mile long strip of rock from the mountainside disappeared during the launch of the eleventh mission. People feared that another such disaster could open up some 'portal' to another dimension sucking in our entire world into it. That was the last nail in the coffin for the entire program.

A dissenting group of scientists, however, fought to keep the **WARGER** system alive, even against the prevailing perception of that time and it is because of them the underground complex of IDP remained intact.

And a mere six months later, after the final launch in that fateful year of 2091, the world itself was blasted out of the reckoning as a planet harboring life.

We owe a lot to the dissenting group of scientists because of whom the IDP infrastructure that we found was still revivable.

In a way, there was some truth there that even the best interstellar traveling science of our time – the **WARGER** science, was not adequate to rescue most of us. It certainly was not **WARGER's** shortcoming, it was our inability to build as many Arks as needed.

Some day, in a far-future we might have a rendezvous with someone from a distant planet in the galaxy Andromeda who once was a or still is a human, how amazing that will be!

Forty - Life is Good, Too Good!

Oh, for sure, life in the *Nuevo Earth* system was good! Way too good! What any man ever wished for all his life had come true here -kind of! The economic system has served everyone well, matching the conditions created by enormous advancement in technology. Humans don't need to do monotonous chores anymore, semi-autonomous robots do all that for them. Common citizens engage in hobbies, recreation, sports, and such activities, which we always had to postpone to the golden part of life. Governance is completely transparent, and each person directly elects the governing council members. All historical prejudices have all fallen apart, long back. Competition continues, and it is good to have that. Most humans are engaged in research kind of activities, at their own pace, the reward for success is fame and rise on a social scoring system (SSC). The SSC score is equated with pride and respect.

In the paradise of the planetoids, humans are unlike we ever were – they are different, very different, in a good sense, and just different. Five and a half thousand years can change a lot. They have different sets of values, different likes and dislikes, as we found out during these eight months that we have been here.

Talk about - 'generational gap'!

That was the abstract side of the gap. On the physical side, that divide is a lot more on the inside than on the outside, in a good sense. They are genetically better prepared to be tough from the instant of conception.

I don't know what level of civilization to call this stage of development.

It is easy to conclude from what I described yet that life was comfortable in Nuevo, but too much comfort is probably not the kind of life I would choose, yet.

Every person is a creature of his time and for us, nothing is like our own time. We can't buy our own time, it is not there for any price. Besides, speaking for myself, I felt that our welcome period was coming to end, we are just still some curious guest from a distant past.

I was beginning to feel a sense that life should be much more than just keep on living in comfort, forever. Life - to me is not about just living, it is about getting that sense of fulfillment and achievement, it is about living it to the fullest and it is about being the best that one can be.

I conferred with the rest of us about it and got a similar vibe.

But you don't get what you don't ask for. In *Nuevo Earth*, replace 'ask' with 'think'. And 'think' we must *to* the council, the council that governs *Nuevo Earth*, and in person, in proximity, of course!

So we filed a request to the council to allow us a trip back to Earth and throttle our starship *Pegasus* again, for another long journey.

The council is proportionally represented by all the planetoids. Our planetoid NERTH-5 also had a few representative councilmen who granted us a time to discuss our formal request.

What transpired in the meeting tested the conviction of our intent - the desire to explore the universes. We were all summoned in front of the governing council. I will save you the detail and shorten it to the main points.

"First of all, the governing council has decided to officially exonerate you all from the accident that your ship had caused in which we lost an entire planetoid.

You have been found innocent on that account!" The councilor in the middle let us know.

"*Thank you councilors! We remain sorry for that mishap!*" Matt reciprocated that message with gratitude!

"*Okay. Now let's get back to your specific petition. Just so you know– We did not abandon* **WARGER** *technology. There were two reasons why after five and a half thousand years you don't see it now.*

The know-how of the **WARGER** *system as kept secured in the vault at IPNES did not survive the double extinctions in its entirety. During the massive turmoil of the decade when we were focused on building the Nuevo Earth's first planetoid and soon after the last launch of 2091, an asteroid strike destroyed a big part of Genève, and with it a treasure trove of information that IPNES had preserved lost. So, a good part of the know-how of this complex technology was lost.*

The reality also was that even after eleven successful launches the technology behind **WARGER** *was never fully understood even by the finest and smartest of all mankind. Even the best minds of that time could not reproduce that know-how from their knowledge or references preserved elsewhere. The science of*

WARGER was **not** meant to be understood in its entirety, as complex as it was for the human brain to grasp.

Secondly, even if we did have the technology in its entirety, we could not have built a port in the scale of the IDP in the small surface area of any of the planetoids. If something were to go wrong, we would lose the entire planetoid. We could not afford to lose a planetoid, it is a generational effort to build one, even for our level of science.

Having said that, the remains of the IDP port on Earth should still be recoverable and made functional. But we lost our confidence to revive it, fearing we might end up doing something very wrong in the process. Besides, we just could not be distracted from our continued work of **Project Atlantis**. Our survival depended on it, literally!"

"What you say does make perfect sense, councilman!" Matt acknowledged.

"Therefore, we will not be able to help you with the revival of the **WARGER** system. Besides, even if you did get it to work, could you replicate that feat on the destination planet that you are aiming for, wherever that is, with just the six of you? So, it leads us to the *question- Do you still want to go on with your program?"* Asked another councilman.

"I hear you, councilman. What you stated are facts, solid facts. But I guess, we still do, despite it all." Matt responded.

"And we should still have enough reserve **WARGER** *power to make three more round trips,"* Mirr spoke and he looked at us, looking for consent or dissent.

We consented.

"We hope that whoever helped us with the **WARGER** *system will help us again, if the need comes to that point and I suspect that they are not helping Nuevo Earth only because you don't need it now. There is no threat to Nuevo Earth now or in any foreseeable future."* Saito made an aspirational comment.

There was some silence at that point as we were given some time to internalize the reality of our decision. The councilor III spoke-

"I suppose your decision also takes into account the time dimension? The next time you all return, seven or eight thousand more years will have passed. It could be a completely different Earth, here and up there in the

old Earth that you will return to. No guarantee how they will view your return. "

"I think that is the unfortunate outcome of any inter-dimensional journey. When we first volunteered to this mission we pretty much had committed to a '**time - independent**' choice of existence for ourselves. We already are in that state of **time-defiant existence**, still alive after five thousand and six hundred plus years!" I don't know why but I ended up saying that spontaneously.

"If I may add to Rex's point, councilor – we learnt that time is kind of an illusion. Every universe has its own. Having traveled across many dimensions across many verses we feel it is only through these journeys that we can live many lives at once. Our journey has changed us. It calls us." Saito summed it up for all of us.

After conferring among themselves the councilor said-

"All right. We understand you completely. We will assist you in finding your true calling.

Also, for your information - we have not given up on Anti-Matter and Fusion reactor technologies although you do not find any on Nuevo Earth. We have an entire colony on Mars devoted to scientific Research and

Developments on Anti-matter and Fusion technologies, which we could not do on the NE system because of the same constraint of space of a planetoid.

*To assist you in a practically useful way, we will install a couple of Anti-Matter producing units and a Thorium purification plant inside your starship. So that whenever you run low on MAM and Fusion fuel reserve, you could mine any rocky planet that comes in your path and use these units to process the raw material obtained from there. However, we could not be of any help for the **WARGER** system."* The councilman spoke.

"Okay then, friends, whenever you are ready for that trip to go back to Earth, let us know and it shall be arranged." The chief councilman concluded.

"Godspeed folks!"

When the meeting ended I kind of felt a sense of relief – don't know why!

As we left the councilors' chamber, Matt asked all of us –

"Have we made a mistake, guys?"

"Thank you for making that decision, Matt! That was the right thing to do! We chose to be immortal!" I expressed my opinion.

Forty One–Checking Out

Days later we were on board on a craft to ancient Earth. This time we took the precaution of flying low so that *C-Mind* wouldn't bolt again if it detected us on its RADAR.

We are back on Earth, the original Earth, the Earth which gave us this life, and of which each cell in our bodies is made of. We have help this time, and we have the benefit of the advanced science from *Nuevo Earth*.

When we attempted to enter our ship after all these months, eleven and a half to be precise, C-*Mind* won't let us in without *interrogating* us at length first.

Once inside, Saito *talked it out* with *C-Mind* **not** to perceive any *Nuevo Earth* craft as a threat anymore.

In less than a couple of weeks, we will launch into the unknown one more time. Two weeks is all we've got to make that happen as the ominous precursors of the return of the deadly Gamma Blast are already manifesting at many locations around the globe.

Let me explain a little more in detail here.

True, the next full blast is still some unknown number of years away but the devastating precursors to the actual blast will begin to hit Earth well in advance of the actual blast. In cosmic timelines 'advance' could be decades or even a century!

Think of a massive hurricane that brewed in the warm water off of the Gulf coasts. The hurricane swirls at an enormous rotational speed around its center, but the translational velocity of the storm itself is very slow which is why it used to take weeks for a category five hurricane to make its landfall. However, the outer fringe of that hurricane is felt much in advance of its landfall, bringing heavy rains and winds over a large area. This gamma blast coming from **Betelgeuse** is loosely comparable to the effect of a hurricane in that sense, except the size and scope of it is in the scale of a planet. In the universe, things happen all the time, and on big scales, just that we, living in our niche corner and our niche little *time*, happen to be blissfully ignorant about them.

Decades in advance to its arrival, rocks, and other materials will come our way, slowly at first and in increasing intensity later.

The fact is the outer fringe of that deadly and massive storm is already teasing us.

We are beginning to witness sporadic meteor showers in many locations worldwide - each week a little worse than the week before.

We need to leave when we can and as soon as we can, or we risk losing all the work we've done so far.

If the forest itself catches fire, we are done! It is the only source of energy we are betting all our chips on.

In addition to the *Anti-Matter producing* and the *Thorium purification* modules, the council has delivered a lot of other useful inventory into our ship. They have sent us a good supply of ready to use Thorium rods for the Fusion reactor engines. Several dozen courier robots called *Druuks* are assisting us in shelving the empty racks of the ship, among other things there will be stock of food supplies worth a decade for the six of us.

We have about ten more days to get everything ready now.

All along, our prodigious children from the future have done an enormous service to see us successful – even after what we had done to one of their planetoids. They have stationed five small crafts at our service!

The incidences of global disturbance are increasing by the day, it is just a matter of time that one or two of them hit us, our ship is like a sitting duck parked on the **IDP** harbor.

And then the day finally arrives. The year 5591, by the *Nuevo Earth*'s calendar, April the 5th.

The launch is slated to happen mid-day, today.

The four crafts from *Nuevo Earth* have left already. They feared for their safety too. Observations from Nuevo Earth warned us of incidences of major forest fires already happening elsewhere in the world, mainly due to large strikes from large stray rocks. One that was particularly fearsome, happened in the former central Asia region of Ulan Bator. A massive shower of celestial rocks and ice, some as large as a neighborhood water tank, bombarded the region only a few hours ago.

In general, the sky these days look pretty dramatic with patches of clear blue next to the patches of thick and dark clouds all in the same hour - surreal.

We are leaving, this time we have no mandate to return- so we don't know if we ever will!

With the power of the **WARGER** energy, we could be anywhere –in any of these galaxies such as the Triangular Galaxy, Sombrero Galaxy, and Andromeda. We could also be in any of these countless others for which we have run short of names in our vocabularies - such as NGC 4216, NGC 4262, NGC 4435, and NGC 4438, to name only a few.

This time we will aim farther much further than **Astraea-B**. We will set our coordinates for a distant planet at one thousand one hundred light-years away -**Kepler 442b**. A super-earth in the constellation of **Lyra**. All data points **Kepler 442b** to be a paradise of our definition. In terms of *habitability rating*, it scores even higher than our good old pre-apocalyptic Earth.

We will rename our starship as *Starship Kepler* from this moment. *C-Mind* is already 'told' about this name change, so it knows.

Eight hours to launch, and each of us is consumed in executing our respective responsibilities to completion.

And then a setback happened. It could not have happened at a worse time.

There was a radiation leak from the Fusion chamber.

"Not good!" I reminded the team as soon as I noticed the reading of one of the Geiger counters placed at the location. It is coming from subsection VR-12. Seemed like a rivet joint in the five-foot thick Lead walls had loosened for some reason. Could be due to material failure.

"What? No!" Matt was not happy.

"I will go down there to have a look and seal it up real hard, real quick. Mirr, please throttle down the Fusion engine to idle." I stood up and headed to grab the special protective suit needed to work in that area.

"Okay," Mirr responded.

*"Wait, Rex. You wait here. I am going there. We need you here to get the MAM and **WARGER** system ready."* Matt interrupted.

"No Matt, I can do both. We still have eight hours. This should take no more than an hour to fix. I am going down!" I insisted. I did not want to jeopardize the life of our Commander. Zone *VR-12* - the entire section of that Fusion Chamber is one dangerous part of the ship, besides, it is not quite in his domain of expertise – it is in mine. I am responsible for it.

"No, Rex! No. We need you here. I am going down. I know the protocol too. Besides, you will be here anyways, to guide me on what to do. Keep the voice channel on." He winked at me, put his big hand on my shoulder, his way of telling me not to worry or not to feel any guilt about it.

Matt went down into the location where the leak was detected. Twenty minutes later he was online.

"Yes, it is just one rivet that failed! I can fix that. Okay... on it..." He was down there speaking to me.

"Great!" I relayed back.

Matt was gone a full hour. I knew it wasn't easy. Certain things may sound easy or look easy until you start doing when you realize that there is more to them than meet the eye.

When he was back at the control an hour later, he appeared weak and tired.

I noticed it immediately, and I instinctively knew that the worst has happened to him. He probably missed one small step in the process and ended up getting hurt.

"Matt, Matt... What's up commander? You don't look so great!"

450

Elea rushed to Matt who just laid on his back on a seat that I reclined all the way for him.

Elea and Greta took him on a stretcher to the medical chamber.

"*Prof, Mirr, and Rex don't worry about me. The work must go on. Please keep doing what you guys are doing.*" Matt spoke as Mirr, Elea and Greta carried him into the Medic Chamber.

Ten minutes into the chamber, Elea came live on the voice channel from the medic chamber, her voice shaking.

"*Team, not looking good for Matt. He took a heavy dose of radiation. His system is failing. We must get help soon.*"

"*O' my!*" was all I could come up with. We all ran up to the medic chamber which is at the other end of the central square of the ship, at the dead-end of a few left and right turns.

"*Matt, I insisted you not to go!*"

"*Don't worry, Rex. I will be alright. You guys go back to what you've been doing. Please.*" Matt responded in his usual self. But toughness cannot fix exposure to nuclear radiation.

"*Let's reach out to the council hotline and ask them what we should do,*" Saito suggested.

Mirr took the suggestion immediately and made the call.

The councilman representing our planetoid appeared on our display.

"*That sounds bad. Luckily for him, we still have one last craft at the outpost. I'll direct it to pick Matt up on its way. He must receive immediate medical attention at NE P-3 medical city, the only location in the entire NE system for such severe cases of radiation illness. While inside the craft, we'll keep him on life support that will keep him alive until he reaches there.*" And the councilman told us in no uncertain terms - "*I am afraid Commander Matteo will not be fit to travel on this journey in any near future. I am sorry!*

The craft will be at your location in twenty minutes. Please bring Commander Matteo out of the ship so we can expedite the pickup." The councilman continued. And in conclusion, he said this -

"*Ladies and gentlemen. The bombardments are intensifying by the hour much ahead of the actual Gamma blast and against our expectations. I strongly suggest that you leave on your scheduled time!*

Goodbye and have a great trip!" He disconnected himself from the live conversation.

It took us some time to digest what we just heard. A mission without Matteo is just unthinkable! Matt heard it all and he slowly spoke –

"Don't worry guys. Don't worry about me! This is how it was destined probably. You all will do just fine without me. I will be here, heart and soul, just not physically." Matt spoke. He already looked pretty frail.

"We need your leadership, Commander. We can postpone this launch. Yes, it is a risk. But, have we not taken more risks than this already?" I implored him.

"No, Rex. No. The councilman is not making up things when he talks about the risk of delaying the launch. You know how the Nuevo folks are. They speak nothing but the truth. They won't say what they said without some concrete facts to back it up. If the forest catches fire, it is all over. There is no way we can postpone this beyond today.

Hear me out my friends. Each of you is capable of commandeering any space ship...each of you. You have each other, all super experts in your respective domain. You have the Plato like the wisdom of Professor Saito, brilliant and quick like Mirr, the best doctor ever – Dr. Elea to keep you and the ship safe, the amazing promise and genius of Greta and you - Rex, the one person that understands all the three technologies- WARGER, MAM, and Fusion like no one else in the universe, who aced all tests that life presented to you in this still young life of yours.

For coordinating things, I agree we need one person to wield that responsibility in an official sense.

So, Rex, It will be my wish that you be the new Commander of this ship from this moment. The Commander of this new starship – Starship Kepler." Having finished that talk, Matteo pulled out a heptagonal badge and another device, from his suit. He handed the two over to me.

"Team, please give a big hand to Commander Rex Song - our new Commander. My Commander!" Matteo managed a smile, even in his condition.

There was soft applause, I did not know how to react. I was sad but understood that it had to be this way.

"From this moment on, Cygnus and all auxiliary systems of this starship will recognize you as the Commander. The ship's systems will recognize you by your biometrics, your personality, and will obey your direct command - of course, all within the purview of

*the two laws that **Cygnus** is governed by."* Matt said his last handing over words.

"I guess it's time to take Commander Matt out, the last craft is due to arrive soon." Saito reminded everyone.

"As soon as I administer a procedure on him... It'll be quick," Elea said.

Just before we took him out, Matt said –

"I have programmed one of the identifying devices with a code, which makes that person the 3rd law from this point onward. No one but only that individual knows that he is the one. That person now has the necessary code to fulfill his duty as the 3rd law! Please respect the role of the 3rd law – we had a situation once – you all know that. We need the 3rd law.

This will be the last time we will ever see each other. Good luck and goodbye friends!"

The craft came just at the time the councilman said it would and we were ready with the stretcher with Matteo on it. We stood firm and stood still, like a team of loyal soldiers that we were, showing our respects for him, saluting, as the small craft took off - with him inside.

Forty- Two – The Unexpected

We were back at the control and a nice surprise was waiting for us.

There was Droon, our guide, and friend who showed us the way through life in *Nuevo Earth*, making us comfortable in that new world all through the eleven months that we spent there.

"Guys, sorry that I did not send you the memo ahead of time. But I will be joining your team. (Pause)... What say? ......No??" Droon was all smiles, his palms open and shoulders raised.

"What on Earth!!" Saito almost lost his balance seeing him appear out of nowhere on the ramp of the main entry to the ship.

"O' my! How did you ... ...Droon?" If I was wearing a pair of jeans, the jeans would have snapped all along both the seams! It was that kind of a surprise to see Droon this way!

"Thought I will give you a surprise! (Pause) but am I in or...?" Droon is still asking and smiling.

"O' my lord! What on Earth is this guy doing here!" Elea who just arrived at the scene spelled out loud in joy at seeing Droon appear in this surprising way.

We all like Droon.

"Nooooooo wayyyy.... what are you doing here?..." Mirr exclaimed too.

"Sorry Guys... wanted to give you all a surprise. I knew your plans from councilman Dez. I spoke to him about my desire to be on this mission. Guess what, he agreed!"

Greta, who arrived last at the scene, almost screamed at seeing Droon. And she screamed one more time knowing that he too will be with us on this mission.

Droon will be a huge asset to this mission.

"Guys, you won't have to teach me much, I know enough already to be dangerous enough and rest I can self-learn - just show me the ship's self-learning system. Btw, during the long associations that I had with you, I have learned a lot about the culture of my future team, and I like it, very, very much. So.... I promise I will be a good fit." Droon had more to say.

"So am I in?"

"Yeshhh, you butt-cheek-from-the-future!" I said and everyone burst out laughing.

"Eeeeeeeeyah! Thanks a lot, guys!"

"..But only if you promised to move your lips and mouth when you speak..!" Saito cracked us up.

"You mean no more ventriloquism? Like this? (He pretended to speak without moving his lips again)" Droon understood us very well, he was already like one of us.

And he said again –

"Okay, deal, no more ventriloquism until all of us are ventriloquists!"

"And no more mind-reading! Until we all have mastered it as well..." Greta added... She was only joking, of course.

"Okay, deal on that too... I will make you all masters of mind-reading by the time we land on the next planet." Droon agreed and he continued.

"I have more surprises guys!"

"What?"

"Two friendly human assist robos – Reno and Rondo also come with us. They are smart and have some sense of humor too."

As soon as Droon was finished Reno and Rondo appeared from their hiding behind the panels. The robots, each made up of two distinct and unconnected thick rings, if you still remembered - one ring levitating over the bigger base ring. The upper ring had two blinking red lights for eyes in its middle and a curved line for the mouth, all physically unconnected to the body of the ring itself in any way. Every time I see them I could not help wondering how such an arrangement works at all. How does its upper ring stay afloat in midair? And how do the eyes and the mouth that are just not connected anywhere to the body-frame of the ring-work?

The two animated smiles appeared on each as Droon introduced them.

I wish we could celebrate this moment longer but we are on the clock. We have only a few hours left.

We owe the people of NE a lot and we hope we can return that favor someday, in some ways. If we could not, we hope we too can save another species facing an imminent extinction to compensate for the help we received.

Time to get ready for departure, first thing first- crank the fusion engine to life. Everything looked good on that front.

It was an hour past mid-day. We are all set. All set to harness the power of nature, the energy of **FWW**, to ingest energy of the order of an entire city's consumption all within a short time into the **WARGER** system. Two Giga Watt per Hour of electrical energy will be injected in a large dose through the control mains.

Three hours later the main **WARGER** storage and the reserve packs were all refilled to capacity.

And just as before the *WARGER **bubble*** started to form all around our ship and just as before in a short twenty-five minutes from that moment we disappeared into nothingness, into the infinity, into the higher dimension.

Forty Three - To Eternity

This, in a relativistic sense, is the present time by starship *Kepler's* clock. We have been living this space-faring life for longer than a hundred and fifty years now - as per our ship's chronograph. Not sure how much time that translates to in the solar time scale on Earth. Must be shockingly long. We left Earth for the second time, the last time, and built a colony on **Kepler 442 B**.

That was a long time ago.

The advanced technology of *Nuevo Earth* gave us a huge head start that enabled us to master most part of our own *evolution* - in the sense that we could now successfully replace and augment our aging body organs, as needed. We have done so a few times during the hundred and fifty years of our explorer-life. Replacing one organ at a time, each time with a much more augmented one, and yet still managed to stay the same person. We have perfected the art and science of *PhysioTranspodics*.

In doing so we have stepped into a timeless existence, a state of near-immortality where we continue to replenish our organs as long as we need to, in perpetuity.

This planet was on our flight-plan to the dwarf galaxy known as the *Large Magellanic Cloud, (LMC)*. In our transit, we are taking the time to survey this planet for potential sources of thorium for future needs. This red rocky planet orbits a white dwarf star located somewhere in the middle of a minor spiral arm of the Milky Way called *Sagittarius-Carina*. This region of the galaxy, located on the opposite side of the galactic center to the solar system is defined by frequent and violent cosmic activities, compared to the region where the solar system is located. Events such as collisions of heavenly bodies, electro-magnetic storms sweeps, meteorite shower bursts and such are tenfold more likely to happen here than in the solar neighborhood by comparison. This dry planet is comparable to Mars in its size and appearance, except it is not as red.

We landed the starship on a suitable ground.

Two hours after landing, Mirr, Droon, Greta and I are on board of a RAVEN to scout this part of the planet, the rest of our crew will stay back in the mother ship. With us is Rondo - the *two-ringed* robot – which Droon brought along from *Nuevo Earth* if you remembered.

Rondo is nothing like you knew from that long past. It can switch among three basic shapes. The two rings can merge into one, which in turn can become larger or smaller in diameter. In its third mode, it morphs into a shiny spherical ball in the size of a soccer ball. In the ring-like mode, it is capable of flight just by spinning rapidly. Its virtual eyes and mouth can completely detach itself from the main body, stay afloat by itself like a small screen, and display graphs and images. It is in its 99th generation of upgrades.

Several scouting trips later what we found in one area was not what we expected to find. A few miles ahead of us laid a massive ruin of something huge.

It was a spaceship in ruin, half-buried in the sand in an inclined orientation to the rocky surface. Parts of it were scattered around for miles out. Clearly, a huge disaster, a terrible one that had happened to this ship. Probably had happened decades or even a century ago - just by an initial look from this far

It will be safe to land the RAVEN here, a few hundred meters from the ruins of the crashed ship. In the low gravity condition of this planet, it takes a good while for the cloud of dust kicked off by our act of landing to settle. As soon as the dust subsided, the three of us stepped out of the RAVEN while Mirr stayed at the control. We cautiously walked toward the crashed ship, each of us armed with a mini F4 gun. Who knows what kind of a belligerent alien life form awaits us inside that ruin! From this point, it still was a good three hundred meters of negotiating through the widely spread out debris until we reached close to the hull of the ruined ship.

A closer approach revealed a part of its hull ripped apart by the crash, leaving an open a gaping hole into the ship's main body. The ship was designed like a huge turtle. Because of the tilted orientation with the ground, its short wingspan on the left side rose hundreds of feet above the ground. A large portion of the entire right side of the ship laid buried deep into the rocky surface. The ship was easily larger than the volume of a football stadium. Layers of sand dumped by many sand storms from the past blanketed the top of everything that was at the ground level.

Just as there are the frequent *dust devils* on Mars, here must be too.

If there were any survivors they probably had abandoned the ship a long time ago.

Greta and I entered the inside of the ship through the ripped hull, followed by Droon. Rondo, the *two-ringed* robot, rolled in swiftly from behind us to be in front of all of us now.

This was an appropriate situation to release the two miniature robotic *dragonfly drones* through the ripped passageway to survey the maze of unknown corridors ahead of us. The two *dragonflies* buzzed their ways through the opening in the hull and into the ship. They should warn us of any possible danger if there was. After several minutes of navigating through the wreckage inside of the ship, we finally arrived at a large chamber that appeared to be the main control room of the ship.

Everything inside the chamber was inclined at about fifteen degrees to the surface just as the entire ship was.

The war zone like inside of the ship was barely illuminated, so we flashed our suit lights ahead of us to get a better visual. Five entryways lead into this chamber from five directions, each large enough for three people to enter at once.

At the mouth of one of those entryways that curved away from the main control chamber was a bony remains of what looked like the skull of a large pachyderm of Earthly origin. A pair of tusks from that

skull rose above the sand. There was another big skull
– looked like that of a one-horned rhino – the rarer
kind, from our time on Earth.

Then something happened, a misstep. As Rondo rolled
ahead of us, it inadvertently lost its balance on the
uneven floor and banged hard into a switch. And
suddenly, the space inside the control chamber got
illuminated by flashing of many hazard lights
accompanied by a haunting sound of distress. That
immediately was followed by someone shooting at us
from somewhere within the chamber. We took cover
to dodge the bullets that were coming from nowhere.

And then everything stopped, everything - the hazard
lights dimmed and the distress wailing sound petered
out.

We got up cautiously, our fingers on the trigger ready
to shoot. But there was no one.

Stealthily and in short cautious steps we proceeded
towards the dashboard area of the main control. There
was nothing there besides the control panels, no signs
of any entity who might have shot at us.

It was probably Rondo's accidental banging on a very
special point on the wall that triggered a defensive
routine of the ship's still alive automated defense

mechanism. That might have been the last gasp of its artificial life.

This main control room will easily be the size of a two-story building by itself, with rows of control panels flushed to the walls all around the circumference. This huge control chamber could easily house forty crew members at once. There were several heavy metal chairs bolted to the floor at predesigned locations and in rows. Each seat had myriads of switches on either sides, the adjacent seats are spaced well apart from each other.

It looked as if there were some figures sitting on the six large chairs facing the opposite direction from where we were approaching. Whoever sat there couldn't be alive now. Except for the two that were well above the surface level and empty, all rest of the chairs were buried some degree into the soil in proportions to their location along the slope of this slanted floor.

On approaching the row of chairs where the figures were seated revealed a horrific sight. Ugh! A chilling sight to see six former crew members still seated there in tilted positions, their helmets still in place over their skulls and the bones inside their suits showing through the tears. The name tags on metal plates were barely clinging to their torn suits. Their lower body portions have petrified inside the bedrock of the planet's surface.

There must have been many such others further to the right, but probably got completely buried inside the rocky surface.

That sight could strike hard for anyone who looked at it.

This starship is huge. Surely there were other people than just these few unfortunate crew members. If there were, they must have abandoned the ship and taken off in one of the many auxiliary ships if they still had the chance in the aftermath. If an escape was not possible, they probably suffered a horrible death out there in the endless desert.

The planet has hardly any atmosphere worth calling as such.

We dusted off the sand from the dashboards and found dozens of switches of some kind. Greta pressed one switch after another, and in one accidental sequence of that press, a part of the control came to life. Amazing that even after all the years, some reserve power still existed.

Slowly a small portion of a huge curved monitor came to life, despite the cracks and the chips all over it. The imagery was flaky. The display started with some geometric patterns, and then an upbeat robotic human female voice came alive, speaking in English – yes, in English.

~ *"Welcome to starship Antarctica. We bring the very best greetings from a species that built an amazing civilization and dreamt of more – to reach many more stars and to befriend all life forms that we would encounter. We called ourselves humans.*

This starship is an Ark, carrying over three thousand humans and as many other fellow creatures from our planet. We are destined for Andromeda.

We intend to adopt a beautiful planet in that galaxy as our new home.

We left Earth in the year 2091 as per our Gregorian calendar, a time tracking system applicable only to our planet. I compute that as 25,610 solar years from this moment into the past." ~

The message then got repeated in dozens of other human languages. After the voice quietened, the vestige of the information system of the ship attempted to display something in mid-air, like a holographic image. But that didn't happen and instead got fizzled out.

It was followed by an attempt where a part of the overhead dome began to display bits and pieces of something. The display was as sketchy as the broken dome was. But even in that blurriness, we could make out that it was attempting to show the location of the solar system in the galactic neighborhood - kind of a cosmic postal address scheme to our old home, in the map-less infinite expanse of the universe.

Year 2091! That is forty-five years after our launch!

That is the eleventh mission – yes, the last one.

The eleventh mission was jinxed to fail from the start, and it failed so very horribly!

The hapless starship *Antarctica* emerged in the wrong place in the **base-dim**. Instead of materializing in empty space, it materialized inside the solid rock of this lonely planet.

A fatal navigational error.

The interstellar *message* of hope that it carried finally had an audience, not exactly **the audience** that it was intended for - but a timeless future self of some from our own species – us, after the passage of a huge time-lapse - 25,610 solar years to be exact.

The irony of that message was the message itself - an upbeat female voice in a ruined spacecraft. We were still dealing with the whole scenario in our minds when Droon spoke to break the silence -

"Commander, you are bruised at two places, on the right side of your torso and on the back of your right shoulder."

I was not even aware of any wounds, so I turned my head to the right and down to look at my torso and turned a little more to look at the back of my right shoulder.

Droon was right, there were several minor damages to my body. A strand of artificial *teres major* on the back of my right shoulder and two of the carbon fiber strands for *abdominal oblique* muscles on the right side of my abdomen had snapped. The wounds were visible through the two-inch-long incisions that ripped up the thick dark suit that I was clad in.

"You are right, I guess my augmented-frame does need some fixing and some replacements!" I agreed.

As soon as I said it, Greta stepped her long right leg forward on an empty chair and pointed us to her wounded spot. Just below her right knee, a thin slit in her suit opened up to reveal some damages to her metallic underframe.

"I got hit as well - here. A fibularis longus carbon fiber got snapped!" She said.

"Looks like you both got shot in that residual automated defense response reaction when that happened."

As we were exploring the inside of the wreckage Rondo slipped out the chamber without us noticing.

Suddenly, we heard this creaking sound, like a metallic door opening and immediately closing. It was followed by another sound like that of a bowling ball rolling down its lane. We stood alert on a possible situation for about half a minute as the rolling sound became louder by the moment. Then it appeared at the entrance to this chamber, a metallic looking sphere of the size of a wrecking ball. It wobbled like a top for a minute before it stabilized right in front of us. Lots of tiny sparkling lights began to display all over it. A tripod leg began to emerge from beneath it at the same time. The tripod grew up vertically, raising the ball up to the height of an average human's waist.

And it spoke to us in a sweet robotic voice with a smiley face drawn in tiny lights on its surface –

<Welcome to starship Antarctica! I bring warm greetings from the great human civilization of planet Earth!>

(Pause and beeps)

<How can I help you?>

<How can I help you?>

<How can I help you?> ....

And it kept on repeating the last line a few more times, as when a malfunction occurs. Then the voice and the lights slowly faded away. It stood on its tripod for a little longer and suddenly the tripod collapsed too causing it to fall with a dull thud on the sandy floor.

Suddenly we experienced a mild tremor, and a very faint low *bloop* kind. Even in the sparse atmosphere as on this dry planet we could hear that *bloop*. The tremor repeated again, and again. It began to increase in magnitude by a little beat each passing time. We looked at each other – apprehension in our minds.

"We will need to dispatch Rondo to check it out!"

"Rondo is not here apparently!"

A short passage of time later, on the device that each of us wear on our right shoulder, a series of beeps signaling an incoming message drew our attention. It was Rondo, sending us a message from the outside.

"Yes, Rondo?"

Commander, a huge storm is coming our way. **I repeat... a huge storm is coming our way**!

A huge storm ......#

We looked at the holographic display that began to materialize in front of us, as Rondo was transmitting what it was seeing outside, in real time.

A wall of dust as high as the Grand Canyon from its bottom most point to the top, and as wide as to cover the entire horizon, was coming towards us, and coming fast.

At the very spear head of that approaching wall of dust was this thing – a huge burrowing wheel of metallic dark slate color with rugged razor sharp blades all around its circumference, as high as the wall of dust itself, shearing through the rocky surface like it was just a piece of old rug!

~ Not THE END ~

(..because there really is no end...)

Extra - A Catalogue of Starship Pegasus' Inventory

· RAVEN – Roving Auxiliary Vehicle (small), five passengers.

· RAVEN (L) – Roving Auxiliary Vehicle (Large), fifteen passengers.

· Aerial Bike (A two-rider bike built on drone technology)

· Robo-Drone – Remotely operated drone.

· TALON – Semi-Autonomous remote operated fighting machine in the shape of animals and birds, such as – Panther, Cheetah, Eagles, and Mountain Lion.

· SKELs – Manually operated Large Exo Skeleton capable of lifting fifty times more weight

· WARGER Reserve Packs

· WARGER Drive System

· Thorium Reserve for FUSION drive

· Fusion Drive

· Matter-Anti-Matter (MAM) Fuel Section

· MAM Drive System

· LAFF4 – Large Automated Force Field Model 4 (FB4 in short)

· AFF4 – Automated Force Field Model 4 (F4 in short)

· AFF4-Mini (F4 in short)

- RS Armed Android

- Rondo – Human Assist, two-ring Advance Patrol Robot

- C-Mind – The autonomous brain of the starship, alias Cygnus

- Galileo – Auxiliary computer System for calculating Galactic positioning

A random note on speed and time in the cosmic scale (source NASA)–

One *Light Year* is 5.8 trillion miles. Man-made probe Voyager 1 traveling at 38000 miles/hour is the farthest anything we have sent out yet. In 43 years of its run, it has covered 13.2 billion miles so far. Even that distance is a mere 0.22 percent of one *Light Year*. At that speed it will take 79,000 Years to reach Proxima B. Parker Solar probe – will reach 430,000 miles an hour in the year 2024 from its current velocity of 244,225 miles an hour. Even at that speed, it will take 1561 years to cover one -light-year, so to cover 4. 2 light-years to Proxima Centauri B it will take - 6556 Years.

The fastest manned spacecraft so far traveled was at 24, 791 miles an hour.

Speed of light is 670 million miles /hour

CPSIA information can be obtained
at www.ICGtesting.com
Printed in the USA
LVHW051428210221
679587LV00004B/358

9 781735 704067